EX LIBRIS

'Wodehouse was quite simply
THE BEE'S KNEES.
And then some'
Joseph Connolly

'Mr Wodehouse's
IDYLLIC WORLD CAN NEVER STALE.
He will continue to release future generations from captivity
that may be more irksome than our own. He has made a
world for us to live in and delight in'
Evelyn Waugh

'**THE ULTIMATE IN COMFORT READING**.
For as long as I'm immersed in a P.G. Wodehouse book, it's
possible to keep the real world at bay and live in a far, far nicer,
funnier one where happy endings are the order of the day'
Marian Keyes

'You should read Wodehouse when you're well
and when you're poorly; when you're travelling,
and when you're not; when you're feeling clever, and when
you're feeling utterly dim. Wodehouse
ALWAYS LIFTS YOUR SPIRITS,
no matter how high they happen to be already'
Lynne Truss

'P. G. Wodehouse remains the greatest chronicler of
A CERTAIN KIND OF ENGLISHNESS,
that no one else has ever captured quite so sharply, or with
quite as much wit and affection'
Julian Fellowes

'Not only the funniest English novelist who
ever wrote but one of our finest stylists.
His world is **PERFECT**, his stories are
PERFECT, his writing is **PERFECT**.'
Susan Hill

P.G. WODEHOUSE

JEEVES

AND THE

YULE-TIDE SPIRIT

AND OTHER STORIES

HUTCHINSON
LONDON

Published by Hutchinson 2014

2 4 6 8 10 9 7 5 3 1

First published in Great Britain in 2014 by
Hutchinson
Random House, 20 Vauxhall Bridge Road,
London SW1V 2SA

www.randomhouse.co.uk

Addresses for companies within The Random House Group Limited can be found at: www.randomhouse.co.uk/offices.htm

The Random House Group Limited Reg. No. 954009

A CIP catalogue record for this book
is available from the British Library

ISBN 9780091959029

The Random House Group Limited supports the Forest Stewardship Council® (FSC®), the leading international forest-certification organisation. Our books carrying the FSC label are printed on FSC®-certified paper. FSC is the only forest-certification scheme supported by the leading environmental organisations, including Greenpeace. Our paper procurement policy can be found at www.randomhouse.co.uk/environment

Typeset by SX Composing DTP, Rayleigh, Essex

Printed and bound in Great Britain by Clays Ltd, St Ives Plc

Contents

Jeeves And The Yule-Tide Spirit

The letter arrived on the morning of the sixteenth. I was pushing a bit of breakfast into the Wooster face at the moment and, feeling fairly well-fortified with coffee and kippers, I decided to break the news to Jeeves without delay. As Shakespeare says, if you're going to do a thing you might just as well pop right at it and get it over. The man would be disappointed, of course, and possibly even chagrined: but, dash it all, a splash of disappointment here and there does a fellow good. Makes him realize that life is stern and life is earnest.

'Oh, Jeeves,' I said.

'Sir?'

'We have here a communication from Lady Wickham. She has written inviting me to Skeldings for the festives. So you will see about bunging the necessaries together. We repair thither on the twenty-third. Plenty of white ties, Jeeves, also a few hearty country suits for use in the daytime. We shall be there some little time, I expect.'

There was a pause. I could feel he was directing a frosty gaze at me, but I dug into the marmalade and refused to meet it.

'I thought I understood you to say, sir, that you proposed to visit Monte Carlo immediately after Christmas.'

'I know. But that's all off. Plans changed.'

'Very good, sir.'

At this point the telephone bell rang, tiding over very nicely what had threatened to be an awkward moment. Jeeves unhooked the receiver.

'Yes? ... Yes, madam ... Very good, madam. Here is Mr Wooster.' He handed me the instrument. 'Mrs Spenser Gregson, sir.'

You know, every now and then I can't help feeling that Jeeves is losing his grip. In his prime it would have been with him the work of a moment to have told Aunt Agatha that I was not at home. I gave him one of those reproachful glances, and took the machine.

'Hullo?' I said. 'Yes? Hullo? Hullo? Bertie speaking. Hullo? Hullo? Hullo?'

'Don't keep on saying Hullo,' yipped the old relative in her customary curt manner. 'You're not a parrot. Sometimes I wish you were, because then you might have a little sense.'

Quite the wrong sort of tone to adopt towards a fellow in the early morning, of course, but what can one do?

'Bertie, Lady Wickham tells me she has invited you to Skeldings for Christmas. Are you going?'

'Rather!'

'Well, mind you behave yourself. Lady Wickham is an old friend of mine.'

I was in no mood for this sort of thing over the telephone. Face to face, I'm not saying, but at the end of a wire, no.

'I shall naturally endeavour, Aunt Agatha,' I replied stiffly, 'to conduct myself in a manner befitting an English gentleman paying a visit—'

'What did you say? Speak up. I can't hear.'

'I said Right-ho.'

'Oh? Well, mind you do. And there's another reason why I particularly wish you to be as little of an imbecile as you can manage while at Skeldings. Sir Roderick Glossop will be there.'

'What!'

'Don't bellow like that. You nearly deafened me.'

'Did you say Sir Roderick Glossop?'

'I did.'

'You don't mean Tuppy Glossop?'

'I mean Sir Roderick Glossop. Which was my reason for saying Sir Roderick Glossop. Now, Bertie, I want you to listen to me attentively. Are you there?'

'Yes. Still here.'

'Well, then, listen. I have at last succeeded, after incredible difficulty, and in face of all the evidence, in almost persuading Sir Roderick that you are not actually insane. He is prepared to suspend judgement until he has seen you once more. On your behaviour at Skeldings, therefore—'

But I had hung up the receiver. Shaken. That's what I was. S. to the core.

Stop me if I've told you this before: but, in case you don't know, let me just mention the facts in the matter of this Glossop. He was a formidable old bird with a bald head and outsize eyebrows, by profession a loony-doctor. How it happened, I couldn't tell you to this day, but I once got engaged to his daughter, Honoria, a ghastly dynamic exhibit who read Nietzsche and had a laugh like waves breaking on a stern and rock-bound coast. The fixture was scratched owing to events occurring which convinced the old boy that I was off my napper; and since then he has always had my name at the top of his list of 'Loonies I have Lunched With'.

It seemed to me that even at Christmas time, with all the peace on earth and goodwill towards men that there is knocking about at that season, a reunion with this bloke was likely to be tough going. If I hadn't had more than one particularly good reason for wanting to go to Skeldings, I'd have called the thing off.

'Jeeves,' I said, all of a twitter, 'do you know what? Sir Roderick Glossop is going to be at Lady Wickham's.'

'Very good, sir. If you have finished breakfast, I will clear away.'

Cold and haughty. No symp. None of the rallying-round spirit which one likes to see. As I had anticipated, the information that we were not going to Monte Carlo had got in amongst him. There is a keen sporting streak in Jeeves, and I knew he had been looking forward to a little flutter at the tables.

We Woosters can wear the mask. I ignored his lack of decent feeling.

'Do so, Jeeves,' I said proudly, 'and with all convenient speed.'

Relations continued pretty fairly strained all through the rest of the week. There was a frigid detachment in the way the man brought me my dollop of tea in the mornings. Going down to Skeldings in the car on the afternoon of the twenty-third, he was aloof and reserved. And before dinner on the first night of my visit he put the studs in my dress-shirt in what I can only call a marked manner. The whole thing was extremely painful, and it seemed to me, as I lay in bed on the morning of the twenty-fourth, that the only step to take was to put the whole facts of the case before him and trust to his native good sense to effect an understanding.

I was feeling considerably in the pink that morning. Everything had gone like a breeze. My hostess, Lady Wickham, was a beaky female built far too closely on the lines of my Aunt Agatha for comfort, but she had seemed matey enough on my arrival. Her daughter, Roberta, had welcomed me with a warmth which, I'm bound to say, had set the old heart-strings fluttering a bit. And Sir Roderick, in the brief moment we had had together, appeared to have let the Yule-Tide Spirit soak into him to the most amazing extent. When he saw me, his mouth sort of flickered at one corner, which I took to be his idea of smiling, and he said 'Ha, young man!' Not particularly chummily, but he said it: and my view was that it practically amounted to the lion lying down with the lamb.

So, all in all, life at this juncture seemed pretty well all to the mustard, and I decided to tell Jeeves exactly how matters stood.

'Jeeves,' I said, as he appeared with the steaming tea.

'Sir?'

'Touching on this business of our being here, I would like to say a few words of explanation. I consider that you have a right to the facts.'

'Sir?'

'I'm afraid scratching that Monte Carlo trip has been a bit of a jar for you, Jeeves.'

'Not at all, sir.'

'Oh, yes, it has. The heart was set on wintering in the world's good old Plague Spot, I know. I saw your eye light up when I said we were due for a visit there. You snorted a bit and your fingers twitched. I know, I know. And now that there has been a change of programme the iron has entered into your soul.'

'Not at all, sir.'

'Oh, yes, it has. I've seen it. Very well, then, what I wish to impress upon you, Jeeves, is that I have not been actuated in this matter by any mere idle whim. It was through no

6

light and airy caprice that I accepted this invitation to Lady Wickham's. I have been angling for it for weeks, prompted by many considerations. In the first place, does one get the Yule-tide spirit at a spot like Monte Carlo?'

'Does one desire the Yule-tide spirit, sir?'

'Certainly one does. I am all for it. Well, that's one thing. Now here's another. It was imperative that I should come to Skeldings for Christmas, Jeeves, because I knew that young Tuppy Glossop was going to be here.'

'Sir Roderick Glossop, sir?'

'His nephew. You may have observed hanging about the place a fellow with light hair and a Cheshire-cat grin. That is Tuppy, and I have been anxious for some time to get to grips with him. I have it in for that man of wrath. Listen to the facts, Jeeves, and tell me if I am not justified in planning a hideous vengeance.' I took a sip of tea, for the mere memory of my wrongs had shaken me. 'In spite of the fact that young Tuppy is the nephew of Sir Roderick Glossop, at whose hands, Jeeves, as you are aware, I have suffered much, I fraternized with him freely, both at the Drones Club and elsewhere. I said to myself that a man is not to be blamed for his relations, and that I would hate to have my pals hold my Aunt Agatha, for instance, against me. Broad-minded, Jeeves, I think?'

'Extremely, sir.'

'Well, then, as I say, I sought this Tuppy out, Jeeves, and hobnobbed, and what do you think he did?'

'I could not say, sir.'

'I will tell you. One night after dinner at the Drones he betted me I wouldn't swing myself across the swimming-bath by the ropes and rings. I took him on and was buzzing along in great style until I came to the last ring. And then I found that this fiend in human shape had looped it back against the rail, thus leaving me hanging in the void with no means of getting ashore to my home and loved ones. There was nothing for it but to drop into the water. He told me that he had often caught fellows that way: and what I maintain, Jeeves, is that, if I can't get back at him somehow at Skeldings – with all the vast resources which a country-house affords at my disposal – I am not the man I was.'

'I see, sir.'

There was still something in his manner which told me that even now he lacked complete sympathy and understanding, so, delicate though the subject was, I decided to put all my cards on the table.

'And now, Jeeves, we come to the most important reason why I had to spend Christmas at Skeldings. Jeeves,' I said, diving into the old cup once more for a moment and bringing myself out wreathed in blushes, 'the fact of the matter is, I'm in love.'

'Indeed, sir?'

'You've seen Miss Roberta Wickham?'

'Yes, sir.'

'Very well, then.'

There was a pause, while I let it sink in.

'During your stay here, Jeeves,' I said, 'you will, no doubt, be thrown a good deal together with Miss Wickham's maid. On such occasions, pitch it strong.'

'Sir?'

'You know what I mean. Tell her I'm rather a good chap. Mention my hidden depths. These things get round. Dwell on the fact that I have a kind heart and was runner-up in the Squash Handicap at the Drones this year. A boost is never wasted, Jeeves.'

'Very good, sir. But—'

'But what?'

'Well, sir—'

'I wish you wouldn't say "Well, sir" in that soupy tone of voice. I have had to speak of this before. The habit is one that is growing upon you. Check it. What's on your mind?'

'I hardly like to take the liberty—'

'Carry on, Jeeves. We are always glad to hear from you, always.'

'What I was about to remark, if you will excuse me, sir, was that I would scarcely have thought Miss Wickham a suitable—'

'Jeeves,' I said coldly, 'if you have anything to say against that lady, it had better not be said in my presence.'

'Very good, sir.'

'Or anywhere else, for that matter. What is your kick against Miss Wickham?'

'Oh, really, sir!'

'Jeeves, I insist. This is a time for plain speaking. You have beefed about Miss Wickham. I wish to know why.'

'It merely crossed my mind, sir, that for a gentleman of your description Miss Wickham is not a suitable mate.'

'What do you mean by a gentleman of my description?'

'Well, sir—'

'Jeeves!'

'I beg your pardon, sir. The expression escaped me inadvertently. I was about to observe that I can only asseverate—'

'Only what?'

'I can only say that, as you have invited my opinion—'

'But I didn't.'

'I was under the impression that you desired to canvass my views on the matter, sir.'

'Oh? Well, let's have them, anyway.'

'Very good, sir. Then briefly, if I may say so, sir, though Miss Wickham is a charming young lady—'

'There, Jeeves, you spoke an imperial quart. What eyes!'

'Yes, sir.'

'What hair!'

'Very true, sir.'

'And what *espièglerie,* if that's the word I want.'

'The exact word, sir.'

'All right, then. Carry on.'

'I grant Miss Wickham the possession of all these desirable qualities, sir. Nevertheless, considered as a matrimonial prospect for a gentleman of your description, I cannot look upon her as suitable. In my opinion Miss Wickham lacks seriousness, sir. She is too volatile and frivolous. To qualify as Miss Wickham's husband, a gentleman would need to possess a commanding personality and considerable strength of character.'

'Exactly!'

'I would always hesitate to recommend as a life's companion a young lady with quite such a vivid shade of red hair. Red hair, sir, in my opinion, is dangerous.'

I eyed the blighter squarely.

'Jeeves,' I said, 'you're talking rot.'

'Very good, sir.'

'Absolute drivel.'

'Very good, sir.'

'Pure mashed potatoes.'

'Very good, sir.'

'Very good, sir – I mean very good Jeeves, that will be all,' I said.

And I drank a modicum of tea, with a good deal of hauteur.

It isn't often that I find myself able to prove Jeeves in the wrong, but by dinnertime that night I was in a position to do so, and I did it without delay.

'Touching on that matter we were touching on, Jeeves,' I said, coming in from the bath and tackling him as he studied the shirt, 'I should be glad if you would give me your careful attention for a moment. I warn you that what I am about to say is going to make you look pretty silly.'

'Indeed, sir?'

'Yes, Jeeves. Pretty dashed silly it's going to make you look. It may lead you to be rather more careful in future about broadcasting these estimates of yours of people's characters. This morning, if I remember rightly, you stated that Miss Wickham was volatile, frivolous and lacking in seriousness. Am I correct?'

'Quite correct, sir.'

'Then what I have to tell you may cause you to alter that opinion. I went for a walk with Miss Wickham this afternoon: and, as we walked, I told her about what young Tuppy Glossop did to me in the swimming-bath at the Drones. She hung upon my words, Jeeves, and was full of sympathy.'

'Indeed, sir?'

'Dripping with it. And that's not all. Almost before I had finished, she was suggesting the ripest, fruitiest, brainiest scheme for bringing young Tuppy's grey hairs in sorrow to the grave that anyone could possibly imagine.'

'That is very gratifying, sir.'

'Gratifying is the word. It appears that at the girls' school where Miss Wickham was educated, Jeeves, it used to become necessary from time to time for the right-thinking element of the community to slip it across certain of the baser sort. Do you know what they did, Jeeves?'

'No, sir.'

'They took a long stick, Jeeves, and – follow me closely here – they tied a darning-needle to the end of it. Then at dead of night, it appears, they sneaked privily into the party of the second part's cubicle and shoved the needle through the bed-clothes and punctured her hot-water bottle. Girls are much subtler in these matters than boys, Jeeves. At my old school one would occasionally heave a jug of water over another bloke during the night watches, but we never thought of effecting the same result in this particularly neat and scientific manner. Well, Jeeves, that was the scheme which Miss Wickham suggested I should work on young Tuppy, and that is the girl you call frivolous and lacking in seriousness. Any girl who can think up a wheeze like that is my idea of a helpmeet. I shall be glad, Jeeves, if by the time I come to bed to-night you have waiting for me in this room a stout stick with a good sharp darning needle attached.'

'Well, sir—'

I raised my hand.

'Jeeves,' I said. 'Not another word. Stick, one, and needle, darning, good, sharp, one, without fail in this room at eleven-thirty to-night.'

'Very good, sir.'

'Have you any idea where young Tuppy sleeps?'

'I could ascertain, sir.'

'Do so, Jeeves.'

In a few minutes he was back with the necessary informash.

'Mr Glossop is established in the Moat Room, sir.'

'Where's that?'

'The second door on the floor below this, sir.'

'Right-ho, Jeeves. Are the studs in my shirt?'

'Yes, sir.'

'And the links also?'

'Yes, sir.'

'Then push me into it.'

The more I thought about this enterprise which a sense of duty and good citizenship had thrust upon me, the better it seemed to me. I am not a vindictive man, but I felt, as anybody would have felt in my place, that if fellows like young Tuppy are allowed to get away with it the whole fabric of Society and Civilization must inevitably crumble. The task to which I had set myself was one that involved hardship and discomfort, for it meant sitting up till well into the small hours and then padding down a cold corridor, but I did not shrink from it. After all, there is a lot to be said for family tradition. We Woosters did our bit in the Crusades.

It being Christmas Eve, there was, as I had foreseen, a good deal of revelry and what not. First, the village choir surged round and sang carols outside the front door, and then somebody suggested a dance, and after that we hung around chatting of this and that, so that it wasn't till past one that I got to my room. Allowing for everything, it didn't seem that it was going to be safe to start my little expedition till half-past two at the earliest: and I'm bound to say that it was only the utmost resolution that kept me from snuggling into the sheets and calling it a day. I'm not much of a lad now for late hours.

However, by half-past two everything appeared to be quiet. I shook off the mists of sleep, grabbed the good old stick-and-needle and toddled off along the corridor. And presently, pausing outside the Moat Room, I turned the handle, found the door wasn't locked, and went in.

I suppose a burglar — I mean a real professional who works at the job six nights a week all the year round — gets so that finding himself standing in the dark in somebody else's bedroom means absolutely nothing to him. But for a bird like me, who has had no previous experience, there's a lot to be said in favour of washing the whole thing out and closing the door gently and popping back to bed again. It was only by summoning up all the old bull-dog courage of the Woosters, and reminding myself that, if I let this opportunity slip another might never occur, that I managed to stick out what you might call the initial minute of the binge. Then the weakness passed, and Bertram was himself again.

At first when I beetled in, the room had seemed as black as a coal-cellar: but after a bit things began to lighten. The curtains weren't quite drawn over the window and I could see a trifle of the scenery here and there. The bed was opposite the window, with the head against the wall and the end where the feet were jutting out towards where I stood, thus rendering it possible after one had sown the seed, so to speak, to make a quick getaway. There only remained now the rather tricky problem of locating the old hot-water bottle. I mean to say, the one thing you can't do if you want to carry a job like this through with secrecy and dispatch is to stand at the end of a fellow's bed, jabbing the blankets at random with a darning-needle. Before proceeding to anything in the nature of definite steps, it is imperative that you locate the bot.

I was a good deal cheered at this juncture to hear a fruity snore from the direction of the pillows. Reason told me that a bloke who could snore like that wasn't going to be awakened by a trifle. I edged forward and ran a hand in a gingerly sort of way over the coverlet. A moment later I had found the bulge.

I steered the good old darning-needle on to it, gripped the stick, and shoved. Then, pulling out the weapon, I sidled towards the door, and in another moment would have been outside, buzzing for home and the good night's rest, when suddenly there was a crash that sent my spine shooting up through the top of my head and the contents of the bed sat up like a jack-in-the-box and said:

'Who's that?'

It just shows how your most careful strategic moves can be the very ones that dish your campaign. In order to facilitate the orderly retreat according to plan I had left the door open, and the beastly thing had slammed like a bomb.

But I wasn't giving much thought to the causes of the explosion, having other things to occupy my mind. What was disturbing me was the discovery that, whoever else the bloke in the bed might be, he was not young Tuppy. Tuppy has one of those high, squeaky voices that sound like the tenor of the village choir failing to hit a high note. This one was something in between the last Trump and a tiger calling for breakfast after being on a diet for a day or two. It was the sort of nasty, rasping voice you hear shouting 'Fore!' when you're one of a slow foursome on the links and are holding up a couple of retired colonels. Among the qualities it lacked were kindliness, suavity and that sort of dove-like cooing note which makes a fellow feel he has found a friend.

I did not linger. Getting swiftly off the mark, I dived for the door-handle and was off and away, banging the door behind me. I may be a chump in many ways, as my Aunt Agatha will freely attest, but I know when and when not to be among those present.

And I was just about to do the stretch of corridor leading to the stairs in a split second under the record time for the course, when something brought me up with a sudden jerk. One moment, I was all dash and fire and speed; the next, an irresistible force had checked me in my stride and was holding me straining at the leash, as it were.

You know, sometimes it seems to me as if Fate were going out of its way to such an extent to snooter you that you wonder if it's worthwhile continuing to struggle. The night being a trifle chillier than the dickens, I had donned for this expedition a dressing-gown. It was the tail of this infernal garment that had caught in the door and pipped me at the eleventh hour.

The next moment the door had opened, light was streaming

through it, and the bloke with the voice had grabbed me by the arm.

It was Sir Roderick Glossop.

The next thing that happened was a bit of a lull in the proceedings. For about three and a quarter seconds or possibly more we just stood there, drinking each other in, so to speak, the old boy still attached with a limpet-like grip to my elbow. If I hadn't been in a dressing-gown and he in pink pyjamas with a blue stripe, and if he hadn't been glaring quite so much as if he were shortly going to commit a murder, the tableau would have looked rather like one of those advertisements you see in the magazines, where the experienced elder is patting the young man's arm, and saying to him, 'My boy, if you subscribe to the Mutt-Jeff Correspondence School of Oswego, Kan., as I did, you may some day, like me, become Third Assistant Vice-President of the Schenectady Consolidated Nail-File and Eyebrow Tweezer Corporation.'

'You!' said Sir Roderick finally. And in this connection I want to state that it's all rot to say you can't hiss a word that hasn't an 's' in it. The way he pushed out that 'You!' sounded like an angry cobra, and I am betraying no secrets when I mention that it did me no good whatsoever.

By rights, I suppose, at this point I ought to have said something. The best I could manage, however, was a faint, soft bleating sound. Even on ordinary social occasions, when meeting this bloke as man to man and with a clear conscience, I could never be completely at my ease: and now those eyebrows seemed to pierce me like a knife.

'Come in here,' he said, lugging me into the room. 'We don't want to wake the whole house. Now,' he said, depositing me on the carpet and closing the door and doing a bit of eyebrow work, 'kindly inform me what is this latest manifestation of insanity?'

It seemed to me that a light and cheery laugh might help the thing along. So I had a pop at one.

'Don't gibber!' said my genial host. And I'm bound to admit that the light and cheery hadn't come out quite as I'd intended.

I pulled myself together with a strong effort.

'Awfully sorry about all this,' I said in a hearty sort of voice. 'The fact is, I thought you were Tuppy.'

'Kindly refrain from inflicting your idiotic slang on me. What do you mean by the adjective "tuppy"?'

'It isn't so much an adjective, don't you know. More of a noun, I should think, if you examine it squarely. What I mean to say is, I thought you were your nephew.'

'You thought I was my nephew? Why should I be my nephew?'

'What I'm driving at is, I thought this was his room.'

'My nephew and I changed rooms. I have a great dislike for sleeping on an upper floor. I am nervous about fire.'

For the first time since this interview had started, I braced up a trifle. The injustice of the whole thing stirred me to such an extent that for a moment I lost that sense of being a toad under the harrow which had been cramping my style up till now. I even went so far as to eye this pink-pyjamaed poltroon with a good deal of contempt and loathing. Just because he had this craven fear of fire and this selfish preference for letting Tuppy be cooked instead of himself should the emergency occur, my nicely-reasoned plans had gone up the spout. I gave him a look, and I think I may even have snorted a bit.

'I should have thought that your man-servant would have informed you,' said Sir Roderick, 'that we contemplated making this change. I met him shortly before luncheon and told him to tell you.'

I reeled. Yes, it is not too much to say that I reeled. This extraordinary statement had taken me amidships without any preparation, and it staggered me. That Jeeves had been aware all along that this old crumb would be the occupant of the bed which I was proposing to prod with darning-needles and had let me rush upon my doom without a word of warning was almost beyond belief. You might say I was aghast. Yes, practically aghast.

'You told Jeeves that you were going to sleep in this room?' I gasped.

'I did. I was aware that you and my nephew were on terms of intimacy, and I wished to spare myself the possibility of a visit from you. I confess that it never occurred to me that such a visit was to be anticipated at three o'clock in the morning. What the devil do you mean,' he barked, suddenly hotting up, 'by prowling about the house at this hour? And what is that thing in your hand?'

I looked down, and found that I was still grasping the stick. I give you my honest word that, what with the maelstrom of emotions into which his revelation about Jeeves had cast me, the discovery came as an absolute surprise.

'This?' I said. 'Oh, yes.'

'What do you mean, "Oh, yes"? What is it?'

'Well, it's a long story—'

'We have the night before us.'

'It's this way. I will ask you to picture me some weeks ago, perfectly peaceful and inoffensive, after dinner at the Drones, smoking a thoughtful cigarette and—'

I broke off. The man wasn't listening. He was goggling in a rapt sort of way at the end of the bed, from which there had now begun to drip on to the carpet a series of drops.

'Good heavens!'

'—thoughtful cigarette and chatting pleasantly of this and that—'

I broke off again. He had lifted the sheets and was gazing at the corpse of the hot-water bottle.

'Did you do this?' he said in a low, strangled sort of voice.

'Er – yes. As a matter of fact, yes. I was just going to tell you—'

'And your aunt tried to persuade me that you were not insane!'

'I'm not. Absolutely not. If you'll just let me explain.'

'I will do nothing of the kind.'

'It all began—'

'Silence!'

'Right-ho.'

He did some deep-breathing exercises through the nose.

'My bed is drenched!'

'The way it all began—'

'Be quiet!' He heaved somewhat for awhile. 'You wretched, miserable idiot,' he said, 'kindly inform me which bedroom you are supposed to be occupying?'

'It's on the floor above. The Clock Room.'

'Thank you. I will find it.'

He gave me the eyebrow.

'I propose,' he said, 'to pass the remainder of the night in your room, where, I presume, there is a bed in a condition to be slept in. You may bestow yourself as comfortably as you can here. I will wish you good-night.'

He buzzed off, leaving me flat.

Well, we Woosters are old campaigners. We can take the rough with the smooth. But to say that I liked the prospect now before me would be paltering with the truth. One glance at the bed told me that any idea of sleeping there was out. A gold-fish could have done it, but not Bertram. After a bit of a look round, I decided that the best chance of getting a sort of night's rest was to doss as well as I could in the arm-chair. I pinched a couple of pillows off the bed, shoved the hearth-rug over my knees, and sat down and started counting sheep.

But it wasn't any good. The old lemon was sizzling much too much to admit of anything in the nature of slumber. This hideous revelation of the blackness of Jeeves's treachery kept coming back to me every time I nearly succeeded in dropping off: and, what's more, it seemed to get colder and colder as the long night wore on. I was just wondering if I would ever get to sleep again in this world when a voice at my elbow said 'Good-morning, sir,' and I sat up with a jerk.

I could have sworn I hadn't so much as dozed off for even a minute, but apparently I had. For the curtains were drawn back and daylight was coming in through the window and there was Jeeves standing beside me with a cup of tea on a tray.

'Merry Christmas, sir!'

I reached out a feeble hand for the restoring brew. I swallowed a mouthful or two, and felt a little better. I was aching in every limb and the dome felt like lead, but I was now able to think with a certain amount of clearness, and I fixed the man with a stony eye and prepared to let him have it.

'You think so, do you?' I said. 'Much, let me tell you, depends on what you mean by the adjective "merry". If, moreover, you suppose that it is going to be merry for you, correct that impression. Jeeves,' I said, taking another half-oz of tea and speaking in a cold, measured voice, 'I wish to ask you one question. Did you or did you not know that Sir Roderick Glossop was sleeping in this room last night?'

'Yes, sir.'

'You admit it!'

'Yes, sir.'

'And you didn't tell me!'

'No, sir. I thought it would be more judicious not to do so.'

'Jeeves——'

'If you will allow me to explain, sir.'

'Explain!'

'I was aware that my silence might lead to something in the nature of an embarrassing contretemps, sir——'

'You thought that, did you?'

'Yes, sir.'

'You were a good guesser,' I said, sucking down further Bohea.

'But it seemed to me, sir, that whatever might occur was all for the best.'

I would have put in a crisp word or two here, but he carried on without giving me the opp.

'I thought that possibly, on reflection, sir, your views being what they are, you would prefer your relations with Sir Roderick Glossop and his family to be distant rather than cordial.'

'My views? What do you mean, my views?'

'As regards a matrimonial alliance with Miss Honoria Glossop, sir.'

Something like an electric shock seemed to zip through me. The man had opened up a new line of thought. I suddenly saw what he was driving at, and realized all in a flash that I had been wronging this faithful fellow. All the while I supposed he had been landing me in the soup, he had really been steering me away from it. It was like those stories one used to read as a kid about the traveller going along on a dark night and his dog grabs him by the leg of his trousers and he says 'Down, sir! What are you doing, Rover?' and the dog hangs on and he gets rather hot under the collar and curses a bit but the dog won't let him go and then suddenly the moon shines through the clouds and he finds he's been standing on the edge of a precipice and one more step would have— well, anyway, you get the idea: and what I'm driving at is that much the same sort of thing seemed to have been happening now.

It's perfectly amazing how a fellow will let himself get off his guard and ignore the perils which surround him. I give you my honest word, it had never struck me till this moment that my Aunt Agatha had been scheming to get me in right with Sir Roderick so that I should eventually be received back into the fold, if you see what I mean, and subsequently pushed off on Honoria.

'My God, Jeeves!' I said, paling.

'Precisely, sir.'

'You think there was a risk?'

'I do, sir. A very grave risk.'

A disturbing thought struck me.

'But, Jeeves, on calm reflection won't Sir Roderick have gathered by now that my objective was young Tuppy and that puncturing his hot-water bottle was just one of those things that occur when the Yule-tide spirit is abroad – one of those things that have to be overlooked and taken with the indulgent smile and the fatherly shake of the head? I mean to say, Young Blood and all that sort of thing? What I mean is he'll realize that I wasn't trying to snooter him, and then all the good work will have been wasted.'

'No, sir. I fancy not. That might possibly have been Sir Roderick's mental reaction, had it not been for the second incident.'

'The second incident?'

'During the night, sir, while Sir Roderick was occupying your bed, somebody entered the room, pierced his hot-water bottle with some sharp instrument, and vanished in the darkness.'

I could make nothing of this.

'What! Do you think I walked in my sleep?'

'No, sir. It was young Mr Glossop who did it. I encountered him this morning, sir, shortly before I came here. He was in cheerful spirits and enquired of me how you were feeling about the incident. Not being aware that his victim had been Sir Roderick.'

'But, Jeeves, what an amazing coincidence!'

'Sir?'

'Why, young Tuppy getting exactly the same idea as I did. Or, rather, as Miss Wickham did. You can't say that's not rummy. A miracle, I call it.'

'Not altogether, sir. It appears that he received the suggestion from the young lady.'

'From Miss Wickham?'

'Yes, sir.'

'You mean to say that, after she had put me up to the scheme of puncturing Tuppy's hot-water bottle, she went away and tipped Tuppy off to puncturing mine?'

'Precisely, sir. She is a young lady with a keen sense of humour, sir.'

I sat there, you might say stunned. When I thought how near I had come to offering the heart and hand to a girl capable of double-crossing a strong man's honest love like that, I shivered.

'Are you cold, sir?'

'No, Jeeves. Just shuddering.'

'The occurrence, if I may take the liberty of saying so, sir, will perhaps lend colour to the view which I put forward yesterday that Miss Wickham, though in many respects a charming young lady—'

I raised the hand.

'Say no more, Jeeves,' I replied. 'Love is dead.'

'Very good, sir.'

I brooded for a while.

'You've seen Sir Roderick this morning, then?'

'Yes, sir.'

'How did he seem?'

'A trifle feverish, sir.'

'Feverish?'

'A little emotional, sir. He expressed a strong desire to meet you, sir.'

'What would you advise?'

'If you were to slip out by the back entrance as soon as you are dressed, sir, it would be possible for you to make your way across the field without being observed and reach the village, where you could hire an automobile to take you to London. I could bring on your effects later in your own car.'

'But London, Jeeves? Is any man safe? My Aunt Agatha is in London.'

'Yes, sir.'

'Well, then?'

He regarded me for a moment with a fathomless eye.

'I think the best plan, sir, would be for you to leave England, which is not pleasant at this time of the year, for some little while. I would not take the liberty of dictating your movements, sir, but as you already have accommodation engaged on the Blue Train for Monte Carlo for the day after to-morrow—'

'But you cancelled the booking?'

'No, sir.'

'I thought you had.'

'No, sir.'

'I told you to.'

'Yes, sir. It was remiss of me, but the matter slipped my mind.'

'Oh?'

'Yes, sir.'

'All right, Jeeves. Monte Carlo ho, then.'

'Very good, sir.'

'It's lucky, as things have turned out, that you forgot to cancel that booking.'

'Very fortunate indeed, sir. If you will wait here, sir, I will return to your room and procure a suit of clothes.'

One Touch of Nature

The feelings of Mr J. Wilmot Birdsey, as he stood wedged in the crowd that moved inch by inch towards the gates of the Chelsea Football Ground, rather resembled those of a starving man who has just been given a meal but realizes that he is not likely to get another for many days. He was full and happy. He bubbled over with the joy of living and a warm affection for his fellow-man. At the back of his mind there lurked the black shadow of future privations, but for the moment he did not allow it to disturb him. On this maddest, merriest day of all the glad New Year he was content to revel in the present and allow the future to take care of itself.

Mr Birdsey had been doing something which he had not done since he left New York five years ago. He had been watching a game of baseball.

New York lost a great baseball fan when Hugo Percy de Wynter Framlinghame, sixth Earl of Carricksteed, married

Mae Elinor, only daughter of Mr and Mrs J. Wilmot Birdsey of East Seventy-Third Street; for scarcely had that internationally important event taken place when Mrs Birdsey, announcing that for the future the home would be in England as near as possible to dear Mae and dear Hugo, scooped J. Wilmot out of his comfortable morris chair as if he had been a clam, corked him up in a swift taxi-cab, and decanted him into a Deck B stateroom on the 'Olympic'. And there he was, an exile.

Mr Birdsey submitted to the worst bit of kidnapping since the days of the old press gang with that delightful amiability which made him so popular among his fellows and such a cypher in his home. At an early date in his married life his position had been clearly defined beyond possibility of mistake. It was his business to make money, and, when called upon, to jump through hoops and sham dead at the bidding of his wife and daughter Mae. These duties he had been performing conscientiously for a matter of twenty years.

It was only occasionally that his humble rôle jarred upon him, for he loved his wife and idolized his daughter. The international alliance had been one of these occasions. He had no objection to Hugo Percy, sixth Earl of Carricksteed. The crushing blow had been the sentence of exile. He loved baseball with a love passing the love of women, and the prospect of never seeing a game again in his life appalled him.

And then, one morning, like a voice from another world, had come the news that the White Sox and the Giants were to give an exhibition in London at the Chelsea Football Ground.

He had counted the days like a child before Christmas.

There had been obstacles to overcome before he could attend the game, but he had overcome them, and had been seated in the front row when the two teams lined up before King George.

And now he was moving slowly from the ground with the rest of the spectators. Fate had been very good to him. It had given him a great game, even unto two home-runs. But its crowning benevolence had been to allot the seats on either side of him to two men of his own mettle, two god-like beings who knew every move on the board, and howled like wolves when they did not see eye to eye with the umpire. Long before the ninth innings he was feeling towards them the affection of a shipwrecked mariner who meets a couple of boyhood's chums on a desert island.

As he shouldered his way towards the gate he was aware of these two men, one on either side of him. He looked at them fondly, trying to make up his mind which of them he liked best. It was sad to think that they must soon go out of his life again for ever.

He came to a sudden resolution. He would postpone the parting. He would ask them to dinner. Over the best that the Savoy Hotel could provide they would fight the afternoon's battle over again. He did not know who they were or anything about them, but what did that matter? They were brother-fans. That was enough for him.

The man on his right was young, clean-shaven, and of a

somewhat vulturine cast of countenance. His face was cold and impassive now, almost forbiddingly so; but only half an hour before it had been a battlefield of conflicting emotions, and his hat still showed the dent where he had banged it against the edge of his seat on the occasion of Mr Daly's home-run. A worthy guest!

The man on Mr Birdsey's left belonged to another species of fan. Though there had been times during the game when he had howled, for the most part he had watched in silence so hungrily tense that a less experienced observer than Mr Birdsey might have attributed his immobility to boredom. But one glance at his set jaw and gleaming eyes had told him that here also was a man and a brother.

This man's eyes were still gleaming, and under their curiously deep tan his bearded cheeks were pale. He was staring straight in front of him with an unseeing gaze.

Mr Birdsey tapped the young man on the shoulder.

'Some game!' he said.

The young man looked at him and smiled.

'You bet,' he said.

'I haven't seen a ball-game in five years.'

'The last one I saw was two years ago next June.'

'Come and have some dinner at my hotel and talk it over,' said Mr Birdsey impulsively.

'Sure!' said the young man.

Mr Birdsey turned and tapped the shoulder of the man on his left.

The result was a little unexpected. The man gave a start that was almost a leap, and the pallor of his face became a sickly white. His eyes, as he swung round, met Mr Birdsey's for an instant before they dropped, and there was panic fear in them. His breath whistled softly through clenched teeth.

Mr Birdsey was taken aback. The cordiality of the clean-shaven young man had not prepared him for the possibility of such a reception. He felt chilled. He was on the point of apologizing with some murmur about a mistake, when the man reassured him by smiling. It was rather a painful smile, but it was enough for Mr Birdsey. This man might be of a nervous temperament, but his heart was in the right place.

He, too, smiled. He was a small, stout, red-faced little man, and he possessed a smile that rarely failed to set strangers at their ease. Many strenuous years on the New York Stock Exchange had not destroyed a certain childlike amiability in Mr Birdsey, and it shone out when he smiled at you.

'I'm afraid I startled you,' he said soothingly. 'I wanted to ask you if you would let a perfect stranger, who also happens to be an exile, offer you dinner tonight.'

The man winced. 'Exile?'

'An exiled fan. Don't you feel that the Polo Grounds are a good long way away? This gentleman is joining me. I have a suite at the Savoy Hotel, and I thought we might all have a quiet little dinner there and talk about the game. I haven't seen a ball-game in five years.'

'Nor have I.'

'Then you must come. You really must. We fans ought to stick to one another in a strange land. Do come.'

'Thank you,' said the bearded man; 'I will.'

When three men, all strangers, sit down to dinner together, conversation, even if they happen to have a mutual passion for baseball, is apt to be for awhile a little difficult. The first fine frenzy in which Mr Birdsey had issued his invitations had begun to ebb by the time the soup was served, and he was conscious of a feeling of embarrassment.

There was some subtle hitch in the orderly progress of affairs. He sensed it in the air. Both of his guests were disposed to silence, and the clean-shaven young man had developed a trick of staring at the man with the beard, which was obviously distressing that sensitive person.

'Wine,' murmured Mr Birdsey to the waiter. 'Wine, wine!'

He spoke with the earnestness of a general calling up his reserves for the grand attack. The success of this little dinner mattered enormously to him. There were circumstances which were going to make it an oasis in his life. He wanted it to be an occasion to which, in grey days to come, he could look back and be consoled. He could not let it be a failure.

He was about to speak when the young man anticipated him. Leaning forward, he addressed the bearded man, who was crumbling bread with an absent look in his eyes.

'Surely we have met before?' he said. 'I'm sure I remember your face.'

The effect of these words on the other was as curious as the effect of Mr Birdsey's tap on the shoulder had been. He looked up like a hunted animal.

He shook his head without speaking.

'Curious,' said the young man. 'I could have sworn to it, and I am positive that it was somewhere in New York. Do you come from New York?'

'Yes.'

'It seems to me,' said Mr Birdsey, 'that we ought to introduce ourselves. Funny it didn't strike any of us before. My name is Birdsey, J. Wilmot Birdsey. I come from New York.'

'My name is Waterall,' said the young man. 'I come from New York.'

The bearded man hesitated.

'My name is Johnson. I – used to live in New York.'

'Where do you live now, Mr Johnson?' asked Waterall.

The bearded man hesitated again. 'Algiers,' he said.

Mr Birdsey was inspired to help matters along with small-talk.

'Algiers,' he said. 'I have never been there, but I understand that it is quite a place. Are you in business there, Mr Johnson?'

'I live there for my health.'

'Have you been there some time?' inquired Waterall.

'Five years.'

'Then it must have been in New York that I saw you, for I have never been to Algiers, and I'm certain I have seen you somewhere. I'm afraid you will think me a bore for sticking to the point like this, but the fact is, the one thing I pride myself on is my memory for faces. It's a hobby of mine. If I think I remember a face, and can't place it, I worry myself into insomnia. It's partly sheer vanity, and partly because in my job a good memory for faces is a mighty fine asset. It has helped me a hundred times.'

Mr Birdsey was an intelligent man, and he could see that Waterall's table-talk was for some reason getting upon Johnson's nerves. Like a good host, he endeavoured to cut in and make things smooth.

'I've heard great accounts of Algiers,' he said helpfully. 'A friend of mine was there in his yacht last year. It must be a delightful spot.'

'It's a hell on earth,' snapped Johnson, and slew the conversation on the spot.

Through a grim silence an angel in human form fluttered in – a waiter bearing a bottle. The pop of the cork was more than music to Mr Birdsey's ears. It was the booming of the guns of the relieving army.

The first glass, as first glasses will, thawed the bearded man, to the extent of inducing him to try and pick up the fragments of the conversation which he had shattered.

'I am afraid you will have thought me abrupt, Mr Birdsey,' he said awkwardly; 'but then you haven't lived in Algiers for five years, and I have.'

Mr Birdsey chirruped sympathetically.

'I liked it at first. It looked mighty good to me. But five

years of it, and nothing else to look forward to till you
die . . .'

He stopped, and emptied his glass. Mr Birdsey was still perturbed. True, conversation was proceeding in a sort of way, but
it had taken a distinctly gloomy turn. Slightly flushed with the
excellent champagne which he had selected for this important
dinner, he endeavoured to lighten it.

'I wonder,' he said, 'which of us three fans had the greatest
difficulty in getting to the bleachers today. I guess none of us
found it too easy.'

The young man shook his head.

'Don't count on me to contribute a romantic story to this
Arabian Night's Entertainment. My difficulty would have
been to stop away. My name's Waterall, and I'm the London
correspondent of the *New York Chronicle*. I had to be there this
afternoon in the way of business.'

Mr Birdsey giggled self-consciously, but not without a
certain impish pride.

'The laugh will be on me when you hear my confession.
My daughter married an English earl, and my wife brought
me over here to mix with his crowd. There was a big dinner-
party tonight, at which the whole gang were to be present, and
it was as much as my life was worth to side-step it. But when
you get the Giants and the White Sox playing ball within fifty
miles of you – Well, I packed a grip and sneaked out the back
way, and got to the station and caught the fast train to London.
And what is going on back there at this moment I don't like

to think. About now,' said Mr Birdsey, looking at his watch, 'I guess they'll be pronging the hors d'œuvres and gazing at the empty chair. It was a shame to do it, but, for the love of Mike, what else could I have done?'

He looked at the bearded man.

'Did you have any adventures, Mr Johnson?'

'No. I – I just came.'

The young man Waterall leaned forward. His manner was quiet, but his eyes were glittering.

'Wasn't that enough of an adventure for you?' he said.

Their eyes met across the table. Seated between them, Mr Birdsey looked from one to the other, vaguely disturbed. Something was happening, a drama was going on, and he had not the key to it.

Johnson's face was pale, and the tablecloth crumpled into a crooked ridge under his fingers, but his voice was steady as he replied:

'I don't understand.'

'Will you understand if I give you your right name, Mr Benyon?'

'What's all this?' said Mr Birdsey feebly.

Waterall turned to him, the vulturine cast of his face more noticeable than ever. Mr Birdsey was conscious of a sudden distaste for this young man.

'It's quite simple, Mr Birdsey. If you have not been enter-taining angels unawares, you have at least been giving a dinner to a celebrity. I told you I was sure I had seen this gentleman before. I have just remembered where, and when. This is Mr John Benyon, and I last saw him five years ago when I was a reporter in New York, and covered his trial.'

'His trial?'

'He robbed the New Asiatic Bank of a hundred thousand dollars, jumped his bail, and was never heard of again.'

'For the love of Mike!'

Mr Birdsey stared at his guest with eyes that grew momently wider. He was amazed to find that deep down in him there was an unmistakable feeling of elation. He had made up his mind, when he left home that morning, that this was to be a day of days. Well, nobody could call this an anti-climax.

'So that's why you have been living in Algiers?'

Benyon did not reply. Outside, the Strand traffic sent a faint murmur into the warm, comfortable room.

Waterall spoke. 'What on earth induced you, Benyon, to run the risk of coming to London, where every second man you meet is a New Yorker, I can't understand. The chances were two to one that you would be recognized. You made a pretty big splash with that little affair of yours five years ago.'

Benyon raised his head. His hands were trembling.

'I'll tell you,' he said with a kind of savage force, which hurt kindly little Mr Birdsey like a blow. 'It was because I was a dead man, and saw a chance of coming to life for a day; because I was sick of the damned tomb I've been living in for five centuries; because I've been aching for New York ever since I've left it – and here was a chance of being back there for a few hours. I knew there was a risk. I took a chance on it. Well?'

Mr Birdsey's heart was almost too full for words. He had found him at last, the Super-Fan, the man who would go through fire and water for a sight of a game of baseball. Till that moment he had been regarding himself as the nearest approach to that dizzy eminence. He had braved great perils to see this game. Even in this moment his mind would not wholly detach itself from speculation as to what his wife would say to him when he slunk back into the fold. But what had he risked compared with this man Benyon? Mr Birdsey glowed. He could not restrain his sympathy and admiration. True, the man was a criminal. He had robbed a bank of a hundred thousand dollars. But, after all, what was that? They would probably have wasted the money in foolishness. And, anyway, a bank which couldn't take care of its money deserved to lose it.

Mr Birdsey felt almost a righteous glow of indignation against the New Asiatic Bank.

He broke the silence which had followed Benyon's words with a peculiarly immoral remark:

'Well, it's lucky it's only us that's recognized you,' he said.

Waterall stared. 'Are you proposing that we should hush this thing up, Mr Birdsey?' he said coldly.

'Oh, well—'

Waterall rose and went to the telephone.

'What are you going to do?'

'Call up Scotland Yard, of course. What did you think?'

Undoubtedly the young man was doing his duty as a citizen, yet it is to be recorded that Mr Birdsey eyed him with unmixed horror.

'You can't! You mustn't!' he cried.

'I certainly shall.'

'But – but – this fellow came all that way to see the ball-game.'

It seemed incredible to Mr Birdsey that this aspect of the affair should not be the one to strike everybody to the exclusion of all other aspects.

'You can't give him up. It's too raw.'

'He's a convicted criminal.'

'He's a fan. Why, say, he's *the* fan.'

Waterall shrugged his shoulders, and walked to the telephone. Benyon spoke.

'One moment.'

Waterall turned, and found himself looking into the muzzle of a small pistol. He laughed.

'I expected that. Wave it about all you want.'

Benyon rested his shaking hand on the edge of the table.

'I'll shoot if you move.'

'You won't. You haven't the nerve. There's nothing to you. You're just a cheap crook, and that's all. You wouldn't find the nerve to pull that trigger in a million years.'

He took off the receiver.

'Give me Scotland Yard,' he said.

He had turned his back to Benyon. Benyon sat motionless.

Then, with a thud, the pistol fell to the ground. The next moment Benyon had broken down. His face was buried in his arms, and he was a wreck of a man, sobbing like a hurt child.

Mr Birdsey was profoundly distressed. He sat tingling and helpless. This was a nightmare.

Waterall's level voice spoke at the telephone.

'Is this Scotland Yard? I am Waterall, of the *New York Chronicle*. Is Inspector Jarvis there? Ask him to come to the 'phone ... Is that you, Jarvis? This is Waterall. I'm speaking from the Savoy, Mr Birdsey's rooms. Birdsey. Listen, Jarvis. There's a man here that's wanted by the American police. Send someone here and get him. Benyon. Robbed the New Asiatic Bank in New York. Yes, you've a warrant out for him, five years old ... All right.'

He hung up the receiver. Benyon sprang to his feet. He stood, shaking, a pitiable sight. Mr Birdsey had risen with him. They stood looking at Waterall.

'You – skunk!' said Mr Birdsey.

'I'm an American citizen,' said Waterall, 'and I happen to have some idea of a citizen's duties. What is more, I'm a newspaper man, and I have some idea of my duty to my paper. Call me what you like, you won't alter that.'

Mr Birdsey snorted.

'You're suffering from ingrowing sentimentality, Mr Birdsey. That's what's the matter with you. Just because this man has escaped justice for five years, you think he ought to be considered quit of the whole thing.'

'But – but—'

'I don't.'

He took out his cigarette case. He was feeling a great deal more strung-up and nervous than he would have had the others suspect. He had had a moment of very swift thinking before he had decided to treat that ugly little pistol in a spirit of contempt. Its production had given him a decided shock, and now he was suffering from reaction. As a consequence, because his nerves were strained, he lit his cigarette very languidly, very carefully, and with an offensive superiority which was to Mr Birdsey the last straw.

These things are matters of an instant. Only an infinitesimal fraction of time elapsed between the spectacle of Mr Birdsey, indignant but inactive, and Mr Birdsey berserk, seeing red, frankly and undisguisedly running amok. The transformation took place in the space of time required for the lighting of a match.

Even as the match gave out its flame, Mr Birdsey sprang.

Aeons before, when the young blood ran swiftly in his veins and life was all before him, Mr Birdsey had played football. Once a footballer, always a potential footballer, even to the grave. Time had removed the flying tackle as a factor in Mr Birdsey's life. Wrath brought it back. He dived at young Mr Waterall's neatly trousered legs as he had dived at other legs, less neatly trousered, thirty years ago. They crashed to the floor together; and with the crash came Mr Birdsey's shout:

'Run! Run, you fool! Run!'

And, even as he clung to his man, breathless, bruised,

feeling as if all the world had dissolved in one vast explosion of dynamite, the door opened, banged to, and feet fled down the passage.

Mr Birdsey disentangled himself, and rose painfully. The shock had brought him to himself. He was no longer berserk. He was a middle-aged gentleman of high respectability who had been behaving in a very peculiar way.

Waterall, flushed and dishevelled, glared at him speechlessly. He gulped. 'Are you crazy?'

Mr Birdsey tested gingerly the mechanism of a leg which lay under suspicion of being broken. Relieved, he put his foot to the ground again. He shook his head at Waterall. He was slightly crumpled, but he achieved a manner of dignified reproof.

'You shouldn't have done it, young man. It was raw work. Oh, yes, I know all about that duty-of-a-citizen stuff. It doesn't go. There are exceptions to every rule, and this was one of them. When a man risks his liberty to come and root at a ball-game, you've got to hand it to him. He isn't a crook. He's a fan. And we exiled fans have got to stick together.'

Waterall was quivering with fury, disappointment, and the peculiar unpleasantness of being treated by an elderly gentleman like a sack of coals. He stammered with rage.

'You damned old fool, do you realize what you've done? The police will be here in another minute.'

'Let them come.'

'But what am I to say to them? What explanation can I give?

What story can I tell them? Can't you see what a hole you've put me in?'

Something seemed to click inside Mr Birdsey's soul. It was the berserk mood vanishing and reason leaping back on to her throne. He was able now to think calmly, and what he thought about filled him with a sudden gloom.

'Young man,' he said, 'don't worry yourself. You've got a cinch. You've only got to hand a story to the police. Any old tale will do for them. I'm the man with the really difficult job – I've got to square myself with my wife!'

The Ordeal of Young Tuppy

'What-ho, Jeeves!' I said, entering the room where he waded knee-deep in suitcases and shirts and winter suitings, like a sea-beast among rocks. 'Packing?'

'Yes, sir,' replied the honest fellow, for there are no secrets between us.

'Pack on!' I said approvingly. 'Pack, Jeeves, pack with care. Pack in the presence of the passenjare.' And I rather fancy I added the words 'Tra-la!' for I was in merry mood.

Every year, starting about the middle of November, there is a good deal of anxiety and apprehension among owners of the better class of country-house throughout England as to who will get Bertram Wooster's patronage for the Christmas holidays. It may be one or it may be another. As my Aunt Dahlia says, you never know where the blow will fall.

This year, however, I had decided early. It couldn't have been later than Nov. 10 when a sigh of relief went up from a dozen stately homes as it became known that the short straw had been drawn by Sir Reginald Witherspoon, Bart, of Bleaching Court, Upper Bleaching, Hants.

In coming to the decision to give this Witherspoon my custom, I had been actuated by several reasons, not counting the fact that, having married Aunt Dahlia's husband's younger sister Katherine, he is by way of being a sort of uncle of mine. In the first place, the Bart does one extraordinarily well, both browsing and sluicing being above criticism. Then, again, his stables always contain something worth riding, which is a consideration. And, thirdly, there is no danger of getting lugged into a party of amateur Waits and having to tramp the countryside in the rain, singing, 'When Shepherds Watched Their Flocks by Night'. Or for the matter of that, 'Noel! Noel!'

All these things counted with me, but what really drew me to Bleaching Court like a magnet was the knowledge that young Tuppy Glossop would be among those present.

I feel sure I have told you before about this black-hearted bird, but I will give you the strength of it once again, just to keep the records straight. He was the fellow, if you remember, who, ignoring a lifelong friendship in the course of which he had frequently eaten my bread and salt, betted me one night at the Drones that I wouldn't swing myself across the swimming-bath by the ropes and rings and then, with almost inconceivable treachery, went and looped back the last ring, causing me to drop into the fluid and ruin one of the nattiest suits of dress-clothes in London.

To execute a fitting vengeance on this bloke had been the ruling passion of my life ever since.

'You are bearing in mind, Jeeves,' I said, 'the fact that Mr Glossop will be at Bleaching?'

'Yes, sir.'

'And, consequently, are not forgetting to put in the Giant Squirt?'

'No, sir.'

'Nor the Luminous Rabbit?'

'No, sir.'

'Good! I am rather pinning my faith on the Luminous Rabbit, Jeeves. I hear excellent reports of it on all sides. You wind it up and put it in somebody's room in the night watches, and it shines in the dark and jumps about, making odd, squeaking noises the while. The whole performance being, I should imagine, well calculated to scare young Tuppy into a decline.'

'Very possibly, sir.'

'Should that fail, there is always the Giant Squirt. We must leave no stone unturned to put it across the man somehow,' I said. 'The Wooster honour is at stake.'

I would have spoken further on this subject, but just then the front-door bell buzzed.

'I'll answer it,' I said. 'I expect it's Aunt Dahlia. She 'phoned that she would be calling this morning.'

It was not Aunt Dahlia. It was a telegraph-boy with telegram. I opened it, read it, and carried it back to the bedroom, the brow a bit knitted.

'Jeeves,' I said. 'A rummy communication has arrived. From Mr Glossop.'

'Indeed, sir?'

'I will read it to you. Handed in at Upper Bleaching. Message runs as follows:

' "When you come to-morrow, bring my football boots. Also, if humanly possible, Irish water-spaniel. Urgent. Regards. Tuppy."

'What do you make of that, Jeeves?'

'As I interpret the document, sir, Mr Glossop wishes you, when you come to-morrow, to bring his football boots. Also, if humanly possible, an Irish water-spaniel. He hints that the matter is urgent, and sends his regards.'

'Yes, that's how I read it, too. But why football boots?'

'Perhaps Mr Glossop wishes to play football, sir.'

I considered this.

'Yes,' I said. 'That may be the solution. But why would a man, staying peacefully at a country-house, suddenly develop a craving to play football?'

'I could not say, sir.'

'And why an Irish water-spaniel?'

'There again I fear I can hazard no conjecture, sir.'

'What *is* an Irish water-spaniel?'

'A water-spaniel of a variety bred in Ireland, sir.'

'You think so?'

'Yes, sir.'

'Well, perhaps you're right. But why should I sweat about the place collecting dogs – of whatever nationality – for young Tuppy? Does he think I'm Santa Claus? Is he under the impression that my feelings towards him, after that Drones Club incident, are those of kindly benevolence? Irish water-spaniels, indeed! Tchah!'

'Sir?'

'Tchah, Jeeves.'

'Very good, sir.'

The front-door bell buzzed again.

'Our busy morning, Jeeves.'

'Yes, sir.'

'All right. I'll go.'

This time it was Aunt Dahlia. She charged in with the air of a woman with something on her mind – giving tongue, in fact, while actually on the very doormat.

'Bertie,' she boomed, in that ringing voice of hers which cracks window-panes and upsets vases, 'I've come about that young hound, Glossop.'

'It's quite all right, Aunt Dahlia,' I replied soothingly. 'I have the situation well in hand. The Giant Squirt and the Luminous Rabbit are even now being packed.'

'I don't know what you're talking about, and I don't for a moment suppose you do, either,' said the relative somewhat brusquely, 'but, if you'll kindly stop gibbering, I'll tell you what I mean. I have had a most disturbing letter from Katherine.

About this reptile. Of course, I haven't breathed a word to Angela. She'd hit the ceiling.'

This Angela is Aunt Dahlia's daughter. She and young Tuppy are generally supposed to be more or less engaged, though nothing definitely 'Morning Posted' yet.

'Why?' I said.

'Why what?'

'Why would Angela hit the ceiling?'

'Well, wouldn't you, if you were practically engaged to a fiend in human shape and somebody told you he had gone off to the country and was flirting with a dog-girl?'

'With a what was that, once again?'

'A dog-girl. One of these dashed open-air flappers in thick boots and tailor-made tweeds who infest the rural districts and go about the place followed by packs of assorted dogs. I used to be one of them myself in my younger days, so I know how dangerous they are. Her name is Dalgleish. Old Colonel Dalgleish's daughter. They live near Bleaching.'

I saw a gleam of daylight.

'Then that must be what his telegram was about. He's just wired, asking me to bring down an Irish water-spaniel. A Christmas present for this girl, no doubt.'

'Probably. Katherine tells me he seems to be infatuated with her. She says he follows her about like one of her dogs, looking like a tame cat and bleating like a sheep.'

'Quite the private Zoo, what?'

'Bertie,' said Aunt Dahlia – and I could see her generous

nature was stirred to its depths – 'one more crack like that out of you, and I shall forget that I am an aunt and hand you one.'

I became soothing. I gave her the old oil.

'I shouldn't worry,' I said. 'There's probably nothing in it. Whole thing no doubt much exaggerated.'

'You think so, eh? Well, you know what he's like. You remember the trouble we had when he ran after that singing-woman.'

I recollected the case. You will find it elsewhere in the archives. Cora Bellinger was the female's name. She was studying for Opera, and young Tuppy thought highly of her. Fortunately, however, she punched him in the eye during Beefy Bingham's clean, bright entertainment in Bermondsey East, and love died.

'Besides,' said Aunt Dahlia, 'there's something I haven't told you. Just before he went to Bleaching, he and Angela quarrelled.'

'They did?'

'Yes. I got it out of Angela this morning. She was crying her eyes out, poor angel. It was something about her last hat. As far as I could gather, he told her it made her look like a Pekingese, and she told him she never wanted to see him again in this world or the next. And he said "Right-ho!" and breezed off. I can see what has happened. This dog-girl has caught him on the rebound, and, unless something is done quick, anything may happen. So place the facts before Jeeves, and tell him to take action the moment you get down there.'

I am always a little piqued, if you know what I mean, at this assumption on the relative's part that Jeeves is so dashed essential on these occasions. My manner, therefore, as I replied, was a bit on the crisp side.

'Jeeves's services will not be required,' I said. 'I can handle this business. The programme which I have laid out will be quite sufficient to take young Tuppy's mind off love-making. It is my intention to insert the Luminous Rabbit in his room at the first opportunity that presents itself. The Luminous Rabbit shines in the dark and jumps about, making odd, squeaking noises. It will sound to young Tuppy like the Voice of Conscience, and I anticipate that a single treatment will make him retire into a nursing-home for a couple of weeks or so. At the end of which period he will have forgotten all about the bally girl.'

'Bertie,' said Aunt Dahlia, with a sort of frozen calm, 'you are the Abysmal Chump. Listen to me. It's simply because I am fond of you and have influence with the Lunacy Commissioners that you weren't put in a padded cell years ago. Bungle this business, and I withdraw my protection. Can't you understand that this thing is far too serious for any fooling about? Angela's whole happiness is at stake. Do as I tell you, and put it up to Jeeves.'

'Just as you say, Aunt Dahlia,' I said stiffly.

'All right, then. Do it now.'

I went back to the bedroom.

'Jeeves,' I said, and I did not trouble to conceal my chagrin, 'you need not pack the Luminous Rabbit.'

'Very good, sir.'

'Nor the Giant Squirt.'

'Very good, sir.'

'They have been subjected to destructive criticism, and the zest has gone. Oh, and, Jeeves.'

'Sir?'

'Mrs Travers wishes you, on arriving at Bleaching Court, to disentangle Mr Glossop from a dog-girl.'

'Very good, sir. I will attend to the matter and will do my best to give satisfaction.'

That Aunt Dahlia had not exaggerated the perilous nature of the situation was made clear to me on the following afternoon. Jeeves and I drove down to Bleaching in the two-seater, and we were tooling along about half-way between the village and the Court when suddenly there appeared ahead of us a sea of dogs and in the middle of it young Tuppy frisking round one of those largish, corn-fed girls. He was bending towards her in a devout sort of way, and even at a considerable distance I could see that his ears were pink. His attitude, in short, was unmistakably that of a man endeavouring to push a good thing along; and when I came closer and noted that the girl wore tailor-made tweeds and thick boots, I had no further doubts.

'You observe, Jeeves?' I said in a low, significant voice.

'Yes, sir.'

'The girl, what?'

'Yes, sir.'

I tootled amiably on the horn and yodelled a bit. They turned – Tuppy, I fancied, not any too pleased.

'Oh, hullo, Bertie,' he said.

'Hullo,' I said.

'My friend, Bertie Wooster,' said Tuppy to the girl, in what seemed to me rather an apologetic manner. You know – as if he would have preferred to hush me up.

'Hullo,' said the girl.

'Hullo,' I said.

'Hullo, Jeeves,' said Tuppy.

'Good afternoon, sir,' said Jeeves.

There was a somewhat constrained silence.

'Well, good-bye, Bertie,' said young Tuppy. 'You'll be wanting to push along, I expect.'

We Woosters can take a hint as well as the next man.

'See you later,' I said.

'Oh, rather,' said Tuppy.

I set the machinery in motion again, and we rolled off.

'Sinister, Jeeves,' I said. 'You noticed that the subject was looking like a stuffed frog?'

'Yes, sir.'

'And gave no indication of wanting us to stop and join the party?'

'No, sir.'

'I think Aunt Dahlia's fears are justified. The thing seems serious.'

'Yes, sir.'

'Well, strain the brain, Jeeves.'

'Very good, sir.'

It wasn't till I was dressing for dinner that night that I saw young Tuppy again. He trickled in just as I was arranging the tie.

'Hullo!' I said.

'Hullo!' said Tuppy.

'Who was the girl?' I asked, in that casual, snaky way of mine – off-hand, I mean.

'A Miss Dalgleish,' said Tuppy, and I noticed that he blushed a spot.

'Staying here?'

'No. She lives in that house just before you come to the gates of this place. Did you bring my football boots?'

'Yes. Jeeves has got them somewhere.'

'And the water-spaniel?'

'Sorry. No water-spaniel.'

'Dashed nuisance. She's set her heart on an Irish water-spaniel.'

'Well, what do you care?'

'I wanted to give her one.'

'Why?'

Tuppy became a trifle haughty. Frigid. The rebuking eye.

'Colonel and Mrs Dalgleish,' he said, 'have been extremely kind to me since I got here. They have entertained me. I naturally wish to make some return for their hospitality. I don't want them to look upon me as one of those ill-mannered modern young men you read about in the papers who grab everything they can lay their hooks on and never buy back. If people ask you to lunch and tea and what not, they appreciate it if you make them some little present in return.'

'Well, give them your football boots. In passing, why did you want the bally things?'

'I'm playing in a match next Thursday.'

'Down here?'

'Yes. Upper Bleaching versus Hockley-cum-Meston. Apparently it's the big game of the year.'

'How did you get roped in?'

'I happened to mention in the course of conversation the other day that, when in London, I generally turn out on Saturdays for the Old Austinians, and Miss Dalgleish seemed rather keen that I should help the village.'

'Which village?'

'Upper Bleaching, of course.'

'Ah, then you're going to play for Hockley?'

'You needn't be funny, Bertie. You may not know it, but I'm pretty hot stuff on the football field. Oh, Jeeves.'

'Sir?' said Jeeves, entering right centre.

'Mr Wooster tells me you have my football boots.'

'Yes, sir. I have placed them in your room.'

'Thanks. Jeeves, do you want to make a bit of money?'

'Yes, sir.'

'Then put a trifle on Upper Bleaching for the annual

encounter with Hockley-cum-Meston next Thursday,' said Tuppy, exiting with swelling bosom.

'Mr Glossop is going to play on Thursday,' I explained as the door closed.

'So I was informed in the Servants' Hall, sir.'

'Oh? And what's the general feeling there about it?'

'The impression I gathered, sir, was that the Servants' Hall considers Mr Glossop ill-advised.'

'Why's that?'

'I am informed by Mr Mulready, Sir Reginald's butler, sir, that this contest differs in some respects from the ordinary football game. Owing to the fact that there has existed for many years considerable animus between the two villages, the struggle is conducted, it appears, on somewhat looser and more primitive lines than is usually the case when two teams meet in friendly rivalry. The primary object of the players, I am given to understand, is not so much to score points as to inflict violence.'

'Good Lord, Jeeves!'

'Such appears to be the case, sir. The game is one that would have a great interest for the antiquarian. It was played first in the reign of King Henry the Eighth, when it lasted from noon till sundown over an area covering several square miles. Seven deaths resulted on that occasion.'

'Seven!'

'Not inclusive of two of the spectators, sir. In recent years, however, the casualties appear to have been confined to broken limbs and other minor injuries. The opinion of the Servants' Hall is that it would be more judicious on Mr Glossop's part, were he to refrain from mixing himself up in the affair.'

I was more or less aghast. I mean to say, while I had made it my mission in life to get back at young Tuppy for that business at the Drones, there still remained certain faint vestiges, if vestiges is the word I want, of the old friendship and esteem. Besides, there are limits to one's thirst for vengeance. Deep as my resentment was for the ghastly outrage he had perpetrated on me, I had no wish to see him toddle unsuspiciously into the arena and get all chewed up by wild villagers. A Tuppy scared stiff by a Luminous Rabbit – yes. Excellent business. The happy ending, in fact. But a Tuppy carried off on a stretcher in half a dozen pieces – no. Quite a different matter. All wrong. Not to be considered for a moment.

Obviously, then, a kindly word of warning, while there was yet time, was indicated. I buzzed off to his room forthwith, and found him toying dreamily with the football boots.

I put him in possession of the facts.

'What you had better do – and the Servants' Hall thinks the same,' I said, 'is fake a sprained ankle on the eve of the match.'

He looked at me in an odd sort of way.

'You suggest that, when Miss Dalgleish is trusting me, relying on me, looking forward with eager, girlish enthusiasm to seeing me help her village on to victory, I should let her down with a thud?'

I was pleased with his ready intelligence.

'That's the idea,' I said.

'Faugh!' said Tuppy – the only time I've ever heard the word.

'How do you mean, "Faugh!"?' I asked.

'Bertie,' said Tuppy, 'what you tell me merely makes me all the keener for the fray. A warm game is what I want. I welcome this sporting spirit on the part of the opposition. I shall enjoy a spot of roughness. It will enable me to go all out and give of my best. Do you realize,' said young Tuppy, vermilion to the gills, 'that She will be looking on? And do you know how that will make me feel? It will make me feel like some knight of old jousting under the eyes of his lady. Do you suppose that Sir Lancelot or Sir Galahad, when there was a tourney scheduled for the following Thursday, went and pretended they had sprained their ankles just because the thing was likely to be a bit rough?'

'Don't forget that in the reign of King Henry the Eighth—'

'Never mind about the reign of King Henry the Eighth. All I care about is that it's Upper Bleaching's turn this year to play in colours, so I shall be able to wear my Old Austinian shirt. Light blue, Bertie, with broad orange stripes. I shall look like something, I tell you.'

'But what?'

'Bertie,' said Tuppy, now becoming purely ga-ga, 'I may as well tell you that I'm in love at last. This is the real thing. I have found my mate. All my life I have dreamed of meeting some sweet, open-air girl with all the glory of the English countryside in her eyes, and I have found her. How different she is, Bertie, from these hot-house, artificial London girls! Would they stand in the mud on a winter afternoon, watching a football match? Would they know what to give an Alsatian for fits? Would they tramp ten miles a day across the fields and come back as fresh as paint? No!'

'Well, why should they?'

'Bertie, I'm staking everything on this game on Thursday. At the moment, I have an idea that she looks on me as something of a weakling, simply because I got a blister on my foot the other afternoon and had to take the bus back from Hockley. But when she sees me going through the rustic opposition like a devouring flame, will that make her think a bit? Will that make her open her eyes? What?'

'What?'

'I said "What?"'

'So did I.'

'I meant, "Won't it?"'

'Oh, rather.'

Here the dinner-gong sounded, not before I was ready for it.

Judicious enquiries during the next couple of days convinced me that the Servants' Hall at Bleaching Court, in advancing the suggestion that young Tuppy, born and bred in the gentler atmosphere of the metropolis, would do well to keep out of local disputes and avoid the football-field on which these were to be settled, had not spoken idly. It had weighed its words and said the sensible thing. Feeling between the two villages undoubtedly ran high, as they say.

You know how it is in these remote rural districts. Life tends at times to get a bit slow. There's nothing much to do in the long winter evenings but listen to the radio and brood on what a tick your neighbour is. You find yourself remembering how Farmer Giles did you down over the sale of your pig, and Farmer Giles finds himself remembering that it was your son, Ernest, who bunged the half-brick at his horse on the second Sunday before Septuagesima. And so on and so forth. How this particular feud had started, I don't know, but the season of peace and good will found it in full blast. The only topic of conversation in Upper Bleaching was Thursday's game, and the citizenry seemed to be looking forward to it in a spirit that can only be described as ghoulish. And it was the same in Hockley-cum-Meston.

I paid a visit to Hockley-cum-Meston on the Wednesday, being rather anxious to take a look at the inhabitants and see how formidable they were. I was shocked to observe that practically every second male might have been the Village Blacksmith's big brother. The muscles of their brawny arms were obviously strong as iron bands, and the way the company at the Green Pig, where I looked in incognito for a spot of beer, talked about the forthcoming sporting contest was enough to chill the blood of anyone who had a pal who proposed to fling himself into the fray. It sounded rather like Attila and a few of his Huns sketching out their next campaign.

I went back to Jeeves with my mind made up.

'Jeeves,' I said, 'you, who had the job of drying and pressing those dress-clothes of mine, are aware that I have suffered much at young Tuppy Glossop's hands. By rights, I suppose, I ought to be welcoming the fact that the Wrath of Heaven is now hovering over him in this fearful manner. But the view I take of it is that Heaven looks like overdoing it. Heaven's idea of a fitting retribution is not mine. In my most unrestrained moments I never wanted the poor blighter assassinated. And the idea in Hockley-cum-Meston seems to be that a good opportunity has arisen of making it a bumper Christmas for the local undertaker. There was a fellow with red hair at the Green Pig this afternoon who might have been the undertaker's partner, the way he talked. We must act, and speedily, Jeeves. We must put a bit of a jerk in it and save young Tuppy in spite of himself.'

'What course would you advocate, sir?'

'I'll tell you. He refuses to do the sensible thing and slide out, because the girl will be watching the game and he imagines, poor lizard, that he is going to shine and impress her. So we must employ guile. You must go up to London to-day, Jeeves, and to-morrow morning you will send a telegram, signed "Angela", which will run as follows. Jot it down. Ready?'

'Yes, sir.'

' "So sorry—" ...' I pondered. 'What would a girl say, Jeeves, who, having had a row with the bird she was practically engaged to because he told her she looked like a Pekingese in her new hat, wanted to extend the olive-branch?'

' "So sorry I was cross", sir, would, I fancy, be the expression.'

'Strong enough, do you think?'

'Possibly the addition of the word "darling" would give the necessary verisimilitude, sir.'

'Right. Resume the jotting. "So sorry I was cross, darling ..." No, wait, Jeeves. Scratch that out. I see where we have gone off the rails. I see where we are missing a chance to make this the real tabasco. Sign the telegram not "Angela" but "Travers".'

'Very good, sir.'

'Or, rather, "Dahlia Travers". And this is the body of the communication. "Please return at once." '

' "Immediately" would be more economical, sir. Only one word. And it has a stronger ring.'

'True. Jot on, then. "Please return immediately. Angela in a hell of a state." '

'I would suggest "seriously ill", sir.'

'All right. "Seriously ill". "Angela seriously ill. Keeps calling for you and says you were quite right about hat." '

'If I might suggest, sir—?'

'Well, go ahead.'

'I fancy the following would meet the case. "Please return immediately. Angela seriously ill. High fever and delirium. Keeps calling your name piteously and saying something about a hat and that you were quite right. Please catch earliest possible train. Dahlia Travers." '

'That sounds all right.'

'Yes, sir.'

'You like that "piteously"? You don't think "incessantly"?'

'No, sir. "Piteously" is the *mot juste*.'

'All right. You know. Well, send it off in time to get here at two-thirty.'

'Yes, sir.'

'Two-thirty, Jeeves. You see the devilish cunning?'

'No, sir.'

'I will tell you. If the telegram arrived earlier, he would get it before the game. By two-thirty, however, he will have started for the ground. I shall hand it to him the moment there is a lull in the battle. By that time he will have begun to get some idea of what a football match between Upper Bleaching and Hockley-cum-Meston is like, and the thing ought to work like magic. I can't imagine anyone who has been sporting awhile with those thugs I saw yesterday not welcoming any excuse to call it a day. You follow me?'

'Yes, sir.'

'Very good, Jeeves.'

'Very good, sir.'

You can always rely on Jeeves. Two-thirty I had said, and two-thirty it was. The telegram arrived almost on the minute. I was going to my room to change into something warmer at the moment, and I took it up with me. Then into the heavy tweeds and off in the car to the field of play. I got there just as the two teams were lining up, and half a minute later the whistle blew and the war was on.

What with one thing and another – having been at a school where they didn't play it and so forth – Rugby football is a game I can't claim absolutely to understand in all its niceties, if you know what I mean. I can follow the broad, general principles, of course. I mean to say, I know that the main scheme is to work the ball down the field somehow and deposit it over the line at the other end, and that, in order to squelch this programme, each side is allowed to put in a certain amount of assault and battery and do things to its fellow-man which, if done elsewhere, would result in fourteen days without the option, coupled with some strong remarks from the Bench. But there I stop. What you might call the science of the thing is to Bertram Wooster a sealed book. However, I am informed by experts that on this occasion there was not enough science for anyone to notice.

There had been a great deal of rain in the last few days, and the going appeared to be a bit sticky. In fact, I have seen swamps that were drier than this particular bit of ground. The red-haired bloke whom I had encountered in the pub paddled up and kicked off amidst cheers from the populace, and the ball went straight to where Tuppy was standing, a pretty colour-scheme in light blue and orange. Tuppy caught it neatly, and hoofed it back, and it was at this point that I understood that an Upper Bleaching versus Hockley-cum-Meston game had certain features not usually seen on the football-field.

For Tuppy, having done his bit, was just standing there, looking modest, when there was a thunder of large feet and the red-haired bird, galloping up, seized him by the neck, hurled him to earth, and fell on him. I had a glimpse of Tuppy's face, as it registered horror, dismay, and a general suggestion of stunned dissatisfaction with the scheme of things, and then he disappeared. By the time he had come to the surface, a sort of mob-warfare was going on at the other side of the field. Two assortments of sons of the soil had got their heads down and were shoving earnestly against each other, with the ball some-where in the middle.

Tuppy wiped a fair portion of Hampshire out of his eye, peered round him in a dazed kind of way, saw the mass-meeting and ran towards it, arriving just in time for a couple of heavyweights to gather him in and give him the mud-treatment again. This placed him in an admirable position for a third heavyweight to kick him in the ribs with a boot like a violin-case. The red-haired man then fell on him. It was all good, brisk play, and looked fine from my side of the ropes.

I saw now where Tuppy had made his mistake. He was too dressy. On occasions such as this it is safest not to be con-spicuous, and that blue and orange shirt rather caught the eye. A sober beige, blending with the colour of the ground, was what his best friends would have recommended. And, in addition to the fact that his costume attracted attention, I rather think that the men of Hockley-cum-Meston resented his being on the field at all. They felt that, as a non-local, he had butted in on a private fight and had no business there.

At any rate, it certainly appeared to me that they were giving him preferential treatment. After each of those shoving-bees to which I have alluded, when the edifice caved in and tons of humanity wallowed in a tangled mass in the juice, the last soul to be excavated always seemed to be Tuppy. And on the rare occasions when he actually managed to stand upright for a moment, somebody – generally the red-haired man – invariably sprang to the congenial task of spilling him again.

In fact, it was beginning to look as though that telegram would come too late to save a human life, when an interruption occurred. Play had worked round close to where I was standing, and there had been the customary collapse of all concerned, with Tuppy at the bottom of the basket, as usual; but this time, when they got up and started to count the survivors, a sizeable cove in what had once been a white shirt remained on the ground. And a hearty cheer went up from a hundred patriotic throats as the news spread that Upper Bleaching had drawn first blood.

The victim was carried off by a couple of his old chums, and the rest of the players sat down and pulled their stockings up and thought of life for a bit. The moment had come, it seemed to me, to remove Tuppy from the *abattoir*, and I hopped over the ropes and toddled to where he sat scraping mud from his wishbone. His air was that of a man who has been passed through a wringer, and his eyes, what you could see of them, had a strange, smouldering gleam. He was so crusted with alluvial deposits that one realized how little a mere bath would ever be able to effect. To fit him to take his place once more in polite society, he would certainly have to be sent to the cleaner's. Indeed, it was a moot point whether it wouldn't be simpler just to throw him away.

'Tuppy, old man,' I said.

'Eh?' said Tuppy.

'A telegram for you.'

'Eh?'

'I've got a wire here that came after you left the house.'

'Eh?' said Tuppy.

I stirred him up a trifle with the ferule of my stick, and he seemed to come to life.

'Be careful what you're doing, you silly ass,' he said, in part. 'I'm one solid bruise. What are you gibbering about?'

'A telegram has come for you. I think it may be important.'

He snorted in a bitter sort of way.

'Do you suppose I've time to read telegrams now?'

'But this one may be frightfully urgent,' I said. 'Here it is.'

But, if you understand me, it wasn't. How I had happened to do it, I don't know, but apparently, in changing the upholstery, I had left it in my other coat.

'Oh, my gosh,' I said, 'I've left it behind.'

'It doesn't matter.'

'But it does. It's probably something you ought to read at once. Immediately, if you know what I mean. If I were you, I'd just say a few words of farewell to the murder-squad and come back to the house right away.'

He raised his eyebrows. At least, I think he must have done, because the mud on his forehead stirred a little, as if something was going on underneath it.

'Do you imagine,' he said, 'that I would slink away under her very eyes? Good God! Besides,' he went on, in a quiet, meditative voice, 'there is no power on earth that could get me off this field until I've thoroughly disembowelled that red-haired bounder. Have you noticed how he keeps tackling me when I haven't got the ball?'

'Isn't that right?'

'Of course it's not right. Never mind! A bitter retribution awaits that bird. I've had enough of it. From now on I assert my personality.'

'I'm a bit foggy as to the rules of this pastime,' I said. 'Are you allowed to bite him?'

'I'll try, and see what happens,' said Tuppy, struck with the idea and brightening a little.

At this point, the pall-bearers returned, and fighting became general again all along the Front.

There's nothing like a bit of rest and what you might call folding of the hands for freshening up the shop-soiled athlete.

The dirty work, resumed after this brief breather, started off with an added vim which it did one good to see. And the life and soul of the party was young Tuppy.

You know, only meeting a fellow at lunch or at the races or loafing round country-houses and so forth, you don't get on to his hidden depths, if you know what I mean. Until this moment, if asked, I would have said that Tuppy Glossop was, on the whole, essentially a pacific sort of bloke, with little or nothing of the tiger of the jungle in him. Yet here he was, running to and fro with fire streaming from his nostrils, a posi-tive danger to traffic.

Yes, absolutely. Encouraged by the fact that the referee was either filled with the spirit of Live and Let Live or else had got his whistle choked up with mud, the result being that he appeared to regard the game with a sort of calm detachment, Tuppy was putting in some very impressive work. Even to me, knowing nothing of the finesse of the thing, it was plain that if Hockley-cum-Meston wanted the happy ending they must eliminate young Tuppy at the earliest possible moment. And I will say for them that they did their best, the red-haired man being particularly assiduous. But Tuppy was made of durable material. Every time the opposition talent ground him into the mire and sat on his head, he rose on stepping-stones of his dead self, if you follow me, to higher things. And in the end it was the red-haired bloke who did the dust-biting.

I couldn't tell you exactly how it happened, for by this time the shades of night were drawing in a bit and there was a dollop of mist rising, but one moment the fellow was haring along, apparently without a care in the world, and then suddenly Tuppy had appeared from nowhere and was sailing through the air at his neck. They connected with a crash and a slither, and a little later the red-haired bird was hopping off, supported by a brace of friends, something having gone wrong with his left ankle.

After that, there was nothing to it. Upper Bleaching, thoroughly bucked, became busier than ever. There was a lot of earnest work in a sort of inland sea down at the Hockley end of the field, and then a kind of tidal wave poured over the line, and when the bodies had been removed and the tumult and the shouting had died, there was young Tuppy lying on the ball. And that, with the exception of a few spots of mayhem in the last five minutes, concluded the proceedings.

I drove back to the Court in rather what you might term a pensive frame of mind. Things having happened as they had happened, there seemed to me a goodish bit of hard thinking to be done. There was a servitor of sorts in the hall, when I arrived, and I asked him to send up a whisky-and-soda, strongish, to my room. The old brain, I felt, needed stimulating. And about ten minutes later there was a knock at the door, and in came Jeeves, bearing tray and materials.

'Hullo, Jeeves,' I said, surprised. 'Are you back?'

'Yes, sir.'

'When did you get here?'

'Some little while ago, sir. Was it an enjoyable game, sir?'

'In a sense, Jeeves,' I said, 'yes. Replete with human interest and all that, if you know what I mean. But I fear that, owing to a touch of carelessness on my part, the worst has happened. I left the telegram in my other coat, so young Tuppy remained in action throughout.'

'Was he injured, sir?'

'Worse than that, Jeeves. He was the star of the game. Toasts, I should imagine, are now being drunk to him at every pub in the village. So spectacularly did he play – in fact, so heartily did he joust – that I can't see the girl not being all over him. Unless I am greatly mistaken, the moment they meet, she will exclaim "My hero!" and fall into his bally arms.'

'Indeed, sir?'

I didn't like the man's manner. Too calm. Unimpressed. A little leaping about with fallen jaw was what I had expected my words to produce, and I was on the point of saying as much when the door opened again and Tuppy limped in.

He was wearing an ulster over his football things, and I wondered why he had come to pay a social call on me instead of proceeding straight to the bathroom. He eyed my glass in a wolfish sort of way.

'Whisky?' he said, in a hushed voice.

'And soda.'

'Bring me one, Jeeves,' said young Tuppy. 'A large one.'

'Very good, sir.'

Tuppy wandered to the window and looked out into the gathering darkness, and for the first time I perceived that he had got a grouch of some description. You can generally tell by a fellow's back. Humped. Bent. Bowed down with weight of woe, if you follow me.

'What's the matter?' I asked.

Tuppy emitted a mirthless laugh.

'Oh, nothing much,' he said. 'My faith in woman is dead, that's all.'

'It is?'

'You jolly well bet it is. Women are a wash-out. I see no future for the sex, Bertie. Blisters, all of them.'

'Er – even the Dogsbody girl?'

'Her name,' said Tuppy, a little stiffly, 'is Dalgleish, if it happens to interest you. And, if you want to know something else, she's the worst of the lot.'

'My dear chap!'

Tuppy turned. Beneath the mud, I could see that his face was drawn and, to put it in a nutshell, wan.

'Do you know what happened, Bertie?'

'What?'

'She wasn't there.'

'Where?'

'At the match, you silly ass.'

'Not at the match?'

'No.'

'You mean, not among the throng of eager spectators?'

'Of course I mean not among the spectators. Did you think I expected her to be playing?'

'But I thought the whole scheme of the thing—'

'So did I. My gosh!' said Tuppy, laughing another of those hollow ones. 'I sweat myself to the bone for her sake. I allow a mob of homicidal maniacs to kick me in the ribs and stroll about on my face. And then, when I have braved a fate worse than death, so to speak, all to please her, I find that she didn't bother to come and watch the game. She got a 'phone-call from London from somebody who said he had located an Irish water-spaniel, and up she popped in her car, leaving me flat. I met her just now outside her house, and she told me. And all she could think of was that she was as sore as a sunburnt neck because she had had her trip for nothing. Apparently it wasn't an Irish water-spaniel at all. Just an ordinary English water-spaniel. And to think I fancied I loved a girl like that. A nice life-partner she would make! "When pain and anguish wring the brow, a ministering angel thou" – I don't think! Why, if a man married a girl like that and happened to get stricken by some dangerous illness, would she smooth his pillow and press cooling drinks on him? Not a chance! She'd be off somewhere trying to buy Siberian eel-hounds. I'm through with women.'

I saw that the moment had come to put in a word for the old firm.

'My cousin Angela's not a bad sort, Tuppy,' I said, in a grave elder-brotherly kind of way. 'Not altogether a bad egg, Angela, if you look at her squarely. I had always been hoping that she and you . . . and I know my Aunt Dahlia felt the same.'

Tuppy's bitter sneer cracked the topsoil.

'Angela!' he woofed. 'Don't talk to me about Angela. Angela's a rag and a bone and a hank of hair and an A1 scourge, if you want to know. She gave me the push. Yes, she did. Simply because I had the manly courage to speak out candidly on the subject of that ghastly lid she was chump enough to buy. It made her look like a Peke, and I told her it made her look like a Peke. And instead of admiring me for my fearless honesty she bunged me out on my ear. Faugh!'

'She did?' I said.

'She jolly well did,' said young Tuppy. At four-sixteen p.m. on Tuesday the seventeenth.'

'By the way, old man,' I said, 'I've found that telegram.'

'What telegram?'

'The one I told you about.'

'Oh, that one?'

'Yes, that's the one.'

'Well, let's have a look at the beastly thing.'

I handed it over, watching him narrowly. And suddenly, as he read, I saw him wobble. Stirred to the core. Obviously.

'Anything important?' I said.

'Bertie,' said young Tuppy, in a voice that quivered with strong emotion, 'my recent remarks *re* your cousin Angela. Wash them out. Cancel them. Look on them as not spoken. I tell you, Bertie, Angela's all right. An angel in human shape, and that's official. Bertie, I've got to get up to London. She's ill.'

77

'Ill?'

'High fever and delirium. This wire's from your aunt. She wants me to come up to London at once. Can I borrow your car?'

'Of course.'

'Thanks,' said Tuppy, and dashed out.

He had only been gone about a second when Jeeves came in with the restorative.

'Mr Glossop's gone, Jeeves.'

'Indeed, sir?'

'To London.'

'Yes, sir?'

'In my car. To see my cousin Angela. The sun is once more shining, Jeeves.'

'Extremely gratifying, sir.'

I gave him the eye.

'Was it you, Jeeves, who 'phoned to Miss What's-her-bally-name about the alleged water-spaniel?'

'Yes, sir.'

'I thought as much.'

'Yes, sir?'

'Yes, Jeeves, the moment Mr Glossop told me that a Mysterious Voice had 'phoned on the subject of Irish water-spaniels, I thought as much. I recognized your touch. I read your motives like an open book. You knew she would come buzzing up.'

'Yes, sir.'

'And you knew how Tuppy would react. If there's one thing that gives a jousting knight the pip, it is to have his audience walk out on him.'

'Yes, sir.'

'But, Jeeves.'

'Sir?'

'There's just one point. What will Mr Glossop say when he finds my cousin Angela full of beans and not delirious?'

'The point had not escaped me, sir. I took the liberty of ringing Mrs Travers up on the telephone and explaining the circumstances. All will be in readiness for Mr Glossop's arrival.'

'Jeeves,' I said, 'you think of everything.'

'Thank you, sir. In Mr Glossop's absence, would you care to drink this whisky-and-soda?'

I shook the head.

'No, Jeeves, there is only one man who must do that. It is you. If ever anyone earned a refreshing snort, you are he. Pour it out, Jeeves, and shove it down.'

'Thank you very much, sir.'

'Cheerio, Jeeves!'

'Cheerio, sir, if I may use the expression.'

Ukridge's Dog College

'Laddie,' said Stanley Featherstonehaugh Ukridge, that much-enduring man, helping himself to my tobacco and slipping the pouch absently into his pocket, 'listen to me, you son of Belial.'

'What?' I said, retrieving the pouch.

'Do you want to make an enormous fortune?'

'I do.'

'Then write my biography. Bung it down on paper, and we'll split the proceeds. I've been making a pretty close study of your stuff lately, old horse, and it's all wrong. The trouble with you is that you don't plumb the wellsprings of human nature and all that. You just think up some rotten yarn about some-dam'-thing-or-other and shove it down. Now, if you tackled my life, you'd have something worth writing about. Pots of money in it, my boy – English serial rights and American serial rights and book rights, and dramatic rights and movie rights – well, you can take it from me that, at a conservative estimate, we should clean up at least fifty thousand pounds apiece.'

'As much as that?'

'Fully that. And listen, laddie, I'll tell you what. You're a good chap and we've been pals for years, so I'll let you have my share of the English serial rights for a hundred pounds down.'

'What makes you think I've got a hundred pounds?'

'Well, then, I'll make it my share of the English *and* American serial rights for fifty.'

'Your collar's come off its stud.'

'How about my complete share of the whole dashed outfit for twenty-five?'

'Not for me, thanks.'

'Then I'll tell you what, old horse,' said Ukridge, inspired. 'Just lend me half a crown to be going on with.'

If the leading incidents of S. F. Ukridge's disreputable career are to be given to the public – and not, as some might suggest, decently hushed up – I suppose I am the man to write them. Ukridge and I have been intimate since the days of school. Together we sported on the green, and when he was expelled no one missed him more than I. An unfortunate business, this expulsion. Ukridge's generous spirit, ever ill-attuned to school rules, caused him eventually to break the solemnest of them all by sneaking out at night to try his skill at the coconut-shies of the local village fair; and his foresight in putting on scarlet whiskers and a false nose for the expedition was completely neutralized by the fact that he absent-mindedly wore his school cap throughout the entire proceedings. He left the next morning, regretted by all.

After this there was a hiatus of some years in our friendship. I was at Cambridge, absorbing culture, and Ukridge, as far as I could gather from his rare letters and the reports of mutual acquaintances, flitting about the world like a snipe. Somebody met him in New York, just off a cattle-ship. Somebody else saw him in Buenos Ayres. Somebody, again, spoke sadly of having been pounced on by him at Monte Carlo and touched for a fiver. It was not until I settled down in London that he came back into my life. We met in Piccadilly one day, and resumed our relations where they had been broken off. Old associations are strong, and the fact that he was about my build and so could wear my socks and shirts drew us very close together.

Then he disappeared again, and it was a month or more before I got news of him.

It was George Tupper who brought the news. George was head of the school in my last year, and he has fulfilled exactly the impeccable promise of those early days. He is in the Foreign Office, doing well and much respected. He has an earnest, pulpy heart and takes other people's troubles very seriously. Often he had mourned to me like a father over Ukridge's erratic progress through life, and now, as he spoke, he seemed to be filled with a solemn joy, as over a reformed prodigal.

'Have you heard about Ukridge?' said George Tupper. 'He has settled down at last. Gone to live with an aunt of his who owns one of those big houses on Wimbledon Common. A very rich woman. I am delighted. It will be the making of the old chap.'

I suppose he was right in a way, but to me this tame subsidence into companionship with a rich aunt in Wimbledon seemed somehow an indecent, almost a tragic, end to a colourful career like that of S. F. Ukridge. And when I met the man a week later my heart grew heavier still.

It was in Oxford Street at the hour when women come up from the suburbs to shop; and he was standing among the dogs and commissionaires outside Selfridge's. His arms were full of parcels, his face was set in a mask of wan discomfort, and he was so beautifully dressed that for an instant I did not recognize him. Everything which the Correct Man wears was assembled on his person, from the silk hat to the patent-leather boots; and, as he confided to me in the first minute, he was suffering the tortures of the damned. The boots pinched him, the hat hurt his forehead, and the collar was worse than the hat and boots combined.

'She makes me wear them,' he said, moodily, jerking his head towards the interior of the store and uttering a sharp howl as the movement caused the collar to gouge his neck.

'Still,' I said, trying to turn his mind to happier things, 'you must be having a great time. George Tupper tells me that your aunt is rich. I suppose you're living off the fat of the land.'

'The browsing and sluicing are good,' admitted Ukridge. 'But it's a wearing life, laddie. A wearing life, old horse.'

'Why don't you come and see me sometimes?'

'I'm not allowed out at night.'

'Well, shall I come and see you?'

A look of poignant alarm shot out from under the silk hat.

'Don't dream of it, laddie,' said Ukridge, earnestly. 'Don't dream of it. You're a good chap – my best pal and all that sort of thing – but the fact is, my standing in the home's none too solid even now, and one sight of you would knock my prestige into hash. Aunt Julia would think you worldly.'

'I'm not worldly.'

'Well, you look worldly. You wear a squash hat and a soft collar. If you don't mind my suggesting it, old horse, I think, if I were you, I'd pop off now before she comes out. Good-bye, laddie.'

'Ichabod!' I murmured sadly to myself as I passed on down Oxford Street. 'Ichabod!'

I should have had more faith. I should have known my Ukridge better. I should have realized that a London suburb could no more imprison that great man permanently than Elba did Napoleon.

One afternoon, as I let myself into the house in Ebury Street of which I rented at that time the bedroom and sitting-room on the first floor, I came upon Bowles, my landlord, standing in listening attitude at the foot of the stairs.

'Good afternoon, sir,' said Bowles. 'A gentleman is waiting to see you. I fancy I heard him calling me a moment ago.'

'Who is he?'

'A Mr Ukridge, sir. He—'

A vast voice boomed out from above.

'Bowles, old horse!'

Bowles, like all other proprietors of furnished apartments in the south-western district of London, was an ex-butler, and about him, as about all ex-butlers, there clung like a garment an aura of dignified superiority which had never failed to crush my spirit. He was a man of portly aspect, with a bald head and prominent eyes of a lightish green – eyes that seemed to weigh me dispassionately and find me wanting. 'H'm!' they seemed to say. 'Young – very young. And not at all what I have been accustomed to in the best places.' To hear this dignitary addressed – and in a shout at that – as 'old horse' affected me with much the same sense of imminent chaos as would afflict a devout young curate if he saw his bishop slapped on the back. The shock, therefore, when he responded not merely mildly but with what almost amounted to camaraderie was numbing.

'Sir?' cooed Bowles.

'Bring me six bones and a corkscrew.'

'Very good, sir.'

Bowles retired, and I bounded upstairs and flung open the door of my sitting-room.

'Great Scott!' I said, blankly.

The place was a sea of Pekingese dogs. Later investigation reduced their numbers to six, but in that first moment there seemed to be hundreds. Goggling eyes met mine wherever I looked. The room was a forest of waving tails. With his back against the mantelpiece, smoking placidly, stood Ukridge.

'Hullo, laddie!' he said, with a genial wave of the hand, as if to make me free of the place. 'You're just in time. I've got to dash off and catch a train in a quarter of an hour. Stop it, you mutts!' he bellowed, and the six Pekingese, who had been barking steadily since my arrival, stopped in mid-yap, and were still. Ukridge's personality seemed to exercise a magnetism over the animal kingdom, from ex-butlers to Pekes, which bordered on the uncanny. 'I'm off to Sheep's Cray, in Kent. Taken a cottage there.'

'Are you going to live there?'

'Yes.'

'But what about your aunt?'

'Oh, I've left her. Life is stern and life is earnest, and if I mean to make a fortune I've got to bustle about and not stay cooped up in a place like Wimbledon.'

'Something in that.'

'Besides which, she told me the very sight of me made her sick and she never wanted to see me again.'

I might have guessed, directly I saw him, that some upheaval had taken place. The sumptuous raiment which had made him such a treat to the eye at our last meeting was gone, and he was back in his pre-Wimbledon costume, which was, as the advertisements say, distinctly individual. Over grey flannel trousers, a golf coat, and a brown sweater he wore like a royal robe a bright yellow mackintosh. His collar had broken free from its stud and showed a couple of inches of bare neck. His hair was disordered, and his masterful nose was topped by a pair of steel-rimmed pince-nez cunningly attached to his flapping ears with ginger-beer wire. His whole appearance spelled revolt.

Bowles manifested himself with a plateful of bones.

'That's right. Chuck 'em down on the floor.'

'Very good, sir.'

'I like that fellow,' said Ukridge, as the door closed. 'We had a dashed interesting talk before you came in. Did you know he had a cousin on the music-halls?'

'He hasn't confided in me much.'

'He's promised me an introduction to him later on. May be useful to be in touch with a man who knows the ropes. You see, laddie, I've hit on the most amazing scheme.' He swept his arm round dramatically, overturning a plaster cast of the Infant Samuel at Prayer. 'All right, all right, you can mend it with glue or something, and anyway, you're probably better without it. Yessir, I've hit on a great scheme. The idea of a thousand years.'

'What's that?'

'I'm going to train dogs.'

'Train dogs?'

'For the music-hall stage. Dog acts, you know. Performing dogs. Pots of money in it. I start in a modest way with these six. When I've taught 'em a few tricks, I sell them to a fellow in the profession for a large sum and buy twelve more. I train those, sell 'em for a large sum, and with the money buy twenty-four more. I train those—'

'Here, wait a minute.' My head was beginning to swim. I

had a vision of England paved with Pekingese dogs, all doing tricks. 'How do you know you'll be able to sell them?'

'Of course I shall. The demand's enormous. Supply can't cope with it. At a conservative estimate I should think I ought to scoop in four or five thousand pounds the first year. That, of course, is before the business really starts to expand.'

'I see.'

'When I get going properly, with a dozen assistants under me and an organized establishment, I shall begin to touch the big money. What I'm aiming at is a sort of Dog's College out in the country somewhere. Big place with a lot of ground. Regular classes and a set curriculum. Large staff, each member of it with so many dogs under his care, me looking on and superintending. Why, once the thing starts moving it'll run itself, and all I shall have to do will be to sit back and endorse the cheques. It isn't as if I would have to confine my operations to England. The demand for performing dogs is universal throughout the civilized world. America wants performing dogs. Australia wants performing dogs. Africa could do with a few, I've no doubt. My aim, laddie, is gradually to get a monopoly of the trade. I want everybody who needs a performing dog of any description to come automatically to me. And I'll tell you what, laddie. If you like to put up a bit of capital, I'll let you in on the ground floor.'

'No, thanks.'

'All right. Have it your own way. Only don't forget that there was a fellow who put nine hundred dollars into the Ford

Car business when it was starting and he collected a cool forty million. I say, is that clock right? Great Scott! I'll be missing my train. Help me mobilize these dashed animals.'

Five minutes later, accompanied by the six Pekingese and bearing about him a pound of my tobacco, three pairs of my socks, and the remains of a bottle of whisky, Ukridge departed in a taxi-cab for Charing Cross Station to begin his life-work.

Perhaps six weeks passed, six quiet Ukridgeless weeks, and then one morning I received an agitated telegram. Indeed, it was not so much a telegram as a cry of anguish. In every word of it there breathed the tortured spirit of a great man who has battled in vain against overwhelming odds. It was the sort of telegram which Job might have sent off after a lengthy session with Bildad the Shuhite:

Come here immediately, laddie. Life and death matter, old horse. Desperate situation. Don't fail me.

It stirred me like a bugle: I caught the next train.

The White Cottage, Sheep's Cray – destined, presumably, to become in future years an historic spot and a Mecca for dog-loving pilgrims – was a small and battered building standing near the main road to London at some distance from the village. I found it without difficulty, for Ukridge seemed to have achieved a certain celebrity in the neighbourhood; but to effect an entry was a harder task. I rapped for a full minute without result, then shouted; and I was about to conclude that

Ukridge was not at home when the door suddenly opened. As I was just giving a final bang at the moment, I entered the house in a manner reminiscent of one of the Ballet Russe practising a new and difficult step.

'Sorry, old horse,' said Ukridge. 'Wouldn't have kept you waiting if I'd known who it was. Thought you were Gooch, the grocer – goods supplied to the value of six pounds three and a penny.'

'I see.'

'He keeps hounding me for his beastly money,' said Ukridge, bitterly, as he led the way into the sitting-room. 'It's a little hard. Upon my Sam it's a little hard. I come down here to inaugurate a vast business and do the natives a bit of good by establishing a growing industry in their midst, and the first thing you know they turn round and bite the hand that was going to feed them. I've been hampered and rattled by these blood-suckers ever since I got here. A little trust, a little sympathy, a little of the good old give-and-take spirit – that was all I asked. And what happened? They wanted a bit on account! Kept bothering me for a bit on account, I'll trouble you, just when I needed all my thoughts and all my energy and every ounce of concentration at my command for my extraordinarily difficult and delicate work, *I* couldn't give them a bit on account. Later on, if they had only exercised reasonable patience, I would no doubt have been in a position to settle their infernal bills fifty times over. But the time was not ripe. I reasoned with the men. I said, "Here am I, a busy man, trying hard to educate six Pekingese dogs for the music-hall stage, and you come distracting my attention and impairing my efficiency by babbling about a bit on account. It isn't the pull-together spirit," I said. "It isn't the spirit that wins to wealth. These narrow petty-cash ideas can never make for success." But no, they couldn't see it. They started calling here at all hours and waylaying me in the public highways till life became an absolute curse. And now what do you think has happened?'

'What?'

'The dogs.'

'Got distemper?'

'No. Worse. My landlord's pinched them as security for his infernal rent! Sneaked the stock. Tied up the assets. Crippled the business at the very outset. Have you ever in your life heard of anything so dastardly? I know I agreed to pay the damned rent weekly and I'm about six weeks behind, but, my gosh! surely a man with a huge enterprise on his hands isn't supposed to have to worry about these trifles when he's occupied with the most delicate – Well, I put all that to old Nickerson, but a fat lot of good it did. So then I wired to you.'

'Ah!' I said, and there was a brief and pregnant pause.

'I thought,' said Ukridge, meditatively, 'that you might be able to suggest somebody I could touch.'

He spoke in a detached and almost casual way, but his eye was gleaming at me significantly, and I avoided it with a sense of guilt. My finances at the moment were in their customary unsettled condition – rather more so, in fact, than usual, owing to unsatisfactory speculations at Kempton Park on the previous Saturday; and it seemed to me that, if ever there was a time for passing the buck, this was it. I mused tensely. It was an occasion for quick thinking.

'George Tupper!' I cried, on the crest of a brainwave.

'George Tupper?' echoed Ukridge, radiantly, his gloom melting like a fog before the sun. 'The very man, by Gad! It's a most amazing thing, but I never thought of him. George Tupper, of course! Big-hearted George, the old school-chum. He'll do it like a shot and won't miss the money. These Foreign Office blokes have always got a spare tenner or two tucked away in the old sock. They pinch it out of the public funds. Rush back to town, laddie, with all speed, get hold of Tuppy, lush him up, and bite his ear for twenty quid. Now is the time for all good men to come to the aid of the party.'

I had been convinced that George Tupper would not fail us, nor did he. He parted without a murmur – even with enthusiasm. The consignment was one that might have been made to order for him. As a boy, George used to write senti-mental poetry for the school magazine, and now he is the sort of man who is always starting subscription lists and getting up memorials and presentations. He listened to my story with the serious official air which these Foreign Office fellows put on when they are deciding whether to declare war on Switzerland or send a firm note to San Marino, and was reaching for his cheque-book before I had been speaking two minutes. Ukridge's sad case seemed to move him deeply.

'Too bad,' said George. 'So he is training dogs, is he? Well, it seems very unfair that, if he has at last settled down to real work, he should be hampered by financial difficulties at the outset. We ought to do something practical for him. After all, a loan of twenty pounds cannot relieve the situation permanently.'

'I think you're a bit optimistic if you're looking on it as a loan.'

'What Ukridge needs is capital.'

'He thinks that, too. So does Gooch, the grocer.'

'Capital,' repeated George Tupper, firmly, as if he were reasoning with the plenipotentiary of some Great Power. 'Every venture requires capital at first.' He frowned thoughtfully. 'Where can we obtain capital for Ukridge?'

'Rob a bank.'

George Tupper's face cleared.

'I have it!' he said. 'I will go straight over to Wimbledon tonight and approach his aunt.'

'Aren't you forgetting that Ukridge is about as popular with her as a cold Welsh rabbit?'

'There may be a temporary estrangement, but if I tell her the facts and impress upon her that Ukridge is really making a genuine effort to earn a living—'

'Well, try it if you like. But she will probably set the parrot on to you.'

'It will have to be done diplomatically, of course. It might be as well if you did not tell Ukridge what I propose to do. I do not wish to arouse hopes which may not be fulfilled.'

A blaze of yellow on the platform of Sheep's Cray Station next morning informed me that Ukridge had come to meet my train. The sun poured down from a cloudless sky, but it took more than sunshine to make Stanley Featherstonehaugh Ukridge discard his mackintosh. He looked like an animated blob of mustard.

When the train rolled in, he was standing in solitary grandeur trying to light his pipe, but as I got out I perceived that he had been joined by a sad-looking man, who, from the rapid and earnest manner in which he talked and the vehemence of his gesticulations, appeared to be ventilating some theme on which he felt deeply. Ukridge was looking warm and harassed, and, as I approached, I could hear his voice booming in reply.

'My dear sir, my dear old horse, do be reasonable, do try to cultivate the big, broad flexible outlook—'

He saw me and broke away – not unwillingly; and, gripping my arm, drew me off along the platform. The sad-looking man followed irresolutely.

'Have you got the stuff, laddie?' inquired Ukridge, in a tense whisper. 'Have you got it?'

'Yes, here it is.'

'Put it back, put it back!' moaned Ukridge in agony, as I felt in my pocket. 'Do you know who that was I was talking to? Gooch, the grocer!'

'Goods supplied to the value of six pounds three and a penny?'

'Absolutely!'

'Well, now's your chance. Fling him a purse of gold. That'll make him look silly.'

'My dear old horse, I can't afford to go about the place squandering my cash simply in order to make grocers look silly. That money is earmarked for Nickerson, my landlord.'

'Oh! I say, I think the six-pounds-three-and-a-penny bird is following us.'

'Then for goodness' sake, laddie, let's get a move on! If that man knew we had twenty quid on us, our lives wouldn't be safe. He'd make one spring.'

He hurried me out of the station and led the way up a shady lane that wound off through the fields, slinking furtively 'like one that on a lonesome road doth walk in fear and dread, and having once looked back walks on and turns no more his head, because he knows a frightful fiend doth close behind him tread'. As a matter of fact, the frightful fiend had given up the pursuit after the first few steps, and a moment later I drew this fact to Ukridge's attention, for it was not the sort of day on which to break walking records unnecessarily.

He halted, relieved, and mopped his spacious brow with a handkerchief which I recognized as having once been my property.

'Thank goodness we've shaken him off,' he said. 'Not a bad chap in his way, I believe — a good husband and father, I'm told, and sings in the church choir. But no vision. That's what he lacks, old horse — vision. He can't understand that all vast industrial enterprises have been built up on a system of liberal and cheerful credit. Won't realize that credit is the life-blood of commerce. Without credit commerce has no elasticity. And if commerce has no elasticity what dam' good is it?'

'I don't know.'

'Nor does anybody else. Well, now that he's gone, you can give me that money. Did old Tuppy cough up cheerfully?'

'Blithely.'

'I knew it,' said Ukridge, deeply moved, 'I knew it. A good fellow. One of the best. I've always liked Tuppy. A man you can rely on. Some day, when I get going on a big scale, he shall have this back a thousandfold. I'm glad you brought small notes.'

'Why?'

'I want to scatter 'em about on the table in front of this Nickerson blighter.'

'Is this where he lives?'

We had come to a red-roofed house, set back from the road amidst trees. Ukridge wielded the knocker forcefully.

'Tell Mr Nickerson,' he said to the maid, 'that Mr Ukridge has called and would like a word.'

About the demeanour of the man who presently entered the room into which we had been shown there was that subtle but well-marked something which stamps your creditor all the world over. Mr Nickerson was a man of medium height, almost completely surrounded by whiskers, and through the shrubbery he gazed at Ukridge with frozen eyes, shooting out waves of deleterious animal magnetism. You could see at a glance that he was not fond of Ukridge. Take him for all in all,

Mr Nickerson looked like one of the less amiable prophets of the Old Testament about to interview the captive monarch of the Amalekites.

'Well?' he said, and I have never heard the word spoken in a more forbidding manner.

'I've come about the rent.'

'Ah!' said Mr Nickerson, guardedly.

'To pay it,' said Ukridge.

'To pay it!' ejaculated Mr Nickerson, incredulously.

'Here!' said Ukridge, and with a superb gesture flung money on the table.

I understood now why the massive-minded man had wanted small notes. They made a brave display. There was a light breeze blowing in through the open window, and so musical a rustling did it set up as it played about the heaped-up wealth that Mr Nickerson's austerity seemed to vanish like breath off a razor-blade. For a moment a dazed look came into his eyes and he swayed slightly; then, as he started to gather up the money, he took on the benevolent air of a bishop blessing pilgrims. As far as Mr Nickerson was concerned, the sun was up.

'Why, thank you, Mr Ukridge, I'm sure,' he said. 'Thank you very much. No hard feelings, I trust?'

'Not on my side, old horse,' responded Ukridge, affably. 'Business is business.'

'Exactly.'

'Well, I may as well take those dogs now,' said Ukridge, helping himself to a cigar from a box which he had just

97

discovered on the mantelpiece and putting a couple more in his pocket in the friendliest way. 'The sooner they're back with me, the better. They've lost a day's education as it is.'

'Why, certainly, Mr Ukridge; certainly. They are in the shed at the bottom of the garden. I will get them for you at once.'

He retreated through the door, babbling ingratiatingly.

'Amazing how fond these blokes are of money,' sighed Ukridge. 'It's a thing I don't like to see. Sordid, I call it. That blighter's eyes were gleaming, positively gleaming, laddie, as he scooped up the stuff. Good cigars these,' he added, pocketing three more.

There was a faltering footstep outside, and Mr Nickerson re-entered the room. The man appeared to have something on his mind. A glassy look was in his whisker-bordered eyes, and his mouth, though it was not easy to see it through the jungle, seemed to me to be sagging mournfully. He resembled a minor prophet who has been hit behind the ear with a stuffed eel-skin.

'Mr Ukridge!'

'Hullo?'

'The – the little dogs!'

'Well?'

'The little dogs!'

'What about them?'

'They have gone!'

'Gone?'

'Run away!'

'Run away? How the devil could they run away?'

'There seems to have been a loose board at the back of the shed. The little dogs must have wriggled through. There is no trace of them to be found.'

Ukridge flung up his arms despairingly. He swelled like a captive balloon. His pince-nez rocked on his nose, his mackintosh flapped menacingly, and his collar sprang off its stud. He brought his fist down with a crash on the table.

'Upon my Sam!'

'I am extremely sorry—'

'Upon my Sam!' cried Ukridge. 'It's hard. It's pretty hard. I come down here to inaugurate a great business, which would eventually have brought trade and prosperity to the whole neighbourhood, and I have hardly had time to turn round and attend to the preliminary details of the enterprise when this man comes and sneaks my dogs. And now he tells me with a light laugh—'

'Mr Ukridge, I assure you—'

'Tells me with a light laugh that they've gone. Gone! Gone where? Why, dash it, they may be all over the county. A fat chance I've got of ever seeing them again. Six valuable Pekingese, already educated practically to the stage where they could have been sold at an enormous profit—'

Mr Nickerson was fumbling guiltily, and now he produced from his pocket a crumpled wad of notes, which he thrust agitatedly upon Ukridge, who waved them away with loathing.

'This gentleman,' boomed Ukridge, indicating me with a sweeping gesture, 'happens to be a lawyer. It is extremely lucky that he chanced to come down today to pay me a visit. Have you followed the proceedings closely?'

I said I had followed them very closely.

'Is it your opinion that an action will lie?'

I said it seemed highly probable, and this expert ruling appeared to put the final touch on Mr Nickerson's collapse. Almost tearfully he urged the notes on Ukridge.

'What's this?' said Ukridge, loftily.

'I – I thought, Mr Ukridge, that, if it were agreeable to you, you might consent to take your money back, and – and consider the episode closed.'

Ukridge turned to me with raised eyebrows.

'Ha!' he cried. 'Ha, ha!'

'Ha, ha!' I chorused, dutifully.

'He thinks that he can close the episode by giving me my money back. Isn't that rich?'

'Fruity,' I agreed.

'Those dogs were worth hundreds of pounds, and he thinks he can square me with a rotten twenty. Would you have believed it if you hadn't heard it with your own ears, old horse?'

'Never!'

'I'll tell you what I'll do,' said Ukridge, after thought. 'I'll take this money.' Mr Nickerson thanked him. 'And there are one or two trifling accounts which want settling with some of the local tradesmen. You will square those—'

'Certainly, Mr Ukridge, certainly.'

'And after that – well, I'll have to think it over. If I decide to institute proceedings my lawyer will communicate with you in due course.'

And we left the wretched man, cowering despicably behind his whiskers.

It seemed to me, as we passed down the tree-shaded lane and out into the white glare of the road, that Ukridge was bearing himself in his hour of disaster with a rather admirable fortitude. His stock-in-trade, the life-blood of his enterprise, was scattered all over Kent, probably never to return, and all that he had to show on the other side of the balance-sheet was the cancelling of a few weeks' back rent and the paying-off of Gooch, the grocer, and his friends. It was a situation which might well have crushed the spirit of an ordinary man, but Ukridge seemed by no means dejected. Jaunty, rather. His eyes shone behind their pince-nez and he whistled a rollicking air. When presently he began to sing, I felt that it was time to create a diversion.

'What are you going to do?' I asked.

'Who, me?' said Ukridge, buoyantly. 'Oh, I'm coming back to town on the next train. You don't mind hoofing it to the next station, do you? It's only five miles. It might be a trifle risky to start from Sheep's Cray.'

'Why risky?'

'Because of the dogs, of course.'

'Dogs?'

Ukridge hummed a gay strain.

'Oh, yes. I forgot to tell you about that. I've got 'em.'

'What?'

'Yes. I went out late last night and pinched them out of the shed.' He chuckled amusedly. 'Perfectly simple. Only needed a clear, level head. I borrowed a dead cat and tied a string to it, legged it to old Nickerson's garden after dark, dug a board out of the back of the shed, and shoved my head down and chirruped. The dogs came trickling out, and I hared off, towing old Colonel Cat on his string. Great run while it lasted, laddie. Hounds picked up the scent right away and started off in a bunch at fifty miles an hour. Cat and I doing a steady fifty-five. Thought every minute old Nickerson would hear and start blazing away with a gun, but nothing happened. I led the pack across country for a run of twenty minutes without a check, parked the dogs in my sitting-room, and so to bed. Took it out of me, by gosh! Not so young as I was.'

I was silent for a moment, conscious of a feeling almost of reverence. This man was undoubtedly spacious. There had always been something about Ukridge that dulled the moral sense.

'Well,' I said at length, 'you've certainly got vision.'

'Yes?' said Ukridge, gratified.

'*And* the big, broad, flexible outlook.'

'Got to, laddie, nowadays. The foundation of a successful business career.'

'And what's the next move?'

We were drawing near to the White Cottage. It stood and broiled in the sunlight, and I hoped that there might be something cool to drink inside it. The window of the sitting-room was open, and through it came the yapping of Pekingese.

'Oh, I shall find another cottage somewhere else,' said Ukridge, eyeing his little home with a certain sentimentality. 'That won't be hard. Lots of cottages all over the place. And then I shall buckle down to serious work. You'll be astounded at the progress I've made already. In a minute I'll show you what those dogs can do.'

'They can bark all right.'

'Yes. They seem excited about something. You know, laddie, I've had a great idea. When I saw you at your rooms my scheme was to specialize in performing dogs for the music-halls – what you might call professional dogs. But I've been thinking it over, and now I don't see why I shouldn't go in for developing amateur talent as well. Say you have a dog – Fido, the household pet – and you think it would brighten the home if he could do a few tricks from time to time. Well, you're a busy man, you haven't the time to give up to teaching him. So you just tie a label to his collar and ship him off for a month to the Ukridge Dog College, and back he comes, thoroughly educated. No trouble, no worry, easy terms. Upon my Sam, I'm not sure there isn't more money in the amateur branch than in the professional. I don't see why eventually dog owners shouldn't send their dogs to me as a regular thing, just as they send their sons to Eton and Winchester. My golly! this idea's beginning to develop. I'll tell you what – how would it be to issue special collars to all dogs which have graduated from my college? Something distinctive which everybody would recognize. See what I mean? Sort of badge of honour. Fellow with a dog entitled to wear the Ukridge collar would be in a position to look down on the bloke whose dog hadn't got one. Gradually it would get so that anybody in a decent social position would be ashamed to be seen out with a non-Ukridge dog. The thing would become a landslide. Dogs would pour in from all corners of the country. More work than I could handle. Have to start branches. The scheme's colossal. Millions in it, my boy! Millions!' He paused with his fingers on the handle of the front door. 'Of course,' he went on, 'just at present it's no good blinking the fact that I'm hampered and handicapped by lack of funds and can only approach the thing on a small scale. What it amounts to, laddie, is that somehow or other I've got to get capital.'

It seemed the moment to spring the glad news.

'I promised him I wouldn't mention it,' I said, 'for fear it might lead to disappointment, but as a matter of fact George Tupper is trying to raise some capital for you. I left him last night starting out to get it.'

'George Tupper!' – Ukridge's eyes dimmed with a not unmanly emotion – 'George Tupper! By Gad, that fellow is the salt of the earth. Good, loyal fellow! A true friend. A man you can rely on. Upon my Sam, if there were more fellows about like old Tuppy, there wouldn't be all this modern pessimism and unrest. Did he seem to have any idea where he could raise a bit of capital for me?'

'Yes. He went round to tell your aunt about your coming down here to train those Pekes, and – What's the matter?'

A fearful change had come over Ukridge's jubilant front. His eyes bulged, his jaw sagged. With the addition of a few feet of grey whiskers he would have looked exactly like the recent Mr Nickerson.

'My aunt?' he mumbled, swaying on the door-handle.

'Yes. What's the matter? He thought, if he told her all about it, she might relent and rally round.'

The sigh of a gallant fighter at the end of his strength forced its way up from Ukridge's mackintosh-covered bosom.

'Of all the dashed, infernal, officious, meddling, muddling, fat-headed, interfering asses,' he said, wanly, 'George Tupper is the worst.'

'What do you mean?'

'The man oughtn't to be at large. He's a public menace.'

'But—'

'Those dogs *belong* to my aunt. I pinched them when she chucked me out!'

Inside the cottage the Pekingese were still yapping industriously.

'Upon my Sam,' said Ukridge, 'it's a little hard.'

I think he would have said more, but at this point a voice spoke with a sudden and awful abruptness from the interior of the cottage. It was a woman's voice, a quiet, steely voice, a voice, it seemed to me, that suggested cold eyes, a beaky nose, and hair like gun-metal.

'Stanley!'

That was all it said, but it was enough. Ukridge's eye met mine in a wild surmise. He seemed to shrink into his mackintosh like a snail surprised while eating lettuce.

'Stanley!'

'Yes, Aunt Julia?' quavered Ukridge.

'Come here. I wish to speak to you.'

'Yes, Aunt Julia.'

I sidled out into the road. Inside the cottage the yapping of the Pekingese had become quite hysterical. I found myself trotting, and then – though it was a warm day – running quite rapidly. I could have stayed if I had wanted to, but somehow I did not want to. Something seemed to tell me that on this holy domestic scene I should be an intruder.

What it was that gave me that impression I do not know – probably vision or the big, broad, flexible outlook.

The Story of William

Miss Postlethwaite, our able and vigilant barmaid, had whispered to us that the gentleman sitting over there in the corner was an American gentleman.

'Comes from America,' added Miss Postlethwaite, making her meaning clearer.

'From America?' echoed we.

'From America,' said Miss Postlethwaite. 'He's an American.'

Mr Mulliner rose with an old-world grace. We do not often get Americans in the bar-parlour of the Angler's Rest. When we do, we welcome them. We make them realize that Hands Across the Sea is no mere phrase.

'Good evening, sir,' said Mr Mulliner. 'I wonder if you would care to join my friend and myself in a little refreshment?'

'Very kind of you, sir.'

'Miss Postlethwaite, the usual. I understand you are from the other side, sir. Do you find our English country-side pleasant?'

'Delightful. Though, of course, if I may say so, scarcely to be compared with the scenery of my home State.'

'What State is that?'

'California,' replied the other, baring his head. 'California, the Jewel State of the Union. With its azure sea, its noble hills, its eternal sunshine, and its fragrant flowers, California stands alone. Peopled by stalwart men and womanly women ...'

'California would be all right,' said Mr Mulliner, 'if it wasn't for the earthquakes.'

Our guest started as though some venomous snake had bitten him.

'Earthquakes are absolutely unknown in California,' he said, hoarsely.

'What about the one in 1906?'

'That was not an earthquake. It was a fire.'

'An earthquake, I always understood,' said Mr Mulliner. 'My Uncle William was out there during it, and many a time has he said to me, "My boy, it was the San Francisco earthquake that won me a bride."'

'Couldn't have been the earthquake. May have been the fire.'

'Well, I will tell you the story, and you shall judge for yourself.'

'I shall be glad to hear your story about the San Francisco fire,' said the Californian, courteously.

*

My Uncle William (said Mr Mulliner) was returning from the East at the time. The commercial interests of the Mulliners have always been far-flung: and he had been over in China looking into the workings of a tea-exporting business in which he held a number of shares. It was his intention to get off the boat at San Francisco and cross the continent by rail. He particularly wanted to see the Grand Canyon of Arizona. And when he found that Myrtle Banks had for years cherished the same desire, it seemed to him so plain a proof that they were twin souls that he decided to offer her his hand and heart without delay.

This Miss Banks had been a fellow-traveller on the boat all the way from Hong-Kong; and day by day William Mulliner had fallen more and more deeply in love with her. So on the last day of the voyage, as they were steaming in at the Golden Gate, he proposed.

I have never been informed of the exact words which he employed, but no doubt they were eloquent. All the Mulliners have been able speakers, and on such an occasion, he would, of course, have extended himself. When at length he finished, it seemed to him that the girl's attitude was distinctly promising. She stood gazing over the rail into the water below in a sort of rapt way. Then she turned.

'Mr Mulliner,' she said, 'I am greatly flattered and honoured by what you have just told me.' These things happened, you will remember, in the days when girls talked like that. 'You have paid me the greatest compliment a man can bestow on a woman. And yet . . .'

William Mulliner's heart stood still. He did not like that 'And yet ...'

'Is there another?' he muttered.

'Well, yes, there is. Mr Franklyn proposed to me this morning. I told him I would think it over.'

There was a silence. William was telling himself that he had been afraid of that bounder Franklyn all along. He might have known, he felt, that Desmond Franklyn would be a menace. The man was one of those lean, keen, hawk-faced, Empire-building sort of chaps you find out East – the kind of fellow who stands on deck chewing his moustache with a far-away look in his eyes, and then, when the girl asks him what he is thinking about, draws a short, quick breath and says he is sorry to be so absent-minded, but a sunset like that always reminds him of the day when he killed the four pirates with his bare hands and saved dear old Tuppy Smithers in the nick of time.

'There is a great glamour about Mr Franklyn,' said Myrtle Banks. 'We women admire men who do things. A girl cannot help but respect a man who once killed three sharks with a Boy Scout pocket-knife.'

'So he says,' growled William.

'He showed me the pocket-knife,' said the girl, simply. 'And on another occasion he brought down two lions with one shot.'

William Mulliner's heart was heavy, but he struggled on.

'Very possibly he may have done these things,' he said, 'but surely marriage means more than this. Personally, if I were a girl, I would go rather for a certain steadiness and stability of character. To illustrate what I mean, did you happen to see me win the Egg-and-Spoon race at the ship's sports? Now there, it seems to me, in what I might call microcosm, was an exhibition of all the qualities a married man most requires – intense coolness, iron resolution, and a quiet, unassuming courage. The man who under test conditions has carried an egg one and a half times round a deck in a small spoon, is a man who can be trusted.'

She seemed to waver, but only for a moment.

'I must think,' she said. 'I must think.'

'Certainly,' said William. 'You will let me see something of you at the hotel, after we have landed?'

'Of course. And if – I mean to say, whatever happens, I shall always look on you as a dear, dear friend.'

'M'yes,' said William Mulliner.

For three days my Uncle William's stay in San Francisco was as pleasant as could reasonably be expected, considering that Desmond Franklyn was also stopping at his and Miss Banks's hotel. He contrived to get the girl to himself to quite a satisfactory extent; and they spent many happy hours together in the Golden Gate Park and at the Cliff House, watching the seals basking on the rocks. But on the evening of the third day the blow fell.

'Mr Mulliner,' said Myrtle Banks, 'I want to tell you something.'

'Anything,' breathed William tenderly, 'except that you are going to marry that perisher Franklyn.'

'But that is exactly what I was going to tell you, and I must not let you call him a perisher, for he is a very brave, intrepid man.'

'When did you decide on this rash act?' asked William dully.

'Scarcely an hour ago. We were talking in the garden, and somehow or other we got on to the subject of rhinoceroses. He then told me how he had once been chased up a tree by a rhinoceros in Africa and escaped by throwing pepper in the brute's eyes. He most fortunately chanced to be eating his lunch when the animal arrived, and he had a hard-boiled egg and the pepper-pot in his hands. When I heard this story, like Desdemona, I loved him for the dangers he had passed, and he loved me that I did pity them. The wedding is to be in June.'

William Mulliner ground his teeth in a sudden access of jealous rage.

'Personally,' he said, 'I consider that the story you have just related reveals this man Franklyn in a very dubious – I might almost say sinister – light. On his own showing, the leading trait in his character appears to be cruelty to animals. The fellow seems totally incapable of meeting a shark or a rhinoceros or any other of our dumb friends without instantly going out of his way to inflict bodily injury on it. The last thing I would wish is to be indelicate, but I cannot refrain from pointing out that, if your union is blessed, your children will probably be the sort of children who kick cats and tie tin cans to dogs' tails. If you take my advice, you will write the man a little note, saying that you are sorry but you have changed your mind.'

The girl rose in a marked manner.

'I do not require your advice, Mr Mulliner,' she said, coldly. 'And I have not changed my mind.'

Instantly William Mulliner was all contrition. There is a certain stage in the progress of a man's love when he feels like curling up in a ball and making little bleating noises if the object of his affections so much as looks squiggle-eyed at him; and this stage my Uncle William had reached. He followed her as she paced proudly away through the hotel lobby, and stammered incoherent apologies. But Myrtle Banks was adamant.

'Leave me, Mr Mulliner,' she said, pointing at the revolving door that led into the street. 'You have maligned a better man than yourself, and I wish to have nothing more to do with you. Go!'

William went, as directed. And so great was the confusion of his mind that he got stuck in the revolving door and had gone round in it no fewer than eleven times before the hall-porter came to extricate him.

'I would have removed you from the machinery earlier, sir,' said the hall-porter deferentially, having deposited him safely in the street, 'but my bet with my mate in there called for ten laps. I waited till you had completed eleven so that there should be no argument.'

William looked at him dazedly.

'Hall-porter,' he said.

'Sir?'

'Tell me, hall-porter,' said William, 'suppose the only girl you have ever loved had gone and got engaged to another, what would you do?'

The hall-porter considered.

'Let me get this right,' he said. 'The proposition is, if I have followed you correctly, what would I do supposing the Jane on whom I had always looked as a steady mamma had handed me the old skimmer and told me to take all the air I needed because she had gotten another sweetie?'

'Precisely.'

'Your question is easily answered,' said the hall-porter. 'I would go around the corner and get me a nice stiff drink at Mike's Place.'

'A drink?'

'Yes, sir. A nice stiff one.'

'At – where did you say?'

'Mike's Place, sir. Just round the corner. You can't miss it.'

William thanked him and walked away. The man's words had started a new, and in many ways interesting, train of thought. A drink? And a nice stiff one? There might be something in it.

William Mulliner had never tasted alcohol in his life. He had promised his late mother that he would not do so until he was either twenty-one or forty-one – he could never remember which. He was at present twenty-nine; but wishing to be on the safe side in case he had got his figures wrong, he had remained a teetotaller. But now, as he walked listlessly along the street towards the corner, it seemed to him that his mother in the special circumstances could not reasonably object if he took a slight snort. He raised his eyes to heaven, as though to ask her if a couple of quick ones might not be permitted; and he fancied that a faint, far-off voice whispered, 'Go to it!'

And at this moment he found himself standing outside a brightly-lighted saloon.

For an instant he hesitated. Then, as a twinge of anguish in the region of his broken heart reminded him of the necessity for immediate remedies, he pushed open the swing doors and went in.

The principal feature of the cheerful, brightly-lit room in which he found himself was a long counter, at which were standing a number of the citizenry, each with an elbow on the woodwork and a foot upon the neat brass rail which ran below. Behind the counter appeared the upper section of one of the most benevolent and kindly-looking men that William had ever seen. He had a large smooth face, and he wore a white coat, and he eyed William, as he advanced, with a sort of reverent joy.

'Is this Mike's Place?' asked William.

'Yes, sir,' replied the white-coated man.

'Are you Mike?'

'No, sir. But I am his representative, and have full authority to act on his behalf. What can I have the pleasure of doing for you?'

The man's whole attitude made him seem so like a

large-hearted elder brother that William felt no diffidence
about confiding in him. He placed an elbow on the counter
and a foot on the rail, and spoke with a sob in his voice.

'Suppose the only girl you had ever loved had gone and got
engaged to another, what in your view would best meet the
case?'

The gentlemanly bar-tender pondered for some moments.

'Well,' he replied at length, 'I advance it, you understand,
as a purely personal opinion, and I shall not be in the least
offended if you decide not to act upon it; but my suggestion –
for what it is worth – is that you try a Dynamite Dew-Drop.'

One of the crowd that had gathered sympathetically round
shook his head. He was a charming man with a black eye, who
had shaved on the preceding Thursday.

'Much better give him a Dreamland Special.'

A second man, in a sweater and a cloth cap, had yet another
theory.

'You can't beat an Undertaker's Joy.'

They were all so perfectly delightful and appeared to have
his interests so unselfishly at heart that William could not bring
himself to choose between them. He solved the problem in
diplomatic fashion by playing no favourites and ordering all
three of the beverages recommended.

The effect was instantaneous and gratifying. As he drained
the first glass, it seemed to him that a torchlight procession, of
whose existence he had hitherto not been aware, had begun to
march down his throat and explore the recesses of his stomach.

The second glass, though slightly too heavily charged with molten lava, was extremely palatable. It helped the torchlight procession along by adding to it a brass band of singular power and sweetness of tone. And with the third somebody began to touch off fireworks inside his head.

William felt better – not only spiritually but physically. He seemed to himself to be a bigger, finer man, and the loss of Myrtle Banks had somehow in a flash lost nearly all its importance. After all, as he said to the man with the black eye, Myrtle Banks wasn't everybody.

'Now what do you recommend?' he asked the man with the sweater, having turned the last glass upside down.

The other mused, one fore-finger thoughtfully pressed against the side of his face.

'Well, I'll tell you,' he said. 'When my brother Elmer lost his girl, he drank straight rye. Yes, sir. That's what he drank – straight rye. "I've lost my girl," he said, "and I'm going to drink straight rye." That's what he said. Yes, sir, straight rye.'

'And was your brother Elmer,' asked William, anxiously, 'a man whose example in your opinion should be followed? Was he a man you could trust?'

'He owned the biggest duck-farm in the southern half of Illinois.'

'That settles it,' said William. 'What was good enough for a duck man who owned half Illinois is good enough for me. Oblige me,' he said to the gentlemanly bar-tender, 'by asking these gentlemen what they will have, and start pouring.'

The bar-tender obeyed, and William, having tried a pint or two of the strange liquid just to see if he liked it, found that he did, and ordered some. He then began to move about among his new friends, patting one on the shoulder, slapping another affably on the back, and asking a third what his Christian name was.

'I want you all,' he said, climbing on to the counter so that his voice should carry better, 'to come and stay with me in England. Never in my life have I met men whose faces I liked so much. More like brothers than anything is the way I regard you. So just you pack up a few things and come along and put up at my little place for as long as you can manage. You particularly, my dear old chap,' he added, beaming at the man in the sweater.

'Thanks,' said the man with the sweater.

'What did you say?' said William.

'I said, "Thanks."'

William slowly removed his coat and rolled up his shirtsleeves.

'I call you gentlemen to witness,' he said, quietly, 'that I have been grossly insulted by this gentleman who has just grossly insulted me. I am not a quarrelsome man, but if anybody wants a row they can have it. And when it comes to being cursed and sworn at by an ugly bounder in a sweater and a cloth cap, it is time to take steps.'

And with these spirited words William Mulliner sprang from the counter, grasped the other by the throat, and bit him sharply on the right ear. There was a confused interval, during which somebody attached himself to the collar of William's waistcoat and the seat of William's trousers, and then a sense of swift movement and rush of cool air.

William discovered that he was seated on the pavement outside the saloon. A hand emerged from the swing door and threw his hat out. And he was alone with the night and his meditations.

These were, as you may suppose, of a singularly bitter nature. Sorrow and disillusionment racked William Mulliner like a physical pain. That his friends inside there, in spite of the fact that he had been all sweetness and light and had not done a thing to them, should have thrown him out into the hard street was the saddest thing he had ever heard of; and for some minutes he sat there, weeping silently.

Presently he heaved himself to his feet and, placing one foot with infinite delicacy in front of the other, and then drawing the other one up and placing it with infinite delicacy in front of that, he began to walk back to his hotel.

At the corner he paused. There were some railings on his right. He clung to them and rested a while.

The railings to which William Mulliner had attached himself belonged to a brownstone house of the kind that seems destined from the first moment of its building to receive guests, both resident and transient, at a moderate weekly rental. It was, in fact, as he would have discovered had he been clear-sighted enough to read the card over the door, Mrs Beulah O'Brien's

Theatrical Boarding-House ('A Home from Home – No Cheques Cashed – This Means You').

But William was not in the best of shape for reading cards. A sort of mist had obscured the world, and he was finding it difficult to keep his eyes open. And presently, his chin wedged into the railings, he fell into a dreamless sleep.

He was awakened by light flashing in his eyes; and, opening them, saw that a window opposite where he was standing had become brightly illuminated. His slumbers had cleared his vision; and he was able to observe that the room into which he was looking was a dining-room. The long table was set for the evening meal; and to William, as he gazed, the sight of that cosy apartment, with the gaslight falling on the knives and forks and spoons, seemed the most pathetic and poignant that he had ever beheld.

A mood of the most extreme sentimentality now had him in its grip. The thought that he would never own a little home like that racked him from stem to stern with an almost unbearable torment. What, argued William, clinging to the railings and crying weakly, could compare, when you came right down to it, with a little home? A man with a little home is all right, whereas a man without a little home is just a bit of flotsam on the ocean of life. If Myrtle Banks had only consented to marry him, he would have had a little home. But she had refused to marry him, so he would never have a little home. What Myrtle Banks wanted, felt William, was a good swift clout on the side of the head.

The thought pleased him. He was feeling physically perfect again now, and seemed to have shaken off completely the slight indisposition from which he had been suffering. His legs had lost their tendency to act independently of the rest of his body. His head felt clearer, and he had a sense of overwhelming strength. If ever, in short, there was a moment when he could administer that clout on the side of the head to Myrtle Banks as it should be administered, that moment was now.

He was on the point of moving off to find her and teach her what it meant to stop a man like himself from having a little home, when someone entered the room into which he was looking, and he paused to make further inspection.

The new arrival was a coloured maid-servant. She staggered to the head of the table beneath the weight of a large tureen containing, so William suspected, hash. A moment later a stout woman with bright golden hair came in and sat down opposite the tureen.

The instinct to watch other people eat is one of the most deeply implanted in the human bosom, and William lingered, intent. There was, he told himself, no need to hurry. He knew which was Myrtle's room in the hotel. It was just across the corridor from his own. He could pop in any time, during the night, and give her that clout. Meanwhile, he wanted to watch these people eat hash.

And then the door opened again, and there filed into the room a little procession. And William, clutching the railings, watched it with bulging eyes.

The procession was headed by an elderly man in a check suit with a carnation in his buttonhole. He was about three feet six in height, though the military jauntiness with which he carried himself made him seem fully three feet seven. He was followed by a younger man who wore spectacles and whose height was perhaps three feet four. And behind these two came, in single file, six others, scaling down by degrees until, bringing up the rear of the procession, there entered a rather stout man in tweeds and bedroom slippers who could not have measured more than two feet eight.

They took their places at the table. Hash was distributed to all. And the man in tweeds, having inspected his plate with obvious relish, removed his slippers and, picking up his knife and fork with his toes, fell to with a keen appetite.

William Mulliner uttered a soft moan, and tottered away.

It was a black moment for my Uncle William. Only an instant before he had been congratulating himself on having shaken off the effects of his first indulgence in alcohol after an abstinence of twenty-nine years; but now he perceived that he was still intoxicated.

Intoxicated? The word did not express it by a mile. He was oiled, boiled, fried, plastered, whiffled, sozzled, and blotto. Only by the exercise of the most consummate caution and address could he hope to get back to his hotel and reach his bedroom without causing an open scandal.

Of course, if his walk that night had taken him a few yards farther down the street than the door of Mike's Place, he would

have seen that there was a very simple explanation of the spectacle which he had just witnessed. A walk so extended would
have brought him to the San Francisco Palace of Varieties, outside which large posters proclaimed the exclusive engagement
for two weeks of

MURPHY'S MIDGETS.
BIGGER AND BETTER THAN EVER.

But of the existence of these posters he was not aware; and
it is not too much to say that the iron entered into William
Mulliner's soul.

That his legs should have become temporarily unscrewed at
the joints was a phenomenon which he had been able to bear
with fortitude. That his head should be feeling as if a good many
bees had decided to use it as a hive was unpleasant, but not
unbearably so. But that his brain should have gone off its castors
and be causing him to see visions was the end of all things.

William had always prided himself on the keenness of his
mental powers. All through the long voyage on the ship, when
Desmond Franklyn had related anecdotes illustrative of his
prowess as a man of Action, William Mulliner had always consoled himself by feeling that in the matter of brain he could
give Franklyn three bisques and a beating any time he chose to
start. And now, it seemed, he had lost even this advantage over
his rival. For Franklyn, dull-witted clod though he might be,
was not such an absolute minus quantity that he would imagine

he had seen a man of two feet eight cutting up hash with his toes. That hideous depth of mental decay had been reserved for William Mulliner.

Moodily he made his way back to his hotel. In a corner of the Palm Room he saw Myrtle Banks deep in conversation with Franklyn, but all desire to give her a clout on the side of the head had now left him. With his chin sunk on his breast, he entered the elevator and was carried up to his room.

Here as rapidly as his quivering fingers would permit, he undressed; and, climbing into the bed as it came round for the second time, lay for a space with wide-open eyes. He had been too shaken to switch his light off, and the rays of the lamp shone on the handsome ceiling which undulated above him. He gave himself up to thought once more.

No doubt, he felt, thinking it over now, his mother had had some very urgent reason for withholding him from alcoholic drink. She must have known of some family secret, sedulously guarded from his infant ears – some dark tale of a fatal Mulliner taint. 'William must never learn of this!' she had probably said when they told her the old legend of how every Mulliner for centuries back had died a maniac, victim at last to the fatal fluid. And to-night, despite her gentle care, he had found out for himself.

He saw now that this derangement of his eyesight was only the first step in the gradual dissolution which was the Mulliner Curse. Soon his sense of hearing would go, then his sense of touch.

He sat up in bed. It seemed to him that, as he gazed at the ceiling, a considerable section of it had parted from the parent body and fallen with a crash to the floor.

William Mulliner stared dumbly. He knew, of course, that it was an illusion. But what a perfect illusion! If he had not had the special knowledge which he possessed, he would have stated without fear of contradiction that there was a gap six feet wide above him and a mass of dust and plaster on the carpet below.

And even as his eyes deceived him, so did his ears. He seemed to be conscious of a babel of screams and shouts. The corridor, he could have sworn, was full of flying feet. The world appeared to be all bangs and crashes and thuds. A cold fear gripped at William's heart. His sense of hearing was playing tricks with him already.

His whole being recoiled from making the final experiment, but he forced himself out of bed. He reached a finger towards the nearest heap of plaster and drew it back with a groan. Yes, it was as he feared, his sense of touch had gone wrong too. That heap of plaster, though purely a figment of his disordered brain, had felt solid.

So there it was. One little moderately festive evening at Mike's Place, and the Curse of the Mulliners had got him. Within an hour of absorbing the first drink of his life, it had deprived him of his sight, his hearing, and his sense of touch. Quick service, felt William Mulliner.

As he climbed back into bed, it appeared to him that two of

the walls fell out. He shut his eyes, and presently sleep, which has been well called Tired Nature's Sweet Restorer, brought oblivion. His last waking thought was that he imagined he had heard another wall go.

William Mulliner was a sound sleeper, and it was many hours before consciousness returned to him. When he awoke, he looked about him in astonishment. The haunting horror of the night had passed; and now, though conscious of a rather severe headache, he knew that he was seeing things as they were.

And yet it seemed odd to think that what he beheld was not the remains of some nightmare. Not only was the world slightly yellow and a bit blurred about the edges, but it had changed in its very essentials overnight. Where eight hours before there had been a wall, only an open space appeared, with bright sunlight streaming through it. The ceiling was on the floor, and almost the only thing remaining of what had been an expensive bedroom in a first-class hotel was the bed. Very strange, he thought, and very irregular.

A voice broke in upon his meditations.

'Why, Mr Mulliner!'

William turned, and being, like all the Mulliners, the soul of modesty, dived abruptly beneath the bed-clothes. For the voice was the voice of Myrtle Banks. And she was in his room!

'Mr Mulliner!'

William poked his head out cautiously. And then he

perceived that the proprieties had not been outraged as he had imagined. Miss Banks was not in his room, but in the corridor. The intervening wall had disappeared. Shaken, but relieved, he sat up in bed, the sheet drawn round his shoulders.

'You don't mean to say you're still in bed?' gasped the girl.

'Why, is it awfully late?' said William.

'Did you actually stay up here all through it?'

'Through what?'

'The earthquake.'

'What earthquake?'

'The earthquake last night.'

'Oh, that earthquake?' said William, carelessly. 'I did notice some sort of an earthquake. I remember seeing the ceiling come down and saying to myself, "I shouldn't wonder if that wasn't an earthquake." And then the walls fell out, and I said, "Yes, I believe it is an earthquake." And then I turned over and went to sleep.'

Myrtle Banks was staring at him with eyes that reminded him partly of twin stars and partly of a snail's.

'You must be the bravest man in the world!'

William gave a curt laugh.

'Oh, well,' he said, 'I may not spend my whole life per-secuting unfortunate sharks with pocket-knives, but I find I generally manage to keep my head fairly well in a crisis. We Mulliners are like that. We do not say much, but we have the right stuff in us.'

He clutched his head. A sharp spasm had reminded him how much of the right stuff he had in him at that moment.

'My hero!' breathed the girl, almost inaudibly.

'And how is your fiancé this bright, sunny morning?' asked William, nonchalantly. It was torture to refer to the man, but he must show her that a Mulliner knew how to take his medicine.

She gave a little shudder.

'I have no fiancé,' she said.

'But I thought you told me you and Franklyn . . .'

'I am no longer engaged to Mr Franklyn. Last night, when the earthquake started, I cried to him to help me; and he with a hasty "Some other time!" over his shoulder, disappeared into the open like something shot out of a gun. I never saw a man run so fast. This morning I broke off the engagement.' She uttered a scornful laugh.

'Sharks and pocket-knives! I don't believe he ever killed a shark in his life.'

'And even if he did,' said William, 'what of it? I mean to say, how infrequently in married life must the necessity for killing sharks with pocket-knives arise! What a husband needs is not some purely adventitious gift like that — a parlour trick, you might almost call it — but a steady character, a warm and generous disposition, and a loving heart.'

'How true!' she murmured, dreamily.

'Myrtle,' said William, 'I would be a husband like that. The steady character, the warm and generous disposition, and the loving heart to which I have alluded are at your disposal. Will you accept them?'

'I will,' said Myrtle Banks.

And that (concluded Mr Mulliner) is the story of my Uncle William's romance. And you will readily understand, having heard it, how his eldest son, my cousin, J. S. F. E. Mulliner, got his name.

'J. S. F. E.?' I said.

'John San Francisco Earthquake Mulliner,' explained my friend.

'There never was a San Francisco earthquake,' said the Californian. 'Only a fire.'

Uncle Fred Flits By

In order that they might enjoy their afternoon luncheon coffee in peace, the Crumpet had taken the guest whom he was entertaining at the Drones Club to the smaller and less frequented of the two smoking-rooms. In the other, he explained, though the conversation always touched an exceptionally high level of brilliance, there was apt to be a good deal of sugar thrown about.

The guest said he understood.

'Young blood, eh?'

'That's right. Young blood.'

'And animal spirits.'

'And animal, as you say, spirits,' agreed the Crumpet. 'We get a fairish amount of those here.'

'The complaint, however, is not, I observe, universal.'

'Eh?'

The other drew his host's attention to the doorway, where

a young man in form-fitting tweeds had just appeared. The aspect of this young man was haggard. His eyes glared wildly and he sucked at an empty cigarette-holder. If he had a mind, there was something on it. When the Crumpet called to him to come and join the party, he merely shook his head in a distraught sort of way and disappeared, looking like a character out of a Greek tragedy pursued by the Fates.

The Crumpet sighed. 'Poor old Pongo!'

'Pongo?'

'That was Pongo Twistleton. He's all broken up about his Uncle Fred.'

'Dead?'

'No such luck. Coming up to London again tomorrow. Pongo had a wire this morning.'

'And that upsets him?'

'Naturally. After what happened last time.'

'What was that?'

'Ah!' said the Crumpet.

'What happened last time?'

'You may well ask.'

'I do ask.'

'Ah!' said the Crumpet.

Poor old Pongo (said the Crumpet) has often discussed his Uncle Fred with me, and if there weren't tears in his eyes when he did so, I don't know a tear in the eye when I see one. In round numbers the Earl of Ickenham, of Ickenham Hall, Ickenham, Hants, he lives in the country most of the year, but from time to time has a nasty way of slipping his collar and getting loose and descending upon Pongo at his flat in the Albany. And every time he does so, the unhappy young blighter is subjected to some soul-testing experience. Because the trouble with this uncle is that, though sixty if a day, he becomes on arriving in the metropolis as young as he feels – which is, apparently, a young-ish twenty-two. I don't know if you happen to know what the word 'excesses' means, but those are what Pongo's Uncle Fred from the country, when in London, invariably commits.

It wouldn't so much matter, mind you, if he would confine his activities to the club premises. We're pretty broad-minded here, and if you stop short of smashing the piano, there isn't much that you can do at the Drones that will cause the raised eyebrow and the sharp intake of breath. The snag is that he will insist on lugging Pongo out in the open and there, right in the public eye, proceeding to step high, wide and plentiful.

So when, on the occasion to which I allude, he stood pink and genial on Pongo's hearth-rug, bulging with Pongo's lunch and wreathed in the smoke of one of Pongo's cigars, and said: 'And now, my boy, for a pleasant and instructive afternoon,' you will readily understand why the unfortunate young clam gazed at him as he would have gazed at two-penn'orth of dynamite, had he discovered it lighting up in his presence.

'A what?' he said, giving at the knees and paling beneath the tan a bit.

'A pleasant and instructive afternoon,' repeated Lord Ickenham, rolling the words round his tongue. 'I propose that you place yourself in my hands and leave the programme entirely to me.'

Now, owing to Pongo's circumstances being such as to necessitate his getting into the aged relative's ribs at intervals and shaking him down for an occasional much-needed tenner or what not, he isn't in a position to use the iron hand with the old buster. But at these words he displayed a manly firmness.

'You aren't going to get me to the dog races again.'

'No, no.'

'You remember what happened last June.'

'Quite,' said Lord Ickenham, 'quite. Though I still think that a wiser magistrate would have been content with a mere reprimand.'

'And I won't—'

'Certainly not. Nothing of that kind at all. What I propose to do this afternoon is to take you to visit the home of your ancestors.'

Pongo did not get this.

'I thought Ickenham was the home of my ancestors.'

'It is one of the homes of your ancestors. They also resided rather nearer the heart of things, at a place called Mitching Hill.'

'Down in the suburbs, do you mean?'

'The neighbourhood is now suburban, true. It is many years since the meadows where I sported as a child were sold and cut up into building lots. But when I was a boy Mitching Hill was open country. It was a vast, rolling estate belonging to your great-uncle, Marmaduke, a man with whiskers of a nature which you with your pure mind would scarcely credit, and I have long felt a sentimental urge to see what the hell the old place looks like now. Perfectly foul, I expect. Still, I think we should make the pious pilgrimage.'

Pongo absolutely-ed heartily. He was all for the scheme. A great weight seemed to have rolled off his mind. The way he looked at it was that even an uncle within a short jump of the loony bin couldn't very well get into much trouble in a suburb. I mean, you know what suburbs are. They don't, as it were, offer the scope. One follows his reasoning, of course.

'Fine!' he said. 'Splendid! Topping!'

'Then put on your hat and rompers, my boy,' said Lord Ickenham, 'and let us be off. I fancy one gets there by omnibuses and things.'

Well, Pongo hadn't expected much in the way of mental uplift from the sight of Mitching Hill, and he didn't get it. Alighting from the bus, he tells me, you found yourself in the middle of rows and rows of semi-detached villas, all looking exactly alike, and you went on and you came to more semi-detached villas, and those all looked exactly alike, too. Nevertheless, he did not repine. It was one of those early spring days which suddenly change to mid-winter and he had come out without his overcoat, and it looked like rain and he hadn't an umbrella, but despite this his mood was one of sober ecstasy. The hours were passing and his uncle had not yet made a goat of himself. At the Dog Races the other had been in the hands of the constabulary in the first ten minutes.

It began to seem to Pongo that with any luck he might be able to keep the old blister pottering harmlessly about here till nightfall, when he could shoot a bit of dinner into him and put him to bed. And as Lord Ickenham had specifically stated that his wife, Pongo's Aunt Jane, had expressed her intention of scalping him with a blunt knife if he wasn't back at the Hall by lunchtime on the morrow, it really looked as if he might get through this visit without perpetrating a single major outrage on the public weal. It is rather interesting to note that as he thought this Pongo smiled, because it was the last time he smiled that day.

All this while, I should mention, Lord Ickenham had been stopping at intervals like a pointing dog and saying that it must have been just about here that he plugged the gardener in the trousers seat with his bow and arrow and that over there he had been sick after his first cigar, and he now paused in front of a villa which for some unknown reason called itself The Cedars. His face was tender and wistful.

'On this very spot, if I am not mistaken,' he said, heaving a bit of a sigh, 'on this very spot, fifty years ago come Lammas Eve, I ... Oh, blast it!'

The concluding remark had been caused by the fact that

the rain, which had held off until now, suddenly began to buzz down like a shower-bath. With no further words, they leaped into the porch of the villa and there took shelter, exchanging glances with a grey parrot which hung in a cage in the window.

Not that you could really call it shelter. They were protected from above all right, but the moisture was now falling with a sort of swivel action, whipping in through the sides of the porch and tickling them up properly. And it was just after Pongo had turned up his collar and was huddling against the door that the door gave way. From the fact that a female of general-servant aspect was standing there he gathered that his uncle must have rung the bell.

This female wore a long mackintosh, and Lord Ickenham beamed upon her with a fairish spot of suavity.

'Good afternoon,' he said.

The female said good afternoon.

'The Cedars?'

The female said yes, it was The Cedars.

'Are the old folks at home?'

The female said there was nobody at home.

'Ah? Well, never mind. I have come,' said Lord Ickenham, edging in, 'to clip the parrot's claws. My assistant, Mr Walkinshaw, who applies the anaesthetic,' he added, indicating Pongo with a gesture.

'Are you from the bird shop?'

'A very happy guess.'

'Nobody told me you were coming.'

'They keep things from you, do they?' said Lord Ickenham, sympathetically. 'Too bad.'

Continuing to edge, he had got into the parlour by now, Pongo following in a sort of dream and the female following Pongo.

'Well, I suppose it's all right,' she said. 'I was just going out. It's my afternoon.'

'Go out,' said Lord Ickenham cordially. 'By all means go out. We will leave everything in order.'

And presently the female, though still a bit on the dubious side, pushed off, and Lord Ickenham lit the gas-fire and drew a chair up.

'So here we are, my boy,' he said. 'A little tact, a little address, and here we are, snug and cosy and not catching our deaths of cold. You'll never go far wrong if you leave things to me.'

'But, dash it, we can't stop here,' said Pongo.

Lord Ickenham raised his eyebrows.

'Not stop here? Are you suggesting that we go out into that rain? My dear lad, you are not aware of the grave issues involved. This morning, as I was leaving home, I had a rather painful disagreement with your aunt. She said the weather was treacherous and wished me to take my woolly muffler. I replied that the weather was not treacherous and that I would be dashed if I took my woolly muffler. Eventually, by the exercise of an iron will, I had my way, and I ask you, my dear boy, to envisage what will happen if I return with a cold in the head.

I shall sink to the level of a fifth-class power. Next time I came to London, it would be with a liver pad and a respirator. No! I shall remain here, toasting my toes at this really excellent fire. I had no idea that a gas-fire radiated such warmth. I feel all in a glow.'

So did Pongo. His brow was wet with honest sweat. He is reading for the Bar, and while he would be the first to admit that he hasn't yet got a complete toe-hold on the Law of Great Britain he had a sort of notion that oiling into a perfect stranger's semi-detached villa on the pretext of pruning the parrot was a tort or misdemeanour, if not actual barratry or soccage in fief or something like that. And apart from the legal aspect of the matter there was the embarrassment of the thing. Nobody is more of a whale on correctness and not doing what's not done than Pongo, and the situation in which he now found himself caused him to chew the lower lip and, as I say, perspire a goodish deal.

'But suppose the blighter who owns this ghastly house comes back?' he asked. 'Talking of envisaging things, try that one over on your pianola.'

And, sure enough, as he spoke, the front-door bell rang.

'There!' said Pongo.

'Don't say "There!" my boy,' said Lord Ickenham reprovingly. 'It's the sort of thing your aunt says. I see no reason for alarm. Obviously this is some casual caller. A ratepayer would have used his latchkey. Glance cautiously out of the window and see if you can see anybody.'

'It's a pink chap,' said Pongo, having done so.

'How pink?'

'Pretty pink.'

'Well, there you are, then. I told you so. It can't be the big chief. The sort of fellows who own houses like this are pale and sallow, owing to working in offices all day. Go and see what he wants.'

'You go and see what he wants.'

'We'll both go and see what he wants,' said Lord Ickenham.

So they went and opened the front door, and there, as Pongo had said, was a pink chap. A small young pink chap, a bit moist about the shoulder-blades.

'Pardon me,' said this pink chap, 'is Mr Roddis in?'

'No,' said Pongo.

'Yes,' said Lord Ickenham. 'Don't be silly, Douglas – of course I'm in. I am Mr Roddis,' he said to the pink chap. 'This, such as he is, is my son Douglas. And you?'

'Name of Robinson.'

'What about it?'

'My name's Robinson.'

'Oh, *your* name's Robinson? Now we've got it straight. Delighted to see you, Mr Robinson. Come right in and take your boots off.'

They all trickled back to the parlour, Lord Ickenham pointing out objects of interest by the wayside to the chap, Pongo gulping for air a bit and trying to get himself abreast of this new twist in the scenario. His heart was becoming more and more bowed down with weight of woe. He hadn't liked being Mr Walkinshaw, the anaesthetist, and he didn't like it any better being Roddis Junior. In brief, he feared the worst. It was only too plain to him by now that his uncle had got it thoroughly up his nose and had settled down to one of his big afternoons, and he was asking himself, as he had so often asked himself before, what would the harvest be?

Arrived in the parlour, the pink chap proceeded to stand on one leg and look coy.

'Is Julia here?' he asked, simpering a bit, Pongo says.

'Is she?' said Lord Ickenham to Pongo.

'No,' said Pongo.

'No,' said Lord Ickenham.

'She wired me she was coming here today.'

'Ah, then we shall have a bridge four.'

The pink chap stood on the other leg.

'I don't suppose you've ever met Julia. Bit of trouble in the family, she gave me to understand.'

'It is often the way.'

'The Julia I mean is your niece Julia Parker. Or, rather, your wife's niece Julia Parker.'

'Any niece of my wife is a niece of mine,' said Lord Ickenham heartily. 'We share and share alike.'

'Julia and I want to get married.'

'Well, go ahead.'

'But they won't let us.'

'Who won't?'

'Her mother and father. And Uncle Charlie Parker and Uncle Henry Parker and the rest of them. They don't think I'm good enough.'

'The morality of the modern young man is notoriously lax.'

'Class enough, I mean. They're a haughty lot.'

'What makes them haughty? Are they earls?'

'No, they aren't earls.'

'Then why the devil,' said Lord Ickenham warmly, 'are they haughty? Only earls have a right to be haughty. Earls are hot stuff. When you get an earl, you've got something.'

'Besides, we've had words. Me and her father. One thing led to another, and in the end I called him a perishing old— Coo!' said the pink chap, breaking off suddenly.

He had been standing by the window, and he now leaped lissomely into the middle of the room, causing Pongo, whose nervous system was by this time definitely down among the wines and spirits and who hadn't been expecting this *adagio* stuff, to bite his tongue with some severity.

'They're on the doorstep! Julia and her mother and father. I didn't know they were all coming.'

'You do not wish to meet them?'

'No, I don't!'

'Then duck behind the settee, Mr Robinson,' said Lord Ickenham, and the pink chap, weighing the advice and finding it good, did so. And as he disappeared the door bell rang.

Once more, Lord Ickenham led Pongo out into the hall.

'I say!' said Pongo, and a close observer might have noted that he was quivering like an aspen.

'Say on, my dear boy.'

'I mean to say, what?'

'What?'

'You aren't going to let these bounders in, are you?'

'Certainly,' said Lord Ickenham. 'We Roddises keep open house. And as they are presumably aware that Mr Roddis has no son, I think we had better return to the old layout. You are the local vet, my boy, come to minister to my parrot. When I return, I should like to find you by the cage, staring at the bird in a scientific manner. Tap your teeth from time to time with a pencil and try to smell of iodoform. It will help to add conviction.'

So Pongo shifted back to the parrot's cage and stared so earnestly that it was only when a voice said 'Well!' that he became aware that there was anybody in the room. Turning, he perceived that Hampshire's leading curse had come back, bringing the gang.

It consisted of a stern, thin, middle-aged woman, a middle-aged man and a girl.

You can generally accept Pongo's estimate of girls, and when he says that this one was a pippin one knows that he uses the term in its most exact sense. She was about nineteen, he thinks, and she wore a black beret, a dark-green leather coat, a shortish tweed skirt, silk stockings and high-heeled shoes. Her eyes were large and lustrous and her face like a dewy rosebud at daybreak on a June morning. So Pongo tells me. Not that I suppose he has ever seen a rosebud at daybreak on a June morning, because it's generally as much as you can do to lug him out of bed in time for nine-thirty breakfast. Still, one gets the idea.

'Well,' said the woman, 'you don't know who I am, I'll be bound. I'm Laura's sister Connie. This is Claude, my husband. And this is my daughter Julia. Is Laura in?'

'I regret to say, no,' said Lord Ickenham.

The woman was looking at him as if he didn't come up to her specifications.

'I thought you were younger,' she said.

'Younger than what?' said Lord Ickenham.

'Younger than you are.'

'You can't be younger than you are, worse luck,' said Lord Ickenham. 'Still, one does one's best, and I am bound to say that of recent years I have made a pretty good go of it.'

The woman caught sight of Pongo, and he didn't seem to please her, either.

'Who's that?'

'The local vet, clustering round my parrot.'

'I can't talk in front of him.'

'It is quite all right,' Lord Ickenham assured her. 'The poor fellow is stone deaf.'

And with an imperious gesture at Pongo, as much as to bid him stare less at girls and more at parrots, he got the company seated.

'Now, then,' he said.

There was silence for a moment, then a sort of muffled sob, which Pongo thinks proceeded from the girl. He couldn't see, of course, because his back was turned and he was looking at the parrot, which looked back at him – most offensively, he says, as parrots will, using one eye only for the purpose. It also asked him to have a nut.

The woman came into action again.

'Although,' she said, 'Laura never did me the honour to invite me to her wedding, for which reason I have not communicated with her for five years, necessity compels me to cross her threshold today. There comes a time when differences must be forgotten and relatives must stand shoulder to shoulder.'

'I see what you mean,' said Lord Ickenham. 'Like the boys of the old brigade.'

'What I say is, let bygones be bygones. I would not have intruded on you, but needs must. I disregard the past and appeal to your sense of pity.'

The thing began to look to Pongo like a touch, and he is convinced that the parrot thought so, too, for it winked and cleared its throat. But they were both wrong. The woman went on.

'I want you and Laura to take Julia into your home for a week or so, until I can make other arrangements for her. Julia is studying the piano, and she sits for her examination in two weeks' time, so until then she must remain in London. The trouble is, she has fallen in love. Or thinks she has.'

'I know I have,' said Julia.

Her voice was so attractive that Pongo was compelled to slew round and take another look at her. Her eyes, he says, were shining like twin stars and there was a sort of Soul's Awakening expression on her face, and what the dickens there was in a pink chap like the pink chap, who even as pink chaps go wasn't much of a pink chap, to make her look like that, was frankly, Pongo says, more than he could understand. The thing baffled him. He sought in vain for a solution.

'Yesterday, Claude and I arrived in London from our Bexhill home to give Julia a pleasant surprise. We stayed, naturally, in the boarding-house where she has been living for the past six weeks. And what do you think we discovered?'

'Insects.'

'Not insects. A letter. From a young man. I found to my horror that a young man of whom I knew nothing was arranging to marry my daughter. I sent for him immediately, and found him to be quite impossible. He jellies eels!'

'Does what?'

'He is an assistant at a jellied eel shop.'

'But surely,' said Lord Ickenham, 'that speaks well for him. The capacity to jelly an eel seems to me to argue intelligence of a high order. It isn't everybody who can do it, by any means. I know if someone came to me and said, "Jelly this eel!" I should be nonplussed. And so, or I am very much mistaken, would Ramsay MacDonald and Winston Churchill.'

The woman did not seem to see eye to eye.

'Tchah!' she said. 'What do you suppose my husband's

brother Charlie Parker would say if I allowed his niece to marry a man who jellies eels?'

'Ah!' said Claude, who, before we go any further, was a tall, drooping bird with a red soup-strainer moustache.

'Or my husband's brother, Henry Parker.'

'Ah!' said Claude. 'Or Cousin Alf Robbins, for that matter.'

'Exactly. Cousin Alfred would die of shame.'

The girl Julia hiccoughed passionately, so much so that Pongo says it was all he could do to stop himself nipping across and taking her hand in his and patting it.

'I've told you a hundred times, Mother, that Wilberforce is only jellying eels till he finds something better.'

'What is better than an eel?' asked Lord Ickenham, who had been following this discussion with the close attention it deserved. 'For jellying purposes, I mean.'

'He is ambitious. It won't be long,' said the girl, 'before Wilberforce suddenly rises in the world.'

She never spoke a truer word. At this very moment, up he came from behind the settee like a leaping salmon.

'Julia!' he cried.

'Wilby!' yipped the girl.

And Pongo says he never saw anything more sickening in his life than the way she flung herself into the blighter's arms and clung there like the ivy on the old garden wall. It wasn't that he had anything specific against the pink chap, but this girl had made a deep impression on him and he resented her glueing herself to another in this manner.

Julia's mother, after just that brief moment which a woman needs in which to recover from her natural surprise at seeing eel-jelliers pop up from behind sofas, got moving and plucked her away like a referee breaking a couple of welterweights.

'Julia Parker,' she said, 'I'm ashamed of you!'

'So am I,' said Claude.

'I blush for you.'

'Me, too,' said Claude. 'Hugging and kissing a man who called your father a perishing old bottle-nosed Gawd-help-us.'

'I think,' said Lord Ickenham, shoving his oar in, 'that before proceeding any further we ought to go into that point. If he called you a perishing old bottle-nosed Gawd-help-us, it seems to me that the first thing to do is to decide whether he was right, and frankly, in my opinion . . .'

'Wilberforce will apologize.'

'Certainly I'll apologize. It isn't fair to hold a remark passed in the heat of the moment against a chap . . .'

'Mr Robinson,' said the woman, 'you know perfectly well that whatever remarks you may have seen fit to pass don't matter one way or the other. If you were listening to what I was saying you will understand . . .'

'Oh, I know, I know. Uncle Charlie Parker and Uncle Henry Parker and Cousin Alf Robbins and all that. Pack of snobs!'

'What!'

'Haughty, stuck-up snobs. Them and their class distinction. Think themselves everybody just because they've got money. I'd like to know how they got it.'

'What do you mean by that?'

'Never mind what I mean.'

'If you are insinuating—'

'Well, of course, you know, Connie,' said Lord Ickenham mildly, 'he's quite right. You can't get away from that.'

I don't know if you have ever seen a bull-terrier embarking on a scrap with an Airedale and just as it was getting down nicely to its work suddenly having an unexpected Kerry Blue sneak up behind it and bite it in the rear quarters. When this happens, it lets go of the Airedale and swivels round and fixes the butting-in animal with a pretty nasty eye. It was exactly the same with the woman Connie when Lord Ickenham spoke these words.

'What!'

'I was only wondering if you had forgotten how Charlie Parker made his pile.'

'What are you talking about?'

'I know it is painful,' said Lord Ickenham, 'and one doesn't mention it as a rule, but, as we are on the subject, you must admit that lending money at two hundred and fifty per cent interest is not done in the best circles. The judge, if you remember, said so at the trial.'

'I never knew that!' cried the girl Julia.

'Ah,' said Lord Ickenham. 'You kept it from the child? Quite right, quite right.'

'It's a lie!'

'And when Henry Parker had all that fuss with the bank

it was touch and go they didn't send him to prison. Between ourselves, Connie, has a bank official, even a brother of your husband, any right to sneak fifty pounds from the till in order to put it on a hundred to one shot for the Grand National? Not quite playing the game, Connie. Not the straight bat. Henry, I grant you, won five thousand of the best and never looked back afterwards, but, though we applaud his judgment of form, we must surely look askance at his financial methods. As for Cousin Alf Robbins ...'

The woman was making rummy stuttering sounds. Pongo tells me he once had a Pommery Seven which used to express itself in much the same way if you tried to get it to take a hill on high. A sort of mixture of gurgles and explosions.

'There is not a word of truth in this,' she gasped at length, having managed to get the vocal cords disentangled. 'Not a single word. I think you must have gone mad.'

Lord Ickenham shrugged his shoulders.

'Have it your own way, Connie. I was only going to say that, while the jury were probably compelled on the evidence submitted to them to give Cousin Alf Robbins the benefit of the doubt when charged with smuggling dope, everybody knew that he had been doing it for years. I am not blaming him, mind you. If a man can smuggle cocaine and get away with it, good luck to him, say I. The only point I am trying to make is that we are hardly a family that can afford to put on dog and sneer at honest suitors for our daughters' hands. Speaking for myself, I consider that we are very lucky to have the chance of marrying even into eel-jellying circles.'

'So do I,' said Julia firmly.

'You don't believe what this man is saying?'

'I believe every word.'

'So do I,' said the pink chap.

The woman snorted. She seemed overwrought.

'Well,' she said, 'goodness knows I have never liked Laura, but I would never have wished her a husband like you!'

'Husband?' said Lord Ickenham, puzzled. 'What gives you the impression that Laura and I are married?'

There was a weighty silence, during which the parrot threw out a general invitation to join it in a nut. Then the girl Julia spoke.

'You'll have to let me marry Wilberforce now,' she said. 'He knows too much about us.'

'I was rather thinking that myself,' said Lord Ickenham. 'Seal his lips, I say.'

'You wouldn't mind marrying into a low family, would you, darling?' asked the girl, with a touch of anxiety.

'No family could be too low for me, dearest, if it was yours,' said the pink chap.

'After all, we needn't see them.'

'That's right.'

'It isn't one's relations that matter: it's oneselves.'

'That's right, too.'

'Wilby!'

'Julia!'

They repeated the old ivy on the garden wall act. Pongo says he didn't like it any better than the first time, but his distaste wasn't in it with the woman Connie's.

'And what, may I ask,' she said, 'do you propose to marry on?'

This seemed to cast a damper. They came apart. They looked at each other. The girl looked at the pink chap, and the pink chap looked at the girl. You could see that a jarring note had been struck.

'Wilberforce is going to be a very rich man some day.'

'Some day!'

'If I had a hundred pounds,' said the pink chap, 'I could buy a half-share in one of the best milk walks in South London tomorrow.'

'If!' said the woman.

'Ah!' said Claude.

'Where are you going to get it?'

'Ah!' said Claude.

'Where,' repeated the woman, plainly pleased with the snappy crack and loath to let it ride without an encore, 'are you going to get it?'

'That,' said Claude, 'is the point. Where are you going to get a hundred pounds?'

'Why, bless my soul,' said Lord Ickenham jovially, 'from me, of course. Where else?'

And before Pongo's bulging eyes he fished out from the

recesses of his costume a crackling bundle of notes and handed it over. And the agony of realizing that the old bounder had had all that stuff on him all this time and that he hadn't touched him for so much as a tithe of it was so keen, Pongo says, that before he knew what he was doing he had let out a sharp, whinnying cry which rang through the room like the yowl of a stepped-on puppy.

'Ah,' said Lord Ickenham. 'The vet wishes to speak to me. Yes, vet?'

This seemed to puzzle the cerise bloke a bit.

'I thought you said this chap was your son.'

'If I had a son,' said Lord Ickenham, a little hurt, 'he would be a good deal better-looking than that. No, this is the local veterinary surgeon. I may have said I *looked* on him as a son. Perhaps that was what confused you.'

He shifted across to Pongo and twiddled his hands enquiringly. Pongo gaped at him, and it was not until one of the hands caught him smartly in the lower ribs that he remembered he was deaf and started to twiddle back. Considering that he wasn't supposed to be dumb, I can't see why he should have twiddled, but no doubt there are moments when twiddling is about all a fellow feels himself equal to. For what seemed to him at least ten hours Pongo had been undergoing great mental stress, and one can't blame him for not being chatty. Anyway, be that as it may, he twiddled.

'I cannot quite understand what he says,' announced Lord Ickenham at length, 'because he sprained a finger this morning and that makes him stammer. But I gather that he wishes to have a word with me in private. Possibly my parrot has got something the matter with it which he is reluctant to mention even in sign language in front of a young unmarried girl. You know what parrots are. We will step outside.'

'*We* will step outside,' said Wilberforce.

'Yes,' said the girl Julia. 'I feel like a walk.'

'And you,' said Lord Ickenham to the woman Connie, who was looking like a female Napoleon at Moscow. 'Do you join the hikers?'

'I shall remain and make myself a cup of tea. You will not grudge us a cup of tea, I hope?'

'Far from it,' said Lord Ickenham cordially. 'This is Liberty Hall. Stick around and mop it up till your eyes bubble.'

Outside, the girl, looking more like a dewy rosebud than ever, fawned on the old buster pretty considerably.

'I don't know how to thank you!' she said. And the pink chap said he didn't, either.

'Not at all, my dear, not at all,' said Lord Ickenham.

'I think you're simply wonderful.'

'No, no.'

'You are. Perfectly marvellous.'

'Tut, tut,' said Lord Ickenham. 'Don't give the matter another thought.'

He kissed her on both cheeks, the chin, the forehead, the right eyebrow, and the tip of the nose, Pongo looking on the while in a baffled and discontented manner. Everybody seemed to be kissing this girl except him.

Eventually the degrading spectacle ceased and the girl and the pink chap shoved off, and Pongo was enabled to take up the matter of that hundred quid.

'Where,' he asked, 'did you get all that money?'

'Now, where did I?' mused Lord Ickenham. 'I know your aunt gave it to me for some purpose. But what? To pay some bill or other, I rather fancy.'

This cheered Pongo up slightly.

'She'll give you the devil when you get back,' he said, with not a little relish. 'I wouldn't be in your shoes for something. When you tell Aunt Jane,' he said, with confidence, for he knew his Aunt Jane's emotional nature, 'that you slipped her entire roll to a girl, and explain, as you will have to explain, that she was an extraordinarily pretty girl – a girl, in fine, who looked like something out of a beauty chorus of the better sort, I should think she would pluck down one of the ancestral battle-axes from the wall and jolly well strike you on the mazzard.'

'Have no anxiety, my dear boy,' said Lord Ickenham. 'It is like your kind heart to be so concerned, but have no anxiety. I shall tell her that I was compelled to give the money to you to enable you to buy back some compromising letters from a Spanish *demi-mondaine*. She will scarcely be able to blame me for rescuing a fondly-loved nephew from the clutches of an adventuress. It may be that she will feel a little vexed with you for a while, and that you may have to allow a certain time to elapse before you visit Ickenham again, but then I shan't be wanting you at Ickenham till the ratting season starts, so all is well.'

At this moment, there came toddling up to the gate of The Cedars a large red-faced man. He was just going in when Lord Ickenham hailed him.

'Mr Roddis?'

'Hey?'

'Am I addressing Mr Roddis?'

'That's me.'

'I am Mr J. G. Bulstrode from down the road,' said Lord Ickenham. 'This is my sister's husband's brother, Percy Frensham, in the lard and imported-butter business.'

The red-faced bird said he was pleased to meet them. He asked Pongo if things were brisk in the lard and imported-butter business, and Pongo said they were all right, and the red-faced bird said he was glad to hear it.

'We have never met, Mr Roddis,' said Lord Ickenham, 'but I think it would be only neighbourly to inform you that a short while ago I observed two suspicious-looking persons in your house.'

'In my house? How on earth did they get there?'

'No doubt through a window at the back. They looked to me like cat burglars. If you creep up, you may be able to see them.'

The red-faced bird crept, and came back not exactly

foaming at the mouth but with the air of a man who for two pins would so foam.

'You're perfectly right. They're sitting in my parlour as cool as dammit, swigging my tea and buttered toast.'

'I thought as much.'

'And they've opened a pot of my raspberry jam.'

'Ah, then you will be able to catch them red-handed. I should fetch a policeman.'

'I will. Thank you, Mr Bulstrode.'

'Only too glad to have been able to render you this little service, Mr Roddis,' said Lord Ickenham. 'Well, I must be moving. I have an appointment. Pleasant after the rain, is it not? Come, Percy.'

He lugged Pongo off.

'So that,' he said, with satisfaction, 'is that. On these visits of mine to the metropolis, my boy, I always make it my aim, if possible, to spread sweetness and light. I look about me, even in a foul hole like Mitching Hill, and I ask myself – How can I leave this foul hole a better and happier foul hole than I found it? And if I see a chance, I grab it. Here is our omnibus. Spring aboard, my boy, and on our way home we will be sketching out rough plans for the evening. If the old Leicester Grill is still in existence, we might look in there. It must be fully thirty-five years since I was last thrown out of the Leicester Grill. I wonder who is the bouncer there now.'

*

Such (concluded the Crumpet) is Pongo Twistleton's Uncle Fred from the country, and you will have gathered by now a rough notion of why it is that when a telegram comes announcing his impending arrival in the great city Pongo blenches to the core and calls for a couple of quick ones.

The whole situation, Pongo says, is very complex. Looking at it from one angle, it is fine that the man lives in the country most of the year. If he didn't, he would have him in his midst all the time. On the other hand, by living in the country he generates, as it were, a store of loopiness which expends itself with frightful violence on his rare visits to the centre of things.

What it boils down to is this – Is it better to have a loopy uncle whose loopiness is perpetually on tap but spread out thin, so to speak, or one who lies low in distant Hants for three hundred and sixty days in the year and does himself proud in London for the other five? Dashed moot, of course, and Pongo has never been able to make up his mind on the point.

Naturally, the ideal thing would be if someone would chain the old hound up permanently and keep him from Jan. One to Dec. Thirty-one where he wouldn't do any harm – viz. among the spuds and tenantry. But this, Pongo admits, is a Utopian dream. Nobody could work harder to that end than his Aunt Jane, and she has never been able to manage it.

How's That, Umpire?

The story of Conky Biddle's great love begins at about six-forty-five on an evening in June in the Marylebone district of London. He had spent the day at Lord's cricket ground watching a cricket match, and driving away at close of play had been held up in a traffic jam. And held up alongside his taxi was a car with a girl at the wheel. And he had just lit a cigarette and was thinking of this and that, when he heard her say:

'Cricket is not a game. It is a mere shallow excuse for walking in your sleep.'

It was at this point that love wound its silken fetters about Conky. He leaped like a jumping bean and the cigarette fell from his nerveless fingers. If a girl who talked like that was not his dream girl, he didn't know a dream girl when he heard one.

You couldn't exactly say that he fell in love at first sight, for owing to the fact that in between him and her, obscuring the visibility, there was sitting a robust blighter in blue flannel with a pin stripe, he couldn't see her. All he had to go on was her voice, but that was ample. It was a charming voice with an American intonation. She was probably, he thought, an American angel who had stepped down from Heaven for a short breather in London.

'If I see another cricket game five thousand years from now,' she said, 'that'll be soon enough.'

Her companion plainly disapproved of these cracks. He said in a stiff, sniffy sort of way that she had not seen cricket at its best that afternoon, play having been greatly interfered with by rain.

'A merciful dispensation,' said the girl. 'Cricket with hardly any cricket going on is a lot better than cricket where the nuisance persists uninterrupted. In my opinion the ideal contest would be one where it rained all day and the rival teams stayed home doing their crossword puzzles.'

The traffic jam then broke up and the car shot forward like a B.29, leaving the taxi nowhere.

The reason why this girl's words had made so deep an impression on the young Biddle was that of all things in existence, with the possible exception of slugs and his uncle Everard, Lord Plumpton, he disliked cricket most. As a boy he had been compelled to play it, and grown to man's estate he was compelled to watch it. And if there was one spectacle that saddened him more than another in a world where the man of sensibility is always being saddened by spectacles, it was that of human beings, the heirs of the ages, waddling about in pads and shouting 'How's that, umpire?'

He had to watch cricket because Lord Plumpton told him to, and he was dependent on the other for his three squares a day. Lord Plumpton was a man who knew the batting averages of every first-class cricketer back to the days when they used to play in top hats and whiskers, and recited them to Conky after dinner. He liked to show Conky with the assistance of an apple (or, in winter, of an orange) how Bodger of Kent got the fingerspin which enabled him to make the ball dip and turn late on a sticky wicket. And frequently when Conky was walking along the street with him and working up to touching him for a tenner, he would break off the conversation at its most crucial point in order to demonstrate with his umbrella how Codger of Sussex made his late cut through the slips.

It was to the home of this outstanding louse, where he had a small bedroom on an upper floor, that Conky was now on his way. Arriving at journey's end, he found a good deal of stir and bustle going on, with doctors coming downstairs with black bags and parlourmaids going upstairs with basins of gruel, and learned from the butler that Lord Plumpton had sprained his ankle.

'No, really?' said Conky, well pleased, for if his uncle had possessed as many ankles as a centipede he would thoroughly have approved of him spraining them all. 'I suppose I had better go up and view the remains.'

He proceeded to the star bedroom and found his uncle propped up with pillows, throwing gruel at the parlourmaid. It was plain that he was in no elfin mood. He was looking like a mass murderer, though his face lacked the genial expression which you often see in mass murderers, and he glared at Conky with the sort of wild regret which sweeps over an irritable man when he sees a loved one approaching his sick bed and realizes that he has used up all the gruel.

'What ho, Uncle Everard,' said Conky. 'The story going the round of the clubs is that you have bust a joint of sorts. What happened?'

Lord Plumpton scowled darkly. He looked now like a mass murderer whose stomach ulcers are paining him.

'I'll tell you what happened. You remember I had to leave you at Lord's to attend a committee meeting at my club. Well, as I was walking back from the club, there were some children playing cricket in the street and one of them skied the ball towards extra cover, so naturally I ran out into the road to catch it. I judged it to a nicety and had just caught it when a homicidal lunatic of a girl came blinding along at ninety miles an hour in her car and knocked me base over apex. One of these days,' said Lord Plumpton, licking his lips, 'I hope to meet that girl again, preferably down a dark alley. I shall skin her very slowly with a blunt knife, dip her in boiling oil, sever her limb from limb, assemble those limbs on the pavement and dance on them.'

'And rightly,' said Conky. 'These girls who bust your ankles and prevent you going to Lord's to-morrow need a sharp lesson.'

'What do you mean, prevent me going to Lord's to-morrow? Do you think a mere sprained ankle will stop me going to a cricket match? I shall be there, with you at my side. And now,' said Lord Plumpton, wearying of these exchanges, 'go to hell!'

Conky did not go to hell, but he went downstairs and out on to the front steps to get a breath of air. He was feeling low and depressed. He had been so certain that he would be able to get to-morrow off. He had turned to go in again when he heard a noise of brakes as a car drew up behind him.

'Excuse me,' said a voice. 'Could I see Lord Plumpton?'

Simple words, but their effect on Conky as he recognized that silvery voice was to make him quiver from stay-combed hair to shoe sole. He uttered a whinnying cry which, as he swivelled round and for the first time was privileged to see her face, became a gasp. The voice had been the voice of an angel. The face measured up to the voice.

Seeing him, she too gasped. This was apt to be the reaction of the other sex on first beholding Conky Biddle, for though his I.Q. was low his outer crust was rather sensational. He was, indeed, a dazzlingly good-looking young man, who out-Caryed Grant and began where Gregory Peck left off.

'I say,' he said, going to the car and placing a foot on the running-board, 'Don't look now, but did I by chance hear you expressing a wish to meet my uncle, Lord Plumpton?'

'That's right. I recently flattened him out with my car, and I was planning to give him some flowers.'

'I wouldn't,' said Conky. 'I really wouldn't. I say this as a friend. Time, the great healer, will have to pull up its socks and spit on its hands quite a bit before it becomes safe for you to enter the presence.'

'I see. Then I'll take the blooms around the corner and have them delivered by a messenger boy. How's that, umpire?'

Conky winced. It was as though he had heard this divine creature sully her lips with something out of a modern historical novel.

'Good God!' he said. 'Where did you pick up that obscene expression?'

'From your uncle. He was chanting it at the top of his voice when I rammed him. A mental case, I imagine. What does it mean?'

'It's what you say at cricket.'

'Cricket!' The girl shuddered strongly. 'Shall I tell you what I think of cricket?'

'I have already heard your views. Your car got stuck abaft my taxi in a traffic block this evening. I was here, if you follow what I mean, and you were there, a few feet to the nor'-nor'east, so I was able to drink in what you were saying about cricket. Would you mind if I thanked you with tears in my eyes?'

'Not at all. But don't you like cricket? I thought all Englishmen loved it.'

'Not this Englishman. It gives me the pip.'

'Me, too. I ought never to have gone near that Lord's place. But in a moment of weakness I let myself be talked into it by my *fiancé*.'

Conky reeled.

'Oh, my sainted aunt! Have you got a *fiancé*?'

'Not now.'

Conky stopped reeling.

'Was he the bloke you were talking to in the car?'

'That's right. Eustace Davenport-Simms. I think he plays for Essex or Sussex or somewhere. My views were too subversive for him, so after kidding back and forth for a while we decided to cancel the order for the wedding cake.'

'I thought he seemed a bit sniffy.'

'He got sniffier.'

'Very sensible of you not to marry a cricketer.'

'So I felt.'

'The upshot, then, when all the smoke has blown away, is that you are once more in circulation?'

'Yes.'

'Well, that's fine,' said Conky. A sudden thought struck him. 'I say, would you object if I pressed your little hand?'

'Some other time, I think.'

'Any time that suits you.'

'You see, I have to hie me back to my hotel and dress. I'm late already, and my father screams like a famished hyaena if he's kept waiting for his rations.'

And with a rapid thrust of her shapely foot she set the

machinery in motion and vanished round the corner on two wheels, leaving Conky staring after her with a growing feeling of desolation. He had just realized that he was unaware of her name, address and telephone number and had had what was probably his last glimpse of her. If the expression 'Ships that pass in the night' had been familiar to him, he would certainly have uttered it, using clenched teeth for the purpose.

It was a Conky with heart bowed down and a general feeling of having been passed through the wringer who accompanied his uncle to Lord's next morning. The thought that a Grade A soulmate had come into his life and buzzed out again, leaving no clue to her identity or whereabouts, was a singularly bitter one. Lord Plumpton on the journey to the Mecca of cricket spoke well and easily of the visit of the Australian team of 1921, but Conky proved a distrait listener; so distrait that Lord Plumpton prodded him irascibly in the ribs and called him an infernal goggle-eyed fathead, which of course he was.

He was still in a sort of trance when they took their seats in the pavilion, but here it was less noticeable, for everybody else was in a sort of trance. The somnambulists out in the field tottered to and fro, and the spectators lay back and let their eyes go glassy. For perhaps an hour nothing happened except that Hodger of Middlesex, waking like Abou ben Adhem from a deep dream of peace, flicked his bat at a rising ball and edged it into the hands of a sleeper dozing in what is technically known as the gully. Then Lord Plumpton, who had been silent except for an occasional 'Nice! Nice!' sat up with a sudden jerk

and an explosive 'Well, I'm dashed!' and glared sideways at the
three shilling seats which adjoined the pavilion. And Conky,
following his gaze, felt his heart execute four separate buck
and wing steps and come to rest quivering like a jelly in a high
wind.

'Well, I'm dashed!' said Lord Plumpton, continuing to
direct at the three shilling seats the kind of look usually associ-
ated with human fiends in mystery stories. 'There's that blasted
girl!'

It was not a description which Conky himself would have
applied to the divinest of her sex, nor one which he enjoyed
hearing applied to her, and for a moment he was in two minds
as to whether to haul off and sock his relative on the beezer.
Wiser counsels prevailed, and he said:

'Yes, there she spouts.'

Lord Plumpton seemed surprised.

'You know her?'

'Just slightly. She ran into me last night.'

'Into you, too? Good gad, the female's a public menace. If
she's allowed to remain at large, the population of London will
be decimated. I've a good mind to go over and tell her what I
think of her.'

'But your uncle, ankle.'

'What the devil are you gibbering about?'

'I mean your ankle, uncle. You mustn't walk about on it.
How would it be if I popped over and acquainted her with your
displeasure?'

Lord Plumpton considered.

'Yes, that's not a bad idea. A surprisingly good idea, in fact, considering what a nitwit you are. But pitch it strong.'

'Oh, I will,' said Conky.

He rose and hurried off, and Lord Plumpton fell into conversation with the barely animate spectator on his left. They were soon deep in an argument as to whether it was at square leg or at extra cover that D. C. L. Wodger of Gloucestershire had fielded in 1904.

If the girl had looked like the better class of angel in the uncertain light of last night, she looked more than ever so in the reasonably bright sunshine of to-day. She was one of those lissom girls of medium height. Her eyes and hair were a browny hazel. The general effect was of a seraph who ate lots of yeast.

'Oh, hullo,' said Conky, lowering himself into a seat beside her. 'We meet again, what?'

She seemed surprised and startled. In her manner, as she gazed at his clean-cut face and then into his frank blue eyes, there was something that might almost be described as fluttering.

'You!' she cried. 'What are you doing here?'

'Just watching cricket.'

'But you told me last night that cricket gave you the pip, which I imagine is something roughly equivalent to the megrims or the heeby-jeebies.'

'Quite. But, you see, it's like this. My uncle is crazy about the ghastly game and I'm dependent on him, so when he says

"Come along and watch cricket", I have to come along and watch it like a lynx.'

The girl frowned. It was as if she had been hurt and disappointed.

'Why are you dependent on your uncle? Why don't you get a job?'

Conky hastened to defend himself.

'I do get a job. I get dozens of jobs. But I lose them all. The trouble is, you see, that I'm not very bright.'

'No?'

'Not very. That's why they call me Conky.'

'Do they call you Conky?'

'Invariably. What started it was an observation one of the masters at school happened to drop one day. He said, addressing me – "To attempt to drive information into your head, Biddle, is no easy task, for Providence, mysterious in its workings, has given you instead of the more customary human brain a skull full of concrete." So after that everyone called me Conky.'

'I see. What sort of jobs have you tried?'

'Practically everything except Chancellor of the Duchy of Lancaster.'

'And you get fired every time?'

'Every time.'

'I'm sorry.'

'It's dashed white of you to be sorry, but as a matter of fact it's all right.'

'How do you mean it's all right?'

Conky hesitated. Then he reflected that if you couldn't confide in an angel in human shape, who could you confide in? He glanced about him. Except for themselves, the three shilling tier of seats was almost empty.

'Well, you'll keep it under your hat, won't you, because it's supposed to be very hush-hush at the moment. I am on the eve of making a stupendous fortune. You know sea water?'

'The stuff that props the ship up when you come over from New York?'

'That's right. Well, you probably aren't aware of it, but it's full of gold, and I'm in with a fellow who's got a secret process for scooping it out. I saw his advertisement in the paper saying that if you dashed along and brassed up quick you could get in on an invention of vast possibilities, so I dashed along and brassed up. He was a nice chap and let me into the thing without a murmur. Bloke of the name of MacSporran. I happened to have scraped up ten quid, so I put that in and he tells me that at a conservative estimate I shall get back about two hundred and fifty thousand. I call that a nice profit.'

'Very nice.'

'Yes, it's all very convenient. And when I say that, I'm not thinking so much of the jolliness of having all that splosh in the old sock, I am alluding more to the difference this has made in what you might call my matrimonial plans. If I want to get married, I mean. What I'm driving at,' said Conky, giving her a melting look, 'is that I am now in a position, when I meet the girl I love, to put the binge on a practical basis.'

'I see.'

'In fact,' said Conky, edging a little closer, 'I might almost start making my plans at once.'

'That's the spirit. Father's slogan is "Do it now", and he's a tycoon.'

'I thought a tycoon was a sort of storm.'

'No, a millionaire.'

'Is your father a millionaire?'

'Yes, and more pouring in all the time.'

'Oh?'

A sudden chill had come over Conky's dashing mood. The one thing he had always vowed he would never do was marry for money. For years his six uncles and seven aunts had been urging him to cash in on his looks and grab something opulent. They had paraded heiresses before him in droves, but he had been firm. He had his principles.

Of course, in the present case it was different. He loved this girl with every fibre of his being. But all the same . . . No, he told himself, better wait till his bank balance was actually bulging.

With a strong effort he changed the conversation.

'Well, as I was saying,' he said, 'I hope to clean up shortly on an impressive scale, and when I do I'll never watch another cricket match as long as I live. Arising from which, what on earth are you doing here, holding the views on cricket which you do?'

A slight shadow of disappointment seemed to pass over the girl's face. It was as if she had been expecting the talk to develop along different lines.

'Oh, I came for a purpose.'

'Eh? What purpose?'

She directed his attention to the rows of living corpses in the pavilion. Lord Plumpton and his friend, having settled the Wodger question, were leaning back with their hats over their eyes. It was difficult to realize that life still animated those rigid limbs.

'When I was here yesterday, I was greatly struck by the spectacle of those stiffs over there. I wondered if it was possible to stir them up into some sort of activity.'

'I doubt it.'

'I'm a little dubious myself. They're like fish on a slab or a Wednesday matinee audience. Still, I thought I would try. Yesterday, of course I hadn't elastic and ammo with me.'

'Elastic? Ammo?'

Conky stared. From the recesses of her costume she had produced a piece of stout elastic and a wad of tin foil. She placed the tin foil on the elastic and then between her teeth. Then, turning, she took careful aim at Lord Plumpton.

For a sighting shot it was an admirable effort. Conky, following the projectile with a rapt gaze, saw his uncle start and put a hand to his ear. There seemed little reason to doubt that he had caught it amidships.

'Good Lord!' he cried. 'Here, after you with that elastic. I used to do that at school, and many was the fine head I secured. I wonder if the old skill still lingers.'

It was some minutes later that Lord Plumpton turned to the friend beside him.

'Wasps very plentiful this year,' he said.

The friend blinked drowsily.

'Watts?'

'Wasps.'

'There was A. R. K. Watts who used to play for Sussex. Ark we used to call him.'

'Not Watts. Wasps.'

'Wasps?'

'Wasps.'

'What about them?'

'They seem very plentiful. One stung me in the ear just now. And now one of them has knocked off my hat. Most extraordinary.'

A man in a walrus moustache who had played for Surrey in 1911 came along, and Lord Plumpton greeted him cordially.

'Hullo, Freddie.'

'Hullo.'

'Good game.'

'Very. Exciting.'

'Wasps are a nuisance, though.'

'Wasps?'

'Wasps.'

'What wasps?'

'I don't know their names. The wasps around here.'

'No wasps around here.'

'Yes.'

'Not in the pavilion at Lord's. You can't get in unless you're a member.'

'Well, one has just knocked off my hat. And look, there goes Jimmy's hat.'

The walrus shook his head. He stooped and picked up a piece of tin foil.

'Someone's shooting this stuff at you. Used to do it myself a long time ago. Ah yes,' he said, peering about him, 'I see where the stuff's coming from. That girl over there in the three shilling seats with your nephew. If you look closely, you'll see she's drawing a bead on you now.

Lord Plumpton looked, started and stiffened.

'That girl again! Is one to be beset by her through all eternity? Send for the attendants! Rouse the attendants and give them their divisional orders. Instruct the attendants to arrest her immediately and bring her to the committee room.

And so it came about that just as Conky was adjusting the elastic to his lips a short while later and preparing to loose off, a heavy hand fell on his shoulder, and there was a stern-faced man in the uniform of a Marylebone Cricket Club attendant. And simultaneously another heavy hand fell on the girl's shoulder, and there was another stern-faced man in the uniform of another Marylebone Cricket Club attendant.

It was a fair cop.

The committee room of the Marylebone Cricket Club is a sombre and impressive apartment. Photographs of bygone cricketers, many of them with long beards, gaze down from the walls — accusingly, or so it seems to the man whose conscience is not as clear as it might be. Only a man with an exceptionally clear conscience can enter this holy of holies without feeling that he is about to be stripped of his M.C.C. tie and formally ticketed as a social leper.

This is particularly so when, as in the present instance the President himself is seated at his desk. It was at Lord Plumpton's request that he was there now. It had seemed to Lord Plumpton that a case of this magnitude could be dealt with adequately only at the very highest levels.

He mentioned this in his opening speech for the prosecution.

'I demand,' said Lord Plumpton, 'the most exemplary punishment for an outrage unparalleled in the annals of the Marylebone Cricket Club, the dear old club we all love so well, if you know what I mean.' Here he paused as if intending to bare his head, but realizing that he had not got his hat on continued, 'I mean to say, taking pot-shots at members with a series of slabs of tin foil, dash it! If that isn't a nice bit of box fruit, what is? Bad enough, if you see what I'm driving at, to take pot-shots at even the *canaille*, as they call them in France, who squash in in the free seats, but when it comes to pot-shotting members in the pavilion, I mean where are we? Personally I would advocate skinning the girl, but if you consider that too extreme I am prepared to settle for twenty years in solitary confinement. A menace to the community, that's what this girl is. Bustling about in her car and knocking people endways with one hand and flicking their hats off with the other, if you follow my drift. She reminds me of . . . who was that woman in the Bible whose work was always so raw? . . . Delilah? . . . No . . . It's on the tip of my tongue . . . Ah yes, Jezebel. She's a modern streamlined Jezebel, dash her insides.'

'Uncle Everard,' said Conky, 'you are speaking of the woman I love.'

The girl gave a little gasp.

'No, really?' she said.

'Absolutely,' said Conky. 'I had intended to mention it earlier. I don't know your name . . .'

'Clarissa. Clarissa Binstead.'

'How many s's?'

'Three, if you count the Binstead.'

'Clarissa, I love you. Will you be my wife?'

'Sure,' said the girl. 'I was hoping you'd suggest it. And what all the fuss is about is more than I can understand. Why when we go to a ball game in America, we throw pop bottles.'

There was a silence.

'Are you an American, madam?' said the President.

'One hundred per cent. Oh, say, can you see . . . No, I never can remember how it goes after that. I could whistle it for you.'

The President had drawn Lord Plumpton aside. His face was grave and anxious.

'My dear Everard,' he said in an urgent undertone, 'we must proceed carefully here, very carefully. I had no notion this girl was American. Somebody should have informed me. The last thing we want is an international incident, particularly at a moment when we are hoping, if all goes well, to get into America's ribs for a bit of the stuff. I can fully appreciate your wounded feelings ...'

'And how about my wounded topper?'

'The club will buy you a new hat, and then, my dear fellow, I would strongly urge that we consider the matter closed.'

'You mean not skin her?'

'No.'

'Not slap her into the cooler for twenty years?'

'No. There might be very unfortunate repercussions.'

'Oh, all right,' said Lord Plumpton sullenly. 'Oh, very well. But,' he proceeded on a brighter note, 'there is one thing I can do, and that is disinherit this frightful object here. Hoy!' he said to Conky.

'Hullo?' said Conky.

'You are no longer a nephew of mine.'

'Well, that's a bit of goose,' said Conky.

As he came out of the committee room, he was informed by an attendant that a gentleman wished to speak to him on the telephone. Excusing himself to Clarissa and bidding her wait for him downstairs, Conky went to the instrument, listened for a few moments, then reeled away, his eyes bulging and his jaw a-droop. He found Clarissa at the spot agreed upon.

'Hullo, there,' said Conky. 'I say, you remember me asking you to be my wife?'

'Yes.'

'You said you would.'

'Yes.'

'Well, the words that spring to the lips are "*Will* you?" Because I'm afraid the whole thing's off. That was MacSporran on the 'phone. He said he'd made a miscalculation, and my tenner won't be enough to start that sea water scheme going. He said he would need another thirty thousand pounds and could I raise it? I said No, and he said "Too bad, too bad". And I said: "Do I get my tenner back?", and he said: "No, you don't get your tenner back." So there you are. I can't marry you.'

Clarissa wrinkled her forehead.

'I don't see it. Father's got it in gobs. He will provide.'

'Not for me, he won't. I always swore I'd never marry a girl for her money.'

'You aren't marrying me for my money. You're marrying me because we're soulmates.'

'That's true. Still, you appear to have a most ghastly lot of the stuff, and I haven't a bean.'

'Suppose you had a job?'

'Oh, if I had a job.'

'That's all right, then. Father runs a gigantic business and he can always find room for another Vice-President.'

'Vice-President?'

'Yes.'

'But I don't know enough to be a Vice-President.'

'It's practically impossible not to know enough to be a Vice-President. All you would have to do would be to attend conferences and say "Yes" when Father made a suggestion.'

'What, in front of a whole lot of people?'

'Well, at least you could nod.'

'Oh yes, I could nod.'

'Then that's settled. Kiss me.'

Their lips met long and lingeringly. Conky came out of the clinch with sparkling eyes and a heightened colour. He raised a hand to heaven.

'How's that, umpire?' he cried.

'Jolly good show, sir,' said Clarissa.

Honeysuckle Cottage

'**D**o you believe in ghosts?' asked Mr Mulliner abruptly.

I weighed the question thoughtfully. I was a little surprised, for nothing in our previous conversation had suggested the topic.

'Well,' I replied, 'I don't like them, if that's what you mean. I was once butted by one as a child.'

'Ghosts. Not goats.'

'Oh, ghosts? Do I believe in ghosts?'

'Exactly.'

'Well, yes – and no.'

'Let me put it another way,' said Mr Mulliner, patiently. 'Do you believe in haunted houses? Do you believe that it is possible for a malign influence to envelop a place and work a spell on all who come within its radius?'

I hesitated.

'Well, no – and yes.'

Mr Mulliner sighed a little. He seemed to be wondering if I was always as bright as this.

'Of course,' I went on, 'one has read stories. Henry James's *Turn of the Screw* . . .'

'I am not talking about fiction.'

'Well, in real life— Well, look here, I once, as a matter of fact, did meet a man who knew a fellow—'

'My distant cousin James Rodman spent some weeks in a haunted house,' said Mr Mulliner, who, if he has a fault, is not a very good listener. 'It cost him five thousand pounds. That is to say, he sacrificed five thousand pounds by not remaining there. Did you ever,' he asked, wandering, it seemed to me, from the subject, 'hear of Leila J. Pinckney?'

Naturally I had heard of Leila J. Pinckney. Her death some years ago has diminished her vogue, but at one time it was impossible to pass a bookshop or a railway bookstall without seeing a long row of her novels. I had never myself actually read any of them, but I knew that in her particular line of literature, the Squashily Sentimental, she had always been regarded by those entitled to judge as pre-eminent. The critics usually headed their reviews of her stories with the words:

ANOTHER PINCKNEY

or sometimes, more offensively:

ANOTHER PINCKNEY!!!

And once, dealing with, I think, *The Love Which Prevails,* the literary expert of the *Scrutinizer* had compressed his entire critique into the single phrase 'Oh, God!'

'Of course,' I said. 'But what about her?'

'She was James Rodman's aunt.'

'Yes?'

'And when she died James found that she had left him five thousand pounds and the house in the country where she had lived for the last twenty years of her life.'

'A very nice little legacy.'

'Twenty years,' repeated Mr Mulliner. 'Grasp that, for it has a vital bearing on what follows. Twenty years, mind you, and Miss Pinckney turned out two novels and twelve short stories regularly every year, besides a monthly page of Advice to Young Girls in one of the magazines. That is to say, forty of her novels and no fewer than two hundred and forty of her short stories were written under the roof of Honeysuckle Cottage.'

'A pretty name.'

'A nasty, sloppy name,' said Mr Mulliner severely, 'which should have warned my distant cousin James from the start. Have you a pencil and a piece of paper?' He scribbled for a while, poring frowningly over columns of figures. 'Yes,' he said, looking up, 'if my calculations are correct, Leila J. Pinckney wrote in all a matter of nine million one hundred and forty thousand words of glutinous sentimentality at Honeysuckle Cottage, and it was a condition of her will that James should reside there for six months in every year. Failing to do this, he was to forfeit the five thousand pounds.'

'It must be great fun making a freak will,' I mused. 'I often wish I was rich enough to do it.'

'This was not a freak will. The conditions are perfectly understandable. James Rodman was a writer of sensational mystery stories, and his aunt Leila had always disapproved of his work. She was a great believer in the influence of environment, and the reason why she inserted that clause in her will was that she wished to compel James to move from London to the country. She considered that living in London hardened him and made his outlook on life sordid. She often asked him if he thought it quite nice to harp so much on sudden death and blackmailers with squints. Surely, she said, there were enough squinting blackmailers in the world without writing about them.

'The fact that Literature meant such different things to these two had, I believe, caused something of a coolness between them, and James had never dreamed that he would be remembered in his aunt's will. For he had never concealed his opinion that Leila J. Pinckney's style of writing revolted him, however dear it might be to her enormous public. He held rigid views on the art of the novel, and always maintained that an artist with a true reverence for his craft should not descend to gooey love stories, but should stick austerely to revolvers, cries in the night, missing papers, mysterious Chinamen and dead bodies — with or without gash in throat. And not even the thought that his aunt had dandled him on her knee as a baby could induce him to stifle his literary conscience to the extent of pretending to enjoy her work. First, last and all the time, James Rodman had held the opinion – and voiced it fearlessly – that Leila J. Pinckney wrote bilge.

'It was a surprise to him, therefore, to find that he had been left this legacy. A pleasant surprise, of course. James was making quite a decent income out of the three novels and eighteen short stories which he produced annually, but an author can always find a use for five thousand pounds. And, as for the cottage, he had actually been looking about for a little place in the country at the very moment when he received the lawyer's letter. In less than a week he was installed at his new residence.'

James's first impressions of Honeysuckle Cottage were, he tells me, wholly favourable. He was delighted with the place. It was a low, rambling, picturesque old house with funny little chimneys and a red roof, placed in the middle of the most charming country. With its oak beams, its trim garden, its trilling birds and its rose-hung porch, it was the ideal spot for a writer. It was just the sort of place, he reflected whimsically, which his aunt had loved to write about in her books. Even the apple-cheeked old housekeeper who attended to his needs might have stepped straight out of one of them.

It seemed to James that his lot had been cast in pleasant

places. He had brought down his books, his pipes and his golf-clubs, and was hard at work finishing the best thing he had ever done. *The Secret Nine* was the title of it; and on the beautiful summer afternoon on which this story opens he was in the study, hammering away at his typewriter, at peace with the world. The machine was running sweetly, the new tobacco he had bought the day before was proving admirable, and he was moving on all six cylinders to the end of a chapter.

He shoved in a fresh sheet of paper, chewed his pipe thoughtfully for a moment, then wrote rapidly:

'For an instant Lester Gage thought that he must have been mistaken. Then the noise came again, faint but unmistakable — a soft scratching on the outer panel.

'His mouth set in a grim line. Silently, like a panther, he made one quick step to the desk, noiselessly opened a drawer, drew out his automatic. After that affair of the poisoned needle, he was taking no chances. Still in dead silence, he tiptoed to the door; then, flinging it suddenly open, he stood there, his weapon poised.

'On the mat stood the most beautiful girl he had ever beheld. A veritable child of Faerie. She eyed him for a moment with a saucy smile; then with a pretty, roguish look of reproof shook a dainty fore-finger at him.

' "I believe you've forgotten me, Mr Gage!" she fluted with a mock severity which her eyes belied.'

James stared at the paper dumbly. He was utterly perplexed. He had not had the slightest intention of writing anything like this. To begin with, it was a rule with him, and one which he never broke, to allow no girls to appear in his stories. Sinister landladies, yes, and naturally any amount of adventuresses with foreign accents, but never under any pretext what may be broadly described as girls. A detective story, he maintained, should have no heroine. Heroines only held up the action and tried to flirt with the hero when he should have been busy looking for clues, and then went and let the villain kidnap them by some childishly simple trick. In his writing, James was positively monastic.

And yet here was this creature with her saucy smile and her dainty fore-finger horning in at the most important point in the story. It was uncanny.

He looked once more at his scenario. No, the scenario was all right.

In perfectly plain words it stated that what happened when the door opened was that a dying man fell in and after gasping, 'The beetle! Tell Scotland Yard that the blue beetle is—' expired on the hearth-rug, leaving Lester Gage not unnaturally some-what mystified. Nothing whatever about any beautiful girls.

In a curious mood of irritation, James scratched out the offending passage, wrote in the necessary corrections and put the cover on the machine. It was at this point that he heard William whining.

The only blot on this paradise which James had so far been able to discover was the infernal dog, William. Belonging nom-inally to the gardener, on the very first morning he had adopted

James by acclamation, and he maddened and infuriated James. He had a habit of coming and whining under the window when James was at work. The latter would ignore this as long as he could; then, when the thing became insupportable, would bound out of his chair, to see the animal standing on the gravel, gazing expectantly up at him with a stone in his mouth. William had a weak-minded passion for chasing stones; and on the first day James, in a rash spirit of camaraderie, had flung one for him. Since then James had thrown no more stones; but he had thrown any number of other solids, and the garden was littered with objects ranging from matchboxes to a plaster statuette of the young Joseph prophesying before Pharaoh. And still William came and whined, an optimist to the last.

The whining, coming now at a moment when he felt irritable and unsettled, acted on James much as the scratching on the door had acted on Lester Gage. Silently, like a panther, he made one quick step to the mantelpiece, removed from it a china mug bearing the legend A Present from Clacton-on-Sea, and crept to the window.

And as he did so a voice outside said, 'Go away, sir, go away!' and there followed a short, high-pitched bark which was certainly not William's. William was a mixture of Airedale, setter, bull terrier, and mastiff; and when in vocal mood, favoured the mastiff side of his family.

James peered out. There on the porch stood a girl in blue. She held in her arms a small fluffy white dog, and she was endeavouring to foil the upward movement toward this of the blackguard William. William's mentality had been arrested some years before at the point where he imagined that everything in the world had been created for him to eat. A bone, a boot, a steak, the back wheel of a bicycle – it was all one to William. If it was there he tried to eat it. He had even made a plucky attempt to devour the remains of the young Joseph prophesying before Pharaoh. And it was perfectly plain now that he regarded the curious wriggling object in the girl's arms purely in the light of a snack to keep body and soul together till dinnertime.

'William!' bellowed James.

William looked courteously over his shoulder with eyes that beamed with the pure light of a life's devotion, wagged the whiplike tail which he had inherited from his bull-terrier ancestor and resumed his intent scrutiny of the fluffy dog.

'Oh, please!' cried the girl. 'This great rough dog is frightening poor Toto.'

The man of letters and the man of action do not always go hand in hand, but practice had made James perfect in handling with a swift efficiency any situation that involved William. A moment later that canine moron, having received the present from Clacton in the short ribs, was scuttling round the corner of the house, and James had jumped through the window and was facing the girl.

She was an extraordinarily pretty girl. Very sweet and fragile she looked as she stood there under the honeysuckle with the breeze ruffling a tendril of golden hair that strayed from beneath her coquettish little hat. Her eyes were very big and very blue, her rose-tinted face becomingly flushed. All wasted on James, though. He disliked all girls, and particularly the sweet, droopy type.

'Did you want to see somebody?' he asked stiffly.

'Just the house,' said the girl, 'if it wouldn't be giving any trouble. I do so want to see the room where Miss Pinckney wrote her books. This is where Leila J. Pinckney used to live, isn't it?'

'Yes; I am her nephew. My name is James Rodman.'

'Mine is Rose Maynard.'

James led the way into the house, and she stopped with a cry of delight on the threshold of the morning-room.

'Oh, how too perfect!' she cried. 'So this was her study?'

'Yes.'

'What a wonderful place it would be for you to think in if you were a writer too.'

James held no high opinion of women's literary taste, but nevertheless he was conscious of an unpleasant shock.

'I am a writer,' he said coldly. 'I write detective stories.'

'I – I'm afraid' – she blushed – 'I'm afraid I don't often read detective stories.'

'You no doubt prefer,' said James, still more coldly, 'the sort of thing my aunt used to write.'

'Oh, I love her stories!' cried the girl, clasping her hands ecstatically. 'Don't you?'

'I cannot say that I do.'

'What?'

'They are pure apple sauce,' said James sternly; 'just nasty blobs of sentimentality, thoroughly untrue to life.'

The girl stared.

'Why, that's just what's so wonderful about them, their trueness to life! You feel they might all have happened. I don't understand what you mean.'

They were walking down the garden now. James held the gate open for her and she passed through into the road.

'Well, for one thing,' he said, 'I decline to believe that a marriage between two young people is invariably preceded by some violent and sensational experience in which they both share.'

'Are you thinking of *Scent o' the Blossom,* where Edgar saves Maud from drowning?'

'I am thinking of every single one of my aunt's books.' He looked at her curiously. He had just got the solution of a mystery which had been puzzling him for some time. Almost from the moment he had set eyes on her she had seemed somehow strangely familiar. It now suddenly came to him why it was that he disliked her so much. 'Do you know,' he said, 'you might be one of my aunt's heroines yourself? You're just the sort of girl she used to love to write about.'

Her face lit up.

'Oh, do you really think so?' She hesitated. 'Do you know what I have been feeling ever since I came here? I've been feeling that you are exactly like one of Miss Pinckney's heroes.'

'No, I say, really!' said James, revolted.

'Oh, but you are! When you jumped through that window it gave me quite a start. You were so exactly like Claude Masterson in *Heather o' the Hills.*'

'I have not read *Heather o' the Hills*,' said James, with a shudder.

'He was very strong and quiet, with deep, dark, sad eyes.'

James did not explain that his eyes were sad because her society gave him a pain in the neck. He merely laughed scornfully.

'So now, I suppose,' he said, 'a car will come and knock you down and I shall carry you gently into the house and lay you— Look out!' he cried.

It was too late. She was lying in a little huddled heap at his feet. Round the corner a large automobile had come bowling, keeping with an almost affected precision to the wrong side of the road. It was now receding into the distance, the occupant of the tonneau, a stout red-faced gentleman in a fur coat, leaning out over the back. He had bared his head – not, one fears, as a pretty gesture of respect and regret, but because he was using his hat to hide the number plate.

The dog Toto was unfortunately uninjured.

James carried the girl gently into the house and laid her on the sofa in the morning-room. He rang the bell and the apple-cheeked housekeeper appeared.

'Send for the doctor,' said James. 'There has been an accident.'

The housekeeper bent over the girl.

'Eh, dearie, dearie!' she said. 'Bless her sweet pretty face!'

The gardener, he who technically owned William, was routed out from among the young lettuces and told to fetch Doctor Brady. He separated his bicycle from William, who was making a light meal of the left pedal, and departed on his mission. Doctor Brady arrived and in due course he made his report.

'No bones broken, but a number of nasty bruises. And, of course, the shock. She will have to stay here for some time, Rodman. Can't be moved.'

'Stay here! But she can't! It isn't proper.'

'Your housekeeper will act as a chaperone.'

The doctor sighed. He was a stolid-looking man of middle age with side-whiskers.

'A beautiful girl, that, Rodman,' he said.

'I suppose so,' said James.

'A sweet, beautiful girl. An elfin child.'

'A what?' cried James, starting.

This imagery was very foreign to Doctor Brady as he knew him. On the only previous occasion on which they had had any extended conversation, the doctor had talked exclusively about the effect of too much protein on the gastric juices.

'An elfin child; a tender, fairy creature. When I was looking at her just now, Rodman, I nearly broke down. Her little hand lay on the coverlet like some white lily floating on the surface of a still pool, and her dear, trusting eyes gazed up at me.'

He pottered off down the garden, still babbling, and James stood staring after him blankly. And slowly, like some cloud athwart a summer sky, there crept over James's heart the chill shadow of a nameless fear.

It was about a week later that Mr Andrew McKinnon, the senior partner in the well-known firm of literary agents, McKinnon & Gooch, sat in his office in Chancery Lane, frowning thoughtfully over a telegram. He rang the bell.

'Ask Mr Gooch to step in here.' He resumed his study of the telegram. 'Oh, Gooch,' he said when his partner appeared, 'I've just had a curious wire from young Rodman. He seems to want to see me very urgently.'

Mr Gooch read the telegram.

'Written under the influence of some strong mental excitement,' he agreed. 'I wonder why he doesn't come to the office if he wants to see you so badly.'

'He's working very hard, finishing that novel for Prodder & Wiggs. Can't leave it, I suppose. Well, it's a nice day. If you will look after things here I think I'll motor down and let him give me lunch.'

As Mr McKinnon's car reached the crossroads a mile from Honeysuckle Cottage, he was aware of a gesticulating figure by the hedge. He stopped the car.

'Morning, Rodman.'

'Thank God, you've come!' said James. It seemed to Mr McKinnon that the young man looked paler and thinner. 'Would you mind walking the rest of the way? There's something I want to speak to you about.'

Mr McKinnon alighted; and James, as he glanced at him, felt cheered and encouraged by the very sight of the man. The literary agent was a grim, hard-bitten person, to whom, when he called at their offices to arrange terms, editors kept their faces turned so that they might at least retain their back collar studs. There was no sentiment in Andrew McKinnon. Editresses of society papers practised their blandishments on him in vain, and many a publisher had waked screaming in the night, dreaming that he was signing a McKinnon contract.

'Well, Rodman,' he said, 'Prodder & Wiggs have agreed to our terms. I was writing to tell you so when your wire arrived. I had a lot of trouble with them, but it's fixed at 20 per cent, rising to 25, and two hundred pounds advance royalties on day of publication.'

'Good!' said James absently. 'Good! McKinnon, do you remember my aunt, Leila J. Pinckney?'

'Remember her? Why, I was her agent all her life.'

'Of course. Then you know the sort of tripe she wrote.'

'No author,' said Mr McKinnon reprovingly, 'who pulls down a steady twenty thousand pounds a year writes tripe.'

'Well anyway, you know her stuff.'

'Who better?'

'When she died she left me five thousand pounds and her house, Honeysuckle Cottage. I'm living there now. McKinnon, do you believe in haunted houses?'

'No.'

'Yet I tell you solemnly that Honeysuckle Cottage is haunted!'

'By your aunt?' said Mr McKinnon, surprised.

'By her influence. There's a malignant spell over the place; a sort of miasma of sentimentalism. Everybody who enters it succumbs.'

'Tut-tut! You mustn't have these fancies.'

'They aren't fancies.'

'You aren't seriously meaning to tell me——'

'Well, how do you account for this? That book you were speaking about, which Prodder & Wiggs are to publish – *The Secret Nine*. Every time I sit down to write it a girl keeps trying to sneak in.'

'Into the room?'

'Into the story.'

'You don't want a love interest in your sort of book,' said Mr McKinnon, shaking his head. 'It delays the action.'

'I know it does. And every day I have to keep shooing this infernal female out. An awful girl, McKinnon. A soppy, soupy, treacly, drooping girl with a roguish smile. This morning she tried to butt in on the scene where Lester Gage is trapped in the den of the mysterious leper.'

'No!'

'She did, I assure you. I had to rewrite three pages before I could get her out of it. And that's not the worst. Do you know, McKinnon, that at this moment I am actually living the plot of a typical Leila May Pinckney novel in just the setting she always used! And I can see the happy ending coming nearer every day! A week ago a girl was knocked down by a car at my door and I've had to put her up, and every day I realize more clearly that sooner or later I shall ask her to marry me.'

'Don't do it,' said Mr McKinnon, a stout bachelor. 'You're too young to marry.'

'So was Methuselah,' said James, a stouter. 'But all the same I know I'm going to do it. It's the influence of this awful house weighing upon me. I feel like an eggshell in a maelstrom. I am being sucked on by a force too strong for me to resist. This morning I found myself kissing her dog!'

'No!'

'I did! And I loathe the little beast. Yesterday I got up at dawn and plucked a nosegay of flowers for her, wet with the dew.'

'Rodman!'

'It's a fact. I laid them at her door and went downstairs kicking myself all the way. And there in the hall was the apple-cheeked housekeeper regarding me archly. If she didn't murmur "Bless their sweet young hearts!" my ears deceived me.'

'Why don't you pack up and leave?'

'If I do I lose the five thousand pounds.'

'Ah!' said Mr McKinnon.

'I can understand what has happened. It's the same with all haunted houses. My aunt's subliminal ether vibrations have woven themselves into the texture of the place, creating an atmosphere which forces the ego of all who come in contact with it to attune themselves to it. It's either that or something to do with the fourth dimension.'

Mr McKinnon laughed scornfully.

'Tut-tut!' he said again. 'This is pure imagination. What has happened is that you've been working too hard. You'll see this precious atmosphere of yours will have no effect on me.'

'That's exactly why I asked you to come down. I hoped you might break the spell.'

'I will that,' said Mr McKinnon jovially.

The fact that the literary agent spoke little at lunch caused James no apprehension. Mr McKinnon was ever a silent trencherman. From time to time James caught him stealing a glance at the girl, who was well enough to come down to meals now, limping pathetically; but he could read nothing in his face. And yet the mere look of his face was a consolation. It was so solid, so matter of fact, so exactly like an unemotional coconut.

'You've done me good,' said James with a sigh of relief, as he escorted the agent down the garden to his car after lunch. 'I felt all along that I could rely on your rugged common sense. The whole atmosphere of the place seems different now.'

Mr McKinnon did not speak for a moment. He seemed to be plunged in thought.

'Rodman,' he said, as he got into his car, 'I've been thinking over that suggestion of yours of putting a love interest into *The Secret Nine*. I think you're wise. The story needs it. After all, what is there greater in the world than love? Love – love – aye, it's the sweetest word in the language. Put in a heroine and let her marry Lester Gage.'

'If,' said James grimly, 'she does succeed in worming her way in she'll jolly well marry the mysterious leper. But look here, I don't understand—'

'It was seeing that girl that changed me,' proceeded Mr McKinnon. And as James stared at him aghast, tears suddenly filled his hard-boiled eyes. He openly snuffled. 'Aye, seeing her sitting there under the roses, with all that smell of honeysuckle and all. And the birdies singing so sweet in the garden and the sun lighting up her bonny face. The puir wee lass!' he muttered, dabbing at his eyes. 'The puir bonny wee lass! Rodman,' he said, his voice quivering, 'I've decided that we're being hard on Prodder & Wiggs. Wiggs has had sickness in his home lately. We mustn't be hard on a man who's had sickness in his home, hey, laddie? No, no! I'm going to take back that contract and alter it to a flat 12 per cent, and no advance royalties.'

'What!'

'But you shan't lose by it, Rodman. No, no, you shan't lose by it, my manny. I am going to waive my commission. The puir bonny wee lass!'

The car rolled off down the road. Mr McKinnon, seated in the back, was blowing his nose violently.

'This is the end!' said James.

It is necessary at this point to pause and examine James Rodman's position with an unbiased eye. The average man, unless he puts himself in James's place, will be unable to appreciate it. James, he will feel, was making a lot of fuss about nothing. Here he was, drawing daily closer and closer to a charming girl with big blue eyes, and surely rather to be envied than pitied.

But we must remember that James was one of Nature's bachelors. And no ordinary man, looking forward dreamily to a little home of his own with a loving wife putting out his slippers and changing the gramophone records, can realize the intensity of the instinct for self-preservation which animates Nature's bachelors in times of peril.

James Rodman had a congenital horror of matrimony. Though a young man, he had allowed himself to develop a great many habits which were as the breath of life to him; and these habits, he knew instinctively, a wife would shoot to pieces within a week of the end of the honeymoon.

James liked to breakfast in bed; and, having breakfasted, to smoke in bed and knock the ashes out on the carpet. What wife would tolerate this practice?

James liked to pass his days in a tennis shirt, grey flannel trousers and slippers. What wife ever rests until she has inclosed her husband in a stiff collar, tight boots and a morning suit and taken him with her to *thés musicales*?

These and a thousand other thoughts of the same kind flashed through the unfortunate young man's mind as the days went by, and every day that passed seemed to draw him nearer to the brink of the chasm. Fate appeared to be taking a malicious pleasure in making things as difficult for him as possible. Now that the girl was well enough to leave her bed, she spent her time sitting in a chair on the sun-sprinkled porch, and James had to read to her – and poetry, at that; and not the jolly, wholesome sort of poetry the boys are turning out nowadays, either – good, honest stuff about sin and gas works and decaying corpses – but the old-fashioned kind with rhymes in it, dealing almost exclusively with love. The weather, moreover, continued superb. The honeysuckle cast its sweet scent on the gentle breeze; the roses over the porch stirred and nodded; the flowers in the garden were lovelier than ever; the birds sang their little throats sore. And every evening there was a magnificent sunset. It was almost as if Nature were doing it on purpose.

At last James intercepted Doctor Brady as he was leaving after one of his visits and put the thing to him squarely:

'When is that girl going?'

The doctor patted him on the arm.

'Not yet, Rodman,' he said in a low, understanding voice. 'No need to worry yourself about that. Mustn't be moved for days and days and days – I might almost say weeks and weeks and weeks.'

'Weeks and weeks!' cried James.

'And weeks,' said Doctor Brady. He prodded James roguishly in the abdomen. 'Good luck to you, my boy, good luck to you,' he said.

It was some small consolation to James that the mushy physician immediately afterward tripped over William on his way down the path and broke his stethoscope. When a man is up against it like James every little helps.

He was walking dismally back to the house after this conversation when he was met by the apple-cheeked housekeeper.

'The little lady would like to speak to you, sir,' said the apple-cheeked exhibit, rubbing her hands.

'Would she?' said James hollowly.

'So sweet and pretty she looks, sir – oh, sir, you wouldn't believe! Like a blessed angel sitting there with her dear eyes all a-shining.'

'Don't do it!' cried James with extraordinary vehemence. 'Don't do it!'

He found the girl propped up on the cushions and thought once again how singularly he disliked her. And yet, even as he thought this, some force against which he had to fight madly was whispering to him, 'Go to her and take that little hand! Breathe into that little ear the burning words that will

make that little face turn away crimsoned with blushes!'
He wiped a bead of perspiration from his forehead and sat
down.

'Mrs Stick-in-the-Mud — what's her name? — says you want
to see me.'

The girl nodded.

'I've had a letter from Uncle Henry. I wrote to him as soon
as I was better and told him what had happened, and he is
coming here to-morrow morning.'

'Uncle Henry?'

'That's what I call him, but he's really no relation. He is my
guardian. He and daddy were officers in the same regiment,
and when daddy was killed, fighting on the Afghan frontier, he
died in Uncle Henry's arms and with his last breath begged him
to take care of me.'

James started. A sudden wild hope had waked in his heart.
Years ago, he remembered, he had read a book of his aunt's
entitled *Rupert's Legacy,* and in that book—

'I'm engaged to marry him,' said the girl quietly.

'Wow!' shouted James.

'What?' asked the girl, startled.

'Touch of cramp,' said James. He was thrilling all over. That
wild hope had been realized.

'It was daddy's dying wish that we should marry' said the
girl.

'And dashed sensible of him, too; dashed sensible,' said
James warmly.

'And yet,' she went on, a little wistfully, 'I sometimes wonder—'

'Don't!' said James. 'Don't! You must respect daddy's dying wish. There's nothing like daddy's dying wish; you can't beat it. So he's coming here to-morrow, is he? Capital, capital! To lunch, I suppose? Excellent! I'll run down and tell Mrs Who-Is-It to lay in another chop.'

It was with a gay and uplifted heart that James strolled the garden and smoked his pipe next morning. A great cloud seemed to have rolled itself away from him. Everything was for the best in the best of all possible worlds. He had finished *The Secret Nine* and shipped it off to Mr McKinnon, and now as he strolled there was shaping itself in his mind a corking plot about a man with only half a face who lived in a secret den and terrorized London with a series of shocking murders. And what made them so shocking was the fact that each of the victims, when discovered, was found to have only half a face too. The rest had been chipped off, presumably by some blunt instrument.

The thing was coming out magnificently, when suddenly his attention was diverted by a piercing scream. Out of the bushes fringing the river that ran beside the garden burst the apple-cheeked housekeeper.

'Oh, sir! Oh, sir! Oh, sir!'

'What is it?' demanded James irritably.

'Oh, sir! Oh, sir! Oh, sir!'

'Yes, and then what?'

'The little dog, sir! He's in the river!'

'Well, whistle him to come out.'

'Oh, sir, do come quick! He'll be drowned!'

James followed her through the bushes, taking off his coat as he went. He was saying to himself, 'I will not rescue this dog. I do not like the dog. It is high time he had a bath, and in any case it would be much simpler to stand on the bank and fish for him with a rake. Only an ass out of a Leila J. Pinckney book would dive into a beastly river to save—'

At this point he dived. Toto, alarmed by the splash, swam rapidly for the bank, but James was too quick for him. Grasping him firmly by the neck, he scrambled ashore and ran for the house, followed by the housekeeper.

The girl was seated on the porch. Over her there bent the tall soldierly figure of a man with keen eyes and greying hair. The housekeeper raced up.

'Oh, miss! Toto! In the river! He saved him! He plunged in and saved him!'

The girl drew a quick breath.

'Gallant, damme! By Jove! By gad! Yes, gallant, by George!' exclaimed the soldierly man.

The girl seemed to wake from a reverie.

'Uncle Henry, this is Mr Rodman. Mr Rodman, my guardian, Colonel Carteret.'

'Proud to meet you, sir,' said the colonel, his honest blue eyes glowing as he fingered his short crisp moustache. 'As fine a thing as I ever heard of, damme!'

'Yes, you are brave – brave,' the girl whispered.

'I am wet – wet,' said James, and went upstairs to change his clothes.

When he came down for lunch, he found to his relief that the girl had decided not to join them, and Colonel Carteret was silent and preoccupied. James, exerting himself in his capacity of host, tried him with the weather, golf, India, the Government, the high cost of living, first-class cricket, the modern dancing craze, and murderers he had met, but the other still preserved that strange, absent-minded silence. It was only when the meal was concluded and James had produced cigarettes that he came abruptly out of his trance.

'Rodman,' he said, 'I should like to speak to you.'

'Yes?' said James, thinking it was about time.

'Rodman,' said Colonel Carteret, 'or rather, George – I may call you George?' he added, with a sort of wistful diffidence that had a singular charm.

'Certainly,' replied James, 'if you wish it. Though my name is James.'

'James, eh? Well, well, it amounts to the same thing, eh, what, damme, by gad?' said the colonel with a momentary return of his bluff soldierly manner. 'Well, then, James, I have something that I wish to say to you. Did Miss Maynard – did Rose happen to tell you anything about myself in er – in connection with herself?'

'She mentioned that you and she were engaged to be married.'

The colonel's tightly drawn lips quivered.

'No longer,' he said.

'What?'

'No, John, my boy.'

'James.'

'No, James, my boy, no longer. While you were upstairs changing your clothes she told me — breaking down, poor child, as she spoke — that she wished our engagement to be at an end.'

James half rose from the table, his cheeks blanched.

'You don't mean that!' he gasped.

Colonel Carteret nodded. He was staring out of the window, his fine eyes set in a look of pain.

'But this is nonsense!' cried James. 'This is absurd! She — she mustn't be allowed to chop and change like this. I mean to say, it — it isn't fair—'

'Don't think of me, my boy.'

'I'm not — I mean, did she give any reason?'

'Her eyes did.'

'Her eyes did?'

'Her eyes, when she looked at you on the porch, as you stood there — young, heroic — having just saved the life of the dog she loves. It is you who won that tender heart, my boy.'

'Now listen,' protested James, 'you aren't going to sit there and tell me that a girl falls in love with a man just because he saves her dog from drowning?'

'Why, surely,' said Colonel Carteret, surprised. 'What better reason could she have?' He sighed. 'It is the old, old story, my boy. Youth to youth. I am an old man. I should have known – I should have foreseen – yes, youth to youth.'

'You aren't a bit old.'

'Yes, yes.'

'No, no.'

'Yes, yes.'

'Don't keep on saying yes, yes!' cried James, clutching at his hair. 'Besides, she wants a steady old buffer – a steady, sensible man of medium age – to look after her.'

Colonel Carteret shook his head with a gentle smile.

'This is mere quixotry, my boy. It is splendid of you to take this attitude; but no, no.'

'Yes, yes.'

'No, no.' He gripped James's hand for an instant, then rose and walked to the door. 'That is all I wished to say, Tom.'

'James.'

'James. I just thought that you ought to know how matters stood. Go to her, my boy, go to her, and don't let any thought of an old man's broken dream keep you from pouring out what is in your heart. I am an old soldier, lad, an old soldier. I have learned to take the rough with the smooth. But I think – I think I will leave you now. I – I should – should like to be alone for a while. If you need me you will find me in the raspberry bushes.'

He had scarcely gone when James also left the room. He took his hat and stick and walked blindly out of the garden, he knew not whither. His brain was numbed. Then, as his powers of reasoning returned, he told himself that he should have foreseen this ghastly thing. If there was one type of character over which Leila J. Pinckney had been wont to spread herself, it was the pathetic guardian who loves his ward but relinquishes her to the younger man. No wonder the girl had broken off the engagement. Any elderly guardian who allowed himself to come within a mile of Honeysuckle Cottage was simply asking for it. And then, as he turned to walk back, a sort of dull defiance gripped James. Why, he asked, should he be put upon in this manner? If the girl liked to throw over this man, why should he be the goat?

He saw his way clearly now. He just wouldn't do it, that was all. And if they didn't like it they could lump it.

Full of a new fortitude, he strode in at the gate. A tall, soldierly figure emerged from the raspberry bushes and came to meet him.

'Well?' said Colonel Carteret.

'Well?' said James defiantly.

'Am I to congratulate you?'

James caught his keen blue eye and hesitated. It was not going to be so simple as he had supposed.

'Well – er—' he said.

Into the keen blue eyes there came a look that James had not seen there before. It was the stern, hard look which – probably

– had caused men to bestow upon this old soldier the name of Cold-Steel Carteret.

'You have not asked Rose to marry you?'

'Er – no; not yet.'

The keen blue eyes grew keener and bluer.

'Rodman,' said Colonel Carteret in a strange, quiet voice, 'I have known that little girl since she was a tiny child. For years she has been all in all to me. Her father died in my arms and with his last breath bade me see that no harm came to his darling. I have nursed her through mumps, measles – aye, and chicken pox – and I live but for her happiness.' He paused, with a significance that made James's toes curl. 'Rodman,' he said, 'do you know what I would do to any man who trifled with that little girl's affections?' He reached in his hip pocket and an ugly-looking revolver glittered in the sunlight. 'I would shoot him like a dog.'

'Like a dog?' faltered James.

'Like a dog,' said Colonel Carteret. He took James's arm and turned him toward the house. 'She is on the porch. Go to her. And if—' He broke off. 'But tut!' he said in a kindlier tone. 'I am doing you an injustice, my boy. I know it.'

'Oh, you are,' said James fervently.

'Your heart is in the right place.'

'Oh, absolutely,' said James.

'Then go to her, my boy. Later on you may have something to tell me. You will find me in the strawberry beds.'

It was very cool and fragrant on the porch. Overhead, little breezes played and laughed among the roses. Somewhere in the distance sheep bells tinkled, and in the shrubbery a thrush was singing its evensong.

Seated in her chair behind a wicker table laden with tea things, Rose Maynard watched James as he shambled up the path.

'Tea's ready,' she called gaily. 'Where is Uncle Henry?' A look of pity and distress flitted for a moment over her flower-like face. 'Oh, I – I forgot,' she whispered.

'He is in the strawberry beds,' said James in a low voice.

She nodded unhappily.

'Of course, of course. Oh, why is life like this?' James heard her whisper.

He sat down. He looked at the girl. She was leaning back with closed eyes, and he thought he had never seen such a little squirt in his life. The idea of passing his remaining days in her society revolted him. He was stoutly opposed to the idea of marrying anyone; but if, as happens to the best of us, he ever were compelled to perform the wedding glide, he had always hoped it would be with some lady golf champion who would help him with his putting, and thus, by bringing his handicap down a notch or two, enable him to save something from the wreck, so to speak. But to link his lot with a girl who read his aunt's books and liked them; a girl who could tolerate the presence of the dog Toto; a girl who clasped her hands in pretty, childish joy when she saw a nasturtium in bloom – it was too much. Nevertheless, he took her hand and began to speak.

'Miss Maynard – Rose—'

She opened her eyes and cast them down. A flush had come into her cheeks. The dog Toto at her side sat up and begged for cake, disregarded.

'Let me tell you a story. Once upon a time there was a lonely man who lived in a cottage all by himself—'

He stopped. Was it James Rodman who was talking this bilge?

'Yes?' whispered the girl.

'– but one day there came to him out of nowhere a little fairy princess. She—'

He stopped again, but this time not because of the sheer shame of listening to his own voice. What caused him to interrupt his tale was the fact that at this moment the tea table suddenly began to rise slowly in the air, tilting as it did so a considerable quantity of hot tea on to the knees of his trousers.

'Ouch!' cried James, leaping.

The table continued to rise, and then fell sideways, revealing the homely countenance of William, who, concealed by the cloth, had been taking a nap beneath it. He moved slowly forward, his eyes on Toto. For many a long day William had been desirous of putting to the test, once and for all, the problem of whether Toto was edible or not. Sometimes he thought yes, at other times no. Now seemed an admirable opportunity for a definite decision. He advanced on the object of his experiment, making a low whistling noise through his nostrils, not unlike a boiling kettle. And Toto, after one long look of incredulous horror, tucked his shapely tail between his legs and, turning, raced for safety. He had laid a course in a bee line for the open garden gate, and William, shaking a dish of marmalade off his head a little petulantly, galloped ponderously after him. Rose Maynard staggered to her feet.

'Oh, save him!' she cried.

Without a word James added himself to the procession. His interest in Toto was but tepid. What he wanted was to get near enough to William to discuss with him that matter of the tea on his trousers. He reached the road and found that the order of the runners had not changed. For so small a dog, Toto was moving magnificently. A cloud of dust rose as he skidded round the corner. William followed. James followed William.

And so they passed Farmer Birkett's barn, Farmer Giles's cow shed, the place where Farmer Willetts' pigsty used to be before the big fire, and the Bunch of Grapes public house, Jno Biggs propr., licensed to sell tobacco, wines and spirits. And it was as they were turning down the lane that leads past Farmer Robinson's chicken run that Toto, thinking swiftly, bolted abruptly into a small drain pipe.

'William!' roared James, coming up at a canter. He stopped to pluck a branch from the hedge and swooped darkly on.

William had been crouching before the pipe, making a noise like a bassoon into its interior; but now he rose and came beamingly to James. His eyes were aglow with chumminess and affection; and placing his forefeet on James's chest, he licked him three times on the face in rapid succession. And as he did so, something seemed to snap in James. The scales seemed to fall from James's eyes. For the first time he saw William as he really was, the authentic type of dog that saves his master from a frightful peril. A wave of emotion swept over him.

'William!' he muttered. 'William!'

William was making an early supper off a half brick he had found in the road. James stooped and patted him fondly.

'William,' he whispered, 'you knew when the time had come to change the conversation, didn't you, old boy!' He straightened himself. 'Come, William,' he said. 'Another four miles and we reach Meadowsweet Junction. Make it snappy and we shall just catch the up express, first stop London.'

William looked up into his face and it seemed to James that he gave a brief nod of comprehension and approval. James turned. Through the trees to the east he could see the red roof of Honeysuckle Cottage, lurking like some evil dragon in ambush.

Then, together, man and dog passed silently into the sunset.

That (concluded Mr Mulliner) is the story of my distant cousin James Rodman. As to whether it is true, that, of course, is an open question. I, personally, am of opinion that it is. There is no doubt that James did go to live at Honeysuckle Cottage and, while there, underwent some experience which has left an ineradicable mark upon him. His eyes to-day have that unmistakable look which is to be seen only in the eyes of confirmed bachelors whose feet have been dragged to the very brink of the pit and who have gazed at close range into the naked face of matrimony.

And, if further proof be needed, there is William. He is now James's inseparable companion. Would any man be habitually seen in public with a dog like William unless he had some solid cause to be grateful to him – unless they were linked together by some deep and imperishable memory? I think not. Myself, when I observe William coming along the street, I cross the road and look into a shop window till he has passed. I am not a snob, but I dare not risk my position in Society by being seen talking to that curious compound.

Nor is the precaution an unnecessary one. There is about William a shameless absence of appreciation of class distinctions which recalls the worst excesses of the French Revolution. I have seen him with these eyes chivvy a pomeranian belonging to a Baroness in her own right from near the Achilles Statue to within a few yards of the Marble Arch.

And yet James walks daily with him in Piccadilly. It is surely significant.

The Spot of Art

I was lunching at my Aunt Dahlia's, and despite the fact that Anatole, her outstanding cook, had rather excelled himself in the matter of the bill-of-fare, I'm bound to say the food was more or less turning to ashes in my mouth. You see, I had some bad news to break to her – always a prospect that takes the edge off the appetite. She wouldn't be pleased, I knew, and when not pleased Aunt Dahlia, having spent most of her youth in the hunting-field, has a crispish way of expressing herself.

However, I supposed I had better have a dash at it and get it over.

'Aunt Dahlia,' I said, facing the issue squarely.

'Hullo?'

'You know that cruise of yours?'

'Yes.'

'That yachting-cruise you are planning?'

'Yes.'

'That jolly cruise in your yacht in the Mediterranean to which you so kindly invited me and to which I have been looking forward with such keen anticipation?'

'Get on, fathead, what about it?'

I swallowed a chunk of *cotelette-suprême-aux-choux-fleurs* and slipped her the distressing info'.

'I'm frightfully sorry, Aunt Dahlia,' I said, 'but I shan't be able to come.'

As I had foreseen, she goggled.

'What!'

'I'm afraid not.'

'You poor, miserable hell-hound, what do you mean, you won't be able to come?'

'Well, I won't.'

'Why not?'

'Matters of the most extreme urgency render my presence in the Metropolis imperative.'

She sniffed.

'I suppose what you really mean is that you're hanging round some unfortunate girl again?'

I didn't like the way she put it, but I admit I was stunned by her penetration, if that's the word I want. I mean the sort of thing detectives have.

'Yes, Aunt Dahlia,' I said, 'you have guessed my secret. I do indeed love.'

'Who is she?'

'A Miss Pendlebury. Christian name, Gwladys. She spells it with a "w".'

'With a "g", you mean.'

'With a "w" *and* a "g".'

'Not Gwladys?'

'That's it.'

The relative uttered a yowl.

'You sit there and tell me you haven't enough sense to steer clear of a girl who calls herself Gwladys? Listen, Bertie,' said Aunt Dahlia earnestly, 'I'm an older woman than you are – well, you know what I mean – and I can tell you a thing or two. And one of them is that no good can come of association with anything labelled Gwladys or Ysobel or Ethyl or Mabelle or Kathryn. But particularly Gwladys. What sort of girl is she?'

'Slightly divine.'

'She isn't that female I saw driving you at sixty miles p.h. in the Park the other day. In a red two-seater?'

'She did drive me in the Park the other day. I thought it rather a hopeful sign. And her Widgeon Seven is red.'

Aunt Dahlia looked relieved.

'Oh well, then, she'll probably break your silly fat neck before she can get you to the altar. That's some consolation. Where did you meet her?'

'At a party in Chelsea. She's an artist.'

'Ye gods!'

'And swings a jolly fine brush, let me tell you. She's painted a portrait of me. Jeeves and I hung it up in the flat this morning. I have an idea Jeeves doesn't like it.'

'Well, if it's anything like you I don't see why he should. An artist! Calls herself Gwladys! And drives a car in the sort of way Segrave would if he were pressed for time.' She brooded awhile. 'Well, it's all very sad, but I can't see why you won't come on the yacht.'

I explained.

'It would be madness to leave the metrop. at this juncture,' I said. 'You know what girls are. They forget the absent face. And I'm not at all easy in my mind about a certain cove of the name of Lucius Pim. Apart from the fact that he's an artist, too, which forms a bond, his hair waves. One must never discount wavy hair, Aunt Dahlia. Moreover, this bloke is one of those strong, masterful men. He treats Gwladys as if she were less than the dust beneath his taxi wheels. He criticizes her hats and says nasty things about her chiaroscuro. For some reason, I've often noticed, this always seems to fascinate girls, and it has sometimes occurred to me that, being myself more the parfait gentle knight, if you know what I mean, I am in grave danger of getting the short end. Taking all these things into consideration, then, I cannot breeze off to the Mediterranean, leaving this Pim a clear field. You must see that?'

Aunt Dahlia laughed. Rather a nasty laugh. Scorn in its *timbre*, or so it seemed to me.

'I shouldn't worry,' she said. 'You don't suppose for a moment that Jeeves will sanction the match?'

I was stung.

'Do you imply, Aunt Dahlia,' I said – and I can't remember if I rapped the table with the handle of my fork or not, but I rather think I did – 'that I allow Jeeves to boss me to the extent of stopping me marrying somebody I want to marry?'

'Well, he stopped you wearing a moustache, didn't he? And purple socks. And soft-fronted shirts with dress-clothes.'

'That is a different matter altogether.'

'Well, I'm prepared to make a small bet with you, Bertie. Jeeves will stop this match.'

'What absolute rot!'

'And if he doesn't like that portrait, he will get rid of it.'

'I never heard such dashed nonsense in my life.'

'And, finally, you wretched, pie-faced wambler, he will present you on board my yacht at the appointed hour. I don't know how he will do it, but you will be there, all complete with yachting-cap and spare pair of socks.'

'Let us change the subject, Aunt Dahlia,' I said coldly.

Being a good deal stirred up by the attitude of the flesh-and-blood at the luncheon-table, I had to go for a bit of a walk in the Park after leaving, to soothe the nervous system. By about four-thirty the ganglions had ceased to vibrate, and I returned to the flat. Jeeves was in the sitting-room, looking at the portrait.

I felt a trifle embarrassed in the man's presence, because just before leaving I had informed him of my intention to scratch the yacht-trip, and he had taken it on the chin a bit. You see, he had been looking forward to it rather. From the moment I had accepted the invitation, there had been a sort of nautical glitter in his eye, and I'm not sure I hadn't heard him trolling Chanties in the kitchen. I think some ancestor of his must have been one of Nelson's tars or something, for he has always had the urge of the salt sea in his blood. I have noticed him on liners, when we were going to America, striding the deck with a sailorly roll and giving the distinct impression of being just about to heave the main-brace or splice the binnacle.

So, though I had explained my reasons, taking the man fully into my confidence and concealing nothing, I knew that he was distinctly peeved; and my first act, on entering, was to do the cheery a bit. I joined him in front of the portrait.

'Looks good, Jeeves, what?'

'Yes, sir.'

'Nothing like a spot of art for brightening the home.'

'No, sir.'

'Seems to lend the room a certain – what shall I say—'

'Yes, sir.'

The responses were all right, but his manner was far from hearty, and I decided to tackle him squarely. I mean, dash it. I mean, I don't know if you have ever had your portrait painted, but if you have you will understand my feelings. The spectacle of one's portrait hanging on the wall creates in one a sort of paternal fondness for the thing: and what you

demand from the outside public is approval and enthusiasm
– not the curling lip, the twitching nostril, and the kind of
supercilious look which you see in the eye of a dead mackerel.
Especially is this so when the artist is a girl for whom you
have conceived sentiments deeper and warmer than those of
ordinary friendship.

'Jeeves,' I said, 'you don't like this spot of art.'

'Oh, yes, sir.'

'No. Subterfuge is useless. I can read you like a book. For
some reason this spot of art fails to appeal to you. What do you
object to about it?'

'Is not the colour-scheme a trifle bright, sir?'

'I had not observed it, Jeeves. Anything else?'

'Well, in my opinion, sir, Miss Pendlebury has given you a
somewhat too hungry expression.'

'Hungry?'

'A little like that of a dog regarding a distant bone, sir.'

I checked the fellow.

'There is no resemblance whatever, Jeeves, to a dog regarding a distant bone. The look to which you allude is wistful and
denotes Soul.'

'I see, sir.'

I proceeded to another subject.

'Miss Pendlebury said she might look in this afternoon to
inspect the portrait. Did she turn up?'

'Yes, sir.'

'But has left?'

'Yes, sir.'

'You mean she's gone, what?'

'Precisely, sir.'

'She didn't say anything about coming back, I suppose?'

'No, sir. I received the impression that it was not Miss Pendlebury's intention to return. She was a little upset, sir, and expressed a desire to go to her studio and rest.'

'Upset? What was she upset about?'

'The accident, sir.'

I didn't actually clutch the brow, but I did a bit of mental brow-clutching, as it were.

'Don't tell me she had an accident!'

'Yes, sir.'

'What sort of accident?'

'Automobile, sir.'

'Was she hurt?'

'No, sir. Only the gentleman.'

'What gentleman?'

'Miss Pendlebury had the misfortune to run over a gentleman in her car almost immediately opposite this building. He sustained a slight fracture of the leg.'

'Too bad! But Miss Pendlebury is all right?'

'Physically, sir, her condition appeared to be satisfactory. She was suffering a certain distress of mind.'

'Of course, with her beautiful, sympathetic nature. Naturally. It's a hard world for a girl, Jeeves, with fellows flinging themselves under the wheels of her car in one long, unending stream. It must have been a great shock to her. What became of the chump?'

'The gentleman, sir?'

'Yes.'

'He is in your spare bedroom, sir.'

'What!'

'Yes, sir.'

'In my spare bedroom?'

'Yes, sir. It was Miss Pendlebury's desire that he should be taken there. She instructed me to telegraph to the gentleman's sister, sir, who is in Paris, advising her of the accident. I also summoned a medical man, who gave it as his opinion that the patient should remain for the time being *in statu quo.*'

'You mean, the corpse is on the premises for an indefinite visit?'

'Yes, sir.'

'Jeeves, this is a bit thick!'

'Yes, sir.'

And I meant it, dash it. I mean to say, a girl can be pretty heftily divine and ensnare the heart and what not, but she's no right to turn a fellow's flat into a morgue. I'm bound to say that for a moment passion ebbed a trifle.

'Well, I suppose I'd better go and introduce myself to the blighter. After all, I am his host. Has he a name?'

'Mr Pim, sir.'

'Pim!'

'Yes, sir. And the young lady addressed him as Lucius. It was owing to the fact that he was on his way here to examine the portrait which she had painted that Mr Pim happened to be in the roadway at the moment when Miss Pendlebury turned the corner.'

I headed for the spare bedroom. I was perturbed to a degree. I don't know if you have ever loved and been handicapped in your wooing by a wavy-haired rival, but one of the things you don't want in such circs is the rival parking himself on the premises with a broken leg. Apart from anything else, the advantage the position gives him is obviously terrific. There he is, sitting up and toying with a grape and looking pale and interesting, the object of the girl's pity and concern, and where do you get off, bounding about the place in morning costume and spats and with the rude flush of health on the cheek? It seemed to me that things were beginning to look pretty mouldy.

I found Lucius Pim lying in bed, draped in a suit of my pyjamas, smoking one of my cigarettes, and reading a detective story. He waved the cigarette at me in what I considered a dashed patronizing manner.

'Ah, Wooster!' he said.

'Not so much of the "Ah, Wooster!" ' I replied brusquely. 'How soon can you be moved?'

'In a week or so, I fancy.'

'In a week!'

'Or so. For the moment, the doctor insists on perfect quiet and repose. So forgive me, old man, for asking you not to raise your voice. A hushed whisper is the stuff to give the troops. And now, Wooster, about this accident. We must come to an understanding.'

'Are you sure you can't be moved?'

'Quite. The doctor said so.'

'I think we ought to get a second opinion.'

'Useless, my dear fellow. He was most emphatic, and evidently a man who knew his job. Don't worry about my not being comfortable here. I shall be quite all right. I like this bed. And now, to return to the subject of this accident. My sister will be arriving to-morrow. She will be greatly upset. I am her favourite brother.'

'You are?'

'I am.'

'How many of you are there?'

'Six.'

'And you're her favourite?'

'I am.'

It seemed to me that the other five must be pretty fairly sub-human, but I didn't say so. We Woosters can curb the tongue.

'She married a bird named Slingsby. Slingsby's Superb Soups. He rolls in money. But do you think I can get him to lend a trifle from time to time to a needy brother-in-law?' said Lucius Pim bitterly. 'No, sir! However, that is neither here nor there. The point is that my sister loves me devotedly: and, this being the case, she might try to prosecute and persecute and generally bite pieces out of poor little Gwladys if she knew that it was she who was driving the car that laid me out. She must never know, Wooster. I appeal to you as a man of honour to keep your mouth shut.'

'Naturally.'

'I'm glad you grasp the point so readily, Wooster. You are not the fool people take you for.'

'Who takes me for a fool?'

The Pim raised his eyebrows slightly.

'Don't people?' he said. 'Well, well. Anyway, that's settled. Unless I can think of something better I shall tell my sister that I was knocked down by a car which drove on without stopping and I didn't get its number. And now perhaps you had better leave me. The doctor made a point of quiet and repose. Moreover, I want to go on with this story. The villain has just dropped a cobra down the heroine's chimney, and I must be at her side. It is impossible not to be thrilled by Edgar Wallace. I'll ring if I want anything.'

I headed for the sitting-room. I found Jeeves there, staring at the portrait in rather a marked manner, as if it hurt him.

'Jeeves,' I said, 'Mr Pim appears to be a fixture.'

'Yes, sir.'

'For the nonce, at any rate. And to-morrow we shall have his sister, Mrs Slingsby, of Slingsby's Superb Soups, in our midst.'

'Yes, sir. I telegraphed to Mrs Slingsby shortly before four. Assuming her to have been at her hotel in Paris at the moment of the telegram's delivery, she will no doubt take a boat early to-morrow afternoon, reaching Dover – or, should she prefer the alternative route, Folkestone – in time to begin the railway journey at an hour which will enable her to arrive in London at about seven. She will possibly proceed first to her London residence—'

'Yes, Jeeves,' I said, 'yes. A gripping story, full of action and human interest. You must have it set to music some time and sing it. Meanwhile, get this into your head. It is imperative that Mrs Slingsby does not learn that it was Miss Pendlebury who broke her brother in two places. I shall require you, therefore, to approach Mr Pim before she arrives, ascertain exactly what tale he intends to tell, and be prepared to back it up in every particular.'

'Very good, sir.'

'And now, Jeeves, what of Miss Pendlebury?'

'Sir?'

'She's sure to call to make enquiries.'

'Yes, sir.'

'Well, she mustn't find me here. You know all about women, Jeeves?'

'Yes, sir.'

'Then tell me this. Am I not right in supposing that if Miss Pendlebury is in a position to go into the sick-room, take a long look at the interesting invalid, and then pop out, with the memory of that look fresh in her mind, and get a square sight of me lounging about in sponge-bag trousers, she will draw damaging comparisons? You see what I mean? Look on this picture and on that – the one romantic, the other not . . . Eh?'

'Very true, sir. It is a point which I had intended to bring to your attention. An invalid undoubtedly exercises a powerful appeal to the motherliness which exists in every woman's heart, sir. Invalids seem to stir their deepest feelings. The poet Scott has put the matter neatly in the lines – "Oh, Woman in our hours of ease uncertain, coy, and hard to please . . . When pain and anguish rack the brow—" '

I held up a hand.

'At some other time, Jeeves,' I said, 'I shall be delighted to hear you say your piece, but just now I am not in the mood. The position being as I have outlined, I propose to clear out early to-morrow morning and not to reappear until nightfall. I shall take the car and dash down to Brighton for the day.'

'Very good, sir.'

'It is better so, is it not, Jeeves?'

'Indubitably, sir.'

'I think so, too. The sea breezes will tone up my system, which sadly needs a dollop of toning. I leave you in charge of the old home.'

'Very good, sir.'

'Convey my regrets and sympathy to Miss Pendlebury and tell her I have been called away on business.'

'Yes, sir.'

'Should the Slingsby require refreshment, feed her in moderation.'

'Very good, sir.'

'And, in poisoning Mr Pim's soup, don't use arsenic, which

is readily detected. Go to a good chemist and get something that leaves no traces.'

I sighed, and cocked an eye at the portrait.

'All this is very wonky, Jeeves.'

'Yes, sir.'

'When that portrait was painted, I was a happy man.'

'Yes, sir.'

'Ah, well, Jeeves!'

'Very true, sir.'

And we left it at that.

It was lateish when I got back on the following evening. What with a bit of ozone-sniffing, a good dinner, and a nice run home in the moonlight with the old car going as sweet as a nut, I was feeling in pretty good shape once more. In fact, coming through Purley, I went so far as to sing a trifle. The spirit of the Woosters is a buoyant spirit, and optimism had begun to reign again in the W. bosom.

The way I looked at it was, I saw I had been mistaken in assuming that a girl must necessarily love a fellow just because he has broken a leg. At first, no doubt, Gwladys Pendlebury would feel strangely drawn to the Pim when she saw him lying there a more or less total loss. But it would not be long before other reflections crept in. She would ask herself if she were wise in trusting her life's happiness to a man who hadn't enough sense to leap out of the way when he saw a car coming. She would tell herself that, if this sort of thing had happened once, who knew that it might not go on happening again and again all down the long years. And she would recoil from a married life which consisted entirely of going to hospitals and taking her husband fruit. She would realize how much better off she would be, teamed up with a fellow like Bertram Wooster, who, whatever his faults, at least walked on the pavement and looked up and down a street before he crossed it.

It was in excellent spirits, accordingly, that I put the car in the garage, and it was with a merry Tra-la on my lips that I let myself into the flat as Big Ben began to strike eleven. I rang the bell and presently, as if he had divined my wishes, Jeeves came in with siphon and decanter.

'Home again, Jeeves,' I said, mixing a spot.

'Yes, sir.'

'What has been happening in my absence? Did Miss Pendlebury call?'

'Yes, sir. At about two o'clock.'

'And left?'

'At about six, sir.'

I didn't like this so much. A four-hour visit struck me as a bit sinister. However, there was nothing to be done about it.

'And Mrs Slingsby?'

'She arrived shortly after eight and left at ten, sir.'

'Ah? Agitated?'

'Yes, sir. Particularly when she left. She was very desirous of seeing you, sir.'

'Seeing me?'

'Yes, sir.'

'Wanted to thank me brokenly, I suppose, for so courteously allowing her favourite brother a place to have his game legs in. Eh?'

'Possibly, sir. On the other hand, she alluded to you in terms suggestive of disapprobation, sir.'

'She – what?'

' "Feckless idiot" was one of the expressions she employed, sir.'

'Feckless idiot?'

'Yes, sir.'

I couldn't make it out. I simply couldn't see what the woman had based her judgement on. My Aunt Agatha has frequently said that sort of thing about me, but she has known me from a boy.

'I must look into this, Jeeves. Is Mr Pim asleep?'

'No, sir. He rang the bell a moment ago to enquire if we had not a better brand of cigarette in the flat.'

'He did, did he?'

'Yes, sir.'

'The accident doesn't seem to have affected his nerve.'

'No, sir.'

I found Lucius Pim sitting propped up among the pillows, reading his detective story.

'Ah, Wooster,' he said. 'Welcome home. I say, in case you were worrying, it's all right about that cobra. The hero had got at it without the villain's knowledge and extracted its poison-fangs. With the result that when it fell down the chimney and started trying to bite the heroine its efforts were null and void. I doubt if a cobra has ever felt so silly.'

'Never mind about cobras.'

'It's no good saying "Never mind about cobras",' said Lucius Pim in a gentle, rebuking sort of voice. 'You've jolly well *got* to mind about cobras, if they haven't had their poison-fangs extracted. Ask anyone. By the way, my sister looked in. She wants to have a word with you.'

'And I want to have a word with her.'

' "Two minds with but a single thought". What she wants to talk to you about is this accident of mine. You remember that story I was to tell her? About the car driving on? Well the understanding was, if you recollect, that I was only to tell it if I couldn't think of something better. Fortunately, I thought of something much better. It came to me in a flash as I lay in bed looking at the ceiling. You see, that driving-on story was thin. People don't knock fellows down and break their legs and go driving on. The thing wouldn't have held water for a minute. So I told her you did it.'

'What!'

'I said it was you who did it in your car. Much more likely. Makes the whole thing neat and well-rounded. I knew you would approve. At all costs we have got to keep it from her that I was outed by Gwladys. I made it as easy for you as I could, saying that you were a bit pickled at the time and so not to be blamed for what you did. Some fellows wouldn't have thought of that. Still,' said Lucius Pim with a sigh, 'I'm afraid she's not any too pleased with you.'

'She isn't, isn't she?'

'No, she is not. And I strongly recommend you, if you want anything like a pleasant interview to-morrow, to sweeten her a bit overnight.'

'How do you mean, sweeten her?'

'I'd suggest you sent her some flowers. It would be a graceful gesture. Roses are her favourites. Shoot her in a few roses – Number Three, Hill Street is the address – and it may make all the difference. I think it my duty to inform you, old man, that my sister Beatrice is rather a tough egg, when roused. My brother-in-law is due back from New York at any moment, and the danger, as I see it, is that Beatrice, unless sweetened, will get at him and make him bring actions against you for torts and malfeasances and what not and get thumping damages. He isn't over-fond of me and, left to himself, would rather approve than otherwise of people who broke my legs: but he's crazy about Beatrice and will do anything she asks him to. So my advice is, Gather ye rose-buds, while ye may and bung them in to Number Three, Hill Street. Otherwise, the case of Slingsby v. Wooster will be on the calendar before you can say "What-ho".'

I gave the fellow a look. Lost on him, of course.

'It's a pity you didn't think of all that before,' I said. And it wasn't so much the actual words, if you know what I mean, as the way I said it.

'I thought of it all right,' said Lucius Pim. 'But, as we were both agreed that at all costs——'

'Oh, all right,' I said. 'All right, all right.'

'You aren't annoyed?' said Lucius Pim, looking at me with a touch of surprise.

'Oh, no!'

'Splendid,' said Lucius Pim, relieved. 'I knew you would feel that I had done the only possible thing. It would have been awful if Beatrice had found out about Gwladys. I daresay you have noticed, Wooster, that when women find themselves in a position to take a running kick at one of their own sex they are twice as rough on her as they would be on a man. Now, you, being of the male persuasion, will find everything made nice and smooth for you. A quart of assorted roses, a few smiles, a tactful word or two, and she'll have melted before you know where you are. Play your cards properly, and you and Beatrice will be laughing merrily and having a game of Round and Round the Mulberry Bush together in about five minutes. Better not let Slingsby's Soups catch you at it, however. He's very jealous where Beatrice is concerned. And now you'll forgive me, old chap, if I send you away. The doctor says I ought not to talk too much for a day or two. Besides, it's time for bye-bye.'

The more I thought it over, the better that idea of sending those roses looked. Lucius Pim was not a man I was fond of – in fact, if I had had to choose between him and a cockroach as a companion for a walking-tour, the cockroach would have had it by a short head – but there was no doubt that he had outlined the right policy. His advice was good, and I decided to follow it. Rising next morning at ten-fifteen, I swallowed a strengthening breakfast and legged it off to that flower-shop in Piccadilly. I couldn't leave the thing to Jeeves. It was essentially a mission that demanded the personal touch. I laid out a couple of quid on a sizeable bouquet, sent it with my card to Hill Street, and then looked in at the Drones for a brief refresher. It is a thing I don't often do in the morning, but this threatened to be rather a special morning.

It was about noon when I got back to the flat. I went into the sitting-room and tried to adjust the mind to the coming interview. It had to be faced, of course, but it wasn't any good my telling myself that it was going to be one of those jolly scenes the memory of which cheer you up as you sit toasting your toes at the fire in your old age. I stood or fell by the roses. If they sweetened the Slingsby, all would be well. If they failed to sweeten her, Bertram was undoubtedly for it.

The clock ticked on, but she did not come. A late riser, I took it, and was slightly encouraged by the reflection. My experience of women has been that the earlier they leave the hay the more vicious specimens they are apt to be. My Aunt Agatha, for instance, is always up with the lark, and look at her.

Still, you couldn't be sure that this rule always worked, and after a while the suspense began to get in amongst me a bit. To divert the mind, I fetched the old putter out of its bag and began to practise putts into a glass. After all, even if the Slingsby turned out to be all that I had pictured her in my gloomier moments, I should have improved my close-to-the-hole work on the green and be that much up, at any rate.

It was while I was shaping for a rather tricky shot that the front-door bell went.

I picked up the glass and shoved the putter behind the settee. It struck me that if the woman found me engaged on what you might call a frivolous pursuit she might take it to indicate lack of remorse and proper feeling. I straightened the collar, pulled down the waistcoat, and managed to fasten on the face a sort of sad half-smile which was welcoming without being actually jovial. It looked all right in the mirror, and I held it as the door opened.

'Mr Slingsby,' announced Jeeves.

And, having spoken these words, he closed the door and left us alone together.

For quite a time there wasn't anything in the way of chit-chat. The shock of expecting Mrs Slingsby and finding myself confronted by something entirely different – in fact, not the same thing at all – seemed to have affected the vocal cords. And the visitor didn't appear to be disposed to make light conversation himself. He stood there looking strong and silent. I suppose you have to be like that if you want to manufacture anything in the nature of a really convincing soup.

Slingsby's Superb Soups was a Roman Emperor-looking sort of bird, with keen, penetrating eyes and one of those jutting chins. The eyes seemed to be fixed on me in a dashed unpleasant stare and, unless I was mistaken, he was grinding his teeth a trifle. For some reason he appeared to have taken a strong dislike to me at sight, and I'm bound to say this rather puzzled me. I don't pretend to have one of those Fascinating Personalities which you get from studying the booklets advertised in the back pages of the magazines, but I couldn't recall another case in the whole of my career where a single glimpse of the old map had been enough to make anyone look as if he wanted to foam at the mouth. Usually, when people meet me for the first time, they don't seem to know I'm there.

However, I exerted myself to play the host.

'Mr Slingsby?'

'That is my name.'

'Just got back from America?'

'I landed this morning.'

'Sooner than you were expected, what?'

'So I imagine.'

'Very glad to see you.'

'You will not be long.'

I took time off to do a bit of gulping. I saw now what had happened. This bloke had been home, seen his wife, heard the story of the accident, and had hastened round to the flat to slip it across me. Evidently those roses had not sweetened the female of the species. The only thing to do now seemed to be to take a stab at sweetening the male.

'Have a drink?' I said.

'No!'

'A cigarette?'

'No!'

'A chair?'

'No!'

I went into the silence once more. These non-drinking, non-smoking non-sitters are hard birds to handle.

'Don't grin at me, sir!'

I shot a glance at myself in the mirror, and saw what he meant. The sad half-smile *had* slopped over a bit. I adjusted it, and there was another pause.

'Now, sir,' said the Superb Souper. 'To business. I think I need scarcely tell you why I am here.'

'No. Of course. Absolutely. It's about that little matter—'

He gave a snort which nearly upset a vase on the mantelpiece.

'Little matter? So you consider it a little matter, do you?'

'Well—'

'Let me tell you, sir, that when I find that during my absence from the country a man has been annoying my wife with his importunities I regard it as anything but a little matter. And I shall endeavour,' said the Souper, the eyes gleaming a trifle brighter as he rubbed his hands together in a hideous, menacing way, 'to make you see the thing in the same light.'

I couldn't make head or tail of this. I simply couldn't follow him. The lemon began to swim.

'Eh?' I said. 'Your wife?'

'You heard me.'

'There must be some mistake.'

'There is. You made it.'

'But I don't know your wife.'

'Ha!'

'I've never even met her.'

'Tchah!'

'Honestly, I haven't.'

'Bah!'

He drank me in for a moment.

'Do you deny you sent her flowers?'

I felt the heart turn a double somersault. I began to catch his drift.

'Flowers!' he proceeded. 'Roses, sir. Great, fat, beastly roses. Enough of them to sink a ship. Your card was attached to them by a small pin—'

His voice died away in a sort of gurgle, and I saw that he was staring at something behind me. I spun round, and there, in the doorway – I hadn't seen it open, because during the last spasm of dialogue I had been backing cautiously towards it – there in the doorway stood a female. One glance was enough to tell me who she was. No woman could look so like Lucius Pim who hadn't the misfortune to be related to him. It was Sister Beatrice, the tough egg. I saw all. She had left home before the flowers had arrived: she had sneaked, unsweetened, into the flat, while I was fortifying the system at the Drones: and here she was.

'Er—' I said.

'Alexander!' said the female.

'Goo!' said the Souper. Or it may have been 'Coo'.

Whatever it was, it was in the nature of a battle-cry or slogan of war. The Souper's worst suspicions had obviously been confirmed. His eyes shone with a strange light. His chin pushed itself out another couple of inches. He clenched and unclenched his fingers once or twice, as if to make sure that they were working properly and could be relied on to do a good, clean job of strangling. Then, once more observing 'Coo!' (or 'Goo!'), he sprang forward, trod on the golf-ball I had been practising putting with, and took one of the finest tosses I have ever witnessed. The purler of a lifetime. For a moment the air seemed to be full of arms and legs, and then, with a thud that nearly dislocated the flat, he made a forced landing against the wall.

And, feeling I had had about all I wanted, I oiled from the room and was in the act of grabbing my hat from the rack in the hall, when Jeeves appeared.

'I fancied I heard a noise, sir,' said Jeeves.

'Quite possibly,' I said. 'It was Mr Slingsby.'

'Sir?'

'Mr Slingsby practising Russian dances,' I explained. 'I rather think he has fractured an assortment of limbs. Better go in and see.'

'Very good, sir.'

'If he is the wreck I imagine, put him in my room and send for the doctor. The flat is filling up nicely with the various units of the Pim family and its connections, eh, Jeeves?'

'Yes, sir.'

'I think the supply is about exhausted, but should any aunts or uncles by marriage come along and break their limbs, bed them out on the Chesterfield.'

'Very good, sir.'

'I, personally, Jeeves,' I said, opening the front door and pausing on the threshold, 'am off to Paris. I will wire you the address. Notify me in due course when the place is free from Pims and completely purged of Slingsbys, and I will return. Oh, and Jeeves.'

'Sir?'

'Spare no effort to mollify these birds. They think – at least, Slingsby (female) thinks, and what she thinks to-day he will think to-morrow – that it was I who ran over Mr Pim in my car. Endeavour during my absence to sweeten them.'

'Very good, sir.'

'And now perhaps you had better be going in and viewing the body. I shall proceed to the Drones, where I shall lunch, subsequently catching the two o'clock train at Charing Cross. Meet me there with an assortment of luggage.'

It was a matter of three weeks or so before Jeeves sent me the 'All clear' signal. I spent the time pottering pretty perturbedly about Paris and environs. It is a city I am fairly fond of, but I was glad to be able to return to the old home. I hopped on to a passing aeroplane and a couple of hours later was bowling through Croydon on my way to the centre of things. It was somewhere down in the Sloane Square neighbourhood that I first caught sight of the posters.

A traffic block had occurred, and I was glancing idly this way and that, when suddenly my eye was caught by something that looked familiar. And then I saw what it was.

Pasted on a blank wall and measuring about a hundred feet each way was an enormous poster, mostly red and blue. At the top of it were the words:

SLINGSBY'S SUPERB SOUPS

and at the bottom:

SUCCULENT AND STRENGTHENING

And, in between, me. Yes, dash it, Bertram Wooster in person. A reproduction of the Pendlebury portrait, perfect in every detail.

It was the sort of thing to make a fellow's eyes flicker, and mine flickered. You might say a mist seemed to roll before them. Then it lifted, and I was able to get a good long look before the traffic moved on.

Of all the absolutely foul sights I have ever seen, this took the biscuit with ridiculous ease. The thing was a bally libel on the Wooster face, and yet it was as unmistakable as if it had had my name under it. I saw now what Jeeves had meant when he said that the portrait had given me a hungry look. In the poster this look had become one of bestial greed. There I sat absolutely slavering through a monocle about six inches in circumference at a plateful of soup, looking as if I hadn't had a meal for weeks. The whole thing seemed to take one straight away into a different and a dreadful world.

I woke from a species of trance or coma to find myself at the door of the block of flats. To buzz upstairs and charge into the home was with me the work of a moment.

Jeeves came shimmering down the hall, the respectful beam of welcome on his face.

'I am glad to see you back, sir.'

'Never mind about that,' I yipped. 'What about—?'

'The posters, sir? I was wondering if you might have observed them.'

'I observed them!'

'Striking, sir?'

'Very striking. Now, perhaps you'll kindly explain—'

'You instructed me, if you recollect, sir, to spare no effort to mollify Mr Slingsby.'

'Yes, but—'

'It proved a somewhat difficult task, sir. For some time Mr Slingsby, on the advice and owing to the persuasion of Mrs Slingsby, appeared to be resolved to institute an action in law against you – a procedure which I knew you would find most distasteful.'

'Yes, but—'

'And then, the first day he was able to leave his bed, he observed the portrait, and it seemed to me judicious to point out to him its possibilities as an advertising medium. He readily fell in with the suggestion and, on my assurance that, should he abandon the projected action in law, you would willingly permit the use of the portrait, he entered into negotiations with Miss Pendlebury for the purchase of the copyright.'

'Oh? Well, I hope she's got something out of it, at any rate?'

'Yes, sir. Mr Pim, acting as Miss Pendlebury's agent, drove, I understand, an extremely satisfactory bargain.'

'He acted as her agent, eh?'

'Yes, sir. In his capacity as fiancé to the young lady, sir.'

'Fiancé!'

'Yes, sir.'

It shows how the sight of that poster had got into my ribs when I state that, instead of being laid out cold by this announcement, I merely said 'Ha!' or 'Ho!' or it may have been 'H'm'. After the poster, nothing seemed to matter.

'After that poster, Jeeves,' I said, 'nothing seems to matter.'

'No, sir?'

'No, Jeeves. A woman has tossed my heart lightly away, but what of it?'

'Exactly, sir.'

'The voice of Love seemed to call to me, but it was a wrong number. Is that going to crush me?'

'No, sir.'

'No, Jeeves. It is not. But what does matter is this ghastly business of my face being spread from end to end of the Metropolis with the eyes fixed on a plate of Slingsby's Superb Soup. I must leave London. The lads at the Drones will kid me without ceasing.'

'Yes, sir. And Mrs Spenser Gregson—'

I paled visibly. I hadn't thought of Aunt Agatha and what she might have to say about letting down the family prestige.

'You don't mean to say she has been ringing up?'

'Several times daily, sir.'

'Jeeves, flight is the only resource.'

'Yes, sir.'

'Back to Paris, what?'

'I should not recommend the move, sir. The posters are, I understand, shortly to appear in that city also, advertising the *Bouillon Suprême*. Mr Slingsby's products command a large sale in France. The sight would be painful for you, sir.'

'Then where?'

'If I might make a suggestion, sir, why not adhere to your original intention of cruising in Mrs Travers' yacht in the Mediterranean? On the yacht you would be free from the annoyance of these advertising displays.'

The man seemed to me to be drivelling.

'But the yacht started weeks ago. It may be anywhere by now.'

'No, sir. The cruise was postponed for a month owing to the illness of Mr Travers' chef, Anatole, who contracted influenza. Mr Travers refused to sail without him.'

'You mean they haven't started?'

'Not yet, sir. The yacht sails from Southampton on Tuesday next.'

'Why, then, dash it, nothing could be sweeter.'

'No, sir.'

'Ring up Aunt Dahlia and tell her we'll be there.'

'I ventured to take the liberty of doing so a few moments before you arrived, sir.'

'You did?'

'Yes, sir. I thought it probable that the plan would meet with your approval.'

'It does! I've wished all along I was going on that cruise.'

'I, too, sir. It should be extremely pleasant.'

'The tang of the salt breezes, Jeeves!'

'Yes, sir.'

'The moonlight on the water!'

'Precisely, sir.'

'The gentle heaving of the waves!'

'Exactly, sir.'

I felt absolutely in the pink. Gwladys – pah! The posters – bah! That was the way I looked at it.

'Yo-ho-ho, Jeeves!' I said, giving the trousers a bit of a hitch.

'Yes, sir.'

'In fact, I will go further. Yo-ho-ho and a bottle of rum!'

'Very good, sir. I will bring it immediately.'

The Heel of Achilles

O n the young man's face, as he sat sipping his ginger-ale
in the club-house smoking-room, there was a look of
disillusionment. 'Never again!' he said.

The Oldest Member glanced up from his paper.

'You are proposing to give up golf once more?' he queried.

'Not golf. Betting on golf.' The Young Man frowned. 'I've
just been let down badly. Wouldn't you have thought I had a
good thing, laying seven to one on McTavish against Robinson?'

'Undoubtedly,' said the Sage. 'The odds, indeed, generous
as they are, scarcely indicate the former's superiority. Do you
mean to tell me that the thing came unstitched?'

'Robinson won in a walk, after being three down at the
turn.'

'Strange! What happened?'

'Why, they looked in at the bar to have a refresher before
starting for the tenth,' said the young man, his voice quivering,

'and McTavish suddenly discovered that there was a hole in his trouser-pocket and sixpence had dropped out. He worried so frightfully about it that on the second nine he couldn't do a thing right. Went completely off his game and didn't win a hole.'

The Sage shook his head gravely.

'If this is really going to be a lesson to you, my boy, never to bet on the result of a golf-match, it will be a blessing in disguise. There is no such thing as a certainty in golf. I wonder if I ever told you a rather curious episode in the career of Vincent Jopp?'

'*The* Vincent Jopp? The American multi-millionaire?'

'The same. You never knew he once came within an ace of winning the American Amateur Championship, did you?'

'I never heard of his playing golf.'

'He played for one season. After that he gave it up and has not touched a club since. Ring the bell and get me a small lime-juice, and I will tell you all.'

It was long before your time (said the Oldest Member) that the events which I am about to relate took place. I had just come down from Cambridge, and was feeling particularly pleased with myself because I had secured the job of private and confidential secretary to Vincent Jopp, then a man in the early thirties, busy in laying the foundations of his present remarkable fortune. He engaged me, and took me with him to Chicago.

Jopp was, I think, the most extraordinary personality I have encountered in a long and many-sided life. He was admirably equipped for success in finance, having the steely eye and square jaw without which it is hopeless for a man to enter that line of business. He possessed also an overwhelming confidence in himself, and the ability to switch a cigar from one corner of his mouth to the other without wiggling his ears, which, as you know, is the stamp of the true Monarch of the Money Market. He was the nearest approach to the financier on the films, the fellow who makes his jaw-muscles jump when he is telephoning, that I have ever seen.

Like all successful men, he was a man of method. He kept a pad on his desk on which he would scribble down his appointments, and it was my duty on entering the office each morning to take this pad and type its contents neatly in a loose-leaved ledger. Usually, of course, these entries referred to business appointments and deals which he was contemplating, but one day I was interested to note, against the date May 3rd, the entry:

Propose to Amelia.

I was interested, as I say, but not surprised. Though a man of steel and iron, there was nothing of the celibate about Vincent Jopp. He was one of those men who marry early and often. On three separate occasions before I joined his service he had jumped off the dock, to scramble back to shore again later by means of the Divorce Court lifebelt. Scattered here and there about the country there were three ex-Mrs Jopps, drawing their monthly envelope, and now, it seemed, he contemplated the addition of a fourth to the platoon.

I was not surprised, I say, at this resolve of his. What did seem a little remarkable to me was the thorough way in which he had thought the thing out. This iron-willed man recked nothing of possible obstacles. Under the date of June 1st was the entry:

Marry Amelia;

while in March of the following year he had arranged to have his first-born christened Thomas Reginald. Later on, the short-coating of Thomas Reginald was arranged for, and there was a note about sending him to school. Many hard things have been said of Vincent Jopp, but nobody has ever accused him of not being a man who looked ahead.

On the morning of May 4th Jopp came into the office, looking, I fancied, a little thoughtful. He sat for some moments staring before him with his brow a trifle furrowed; then he seemed to come to himself. He rapped his desk.

'Hi! You!' he said. It was thus that he habitually addressed me.

'Mr Jopp?' I replied.

'What's golf?'

I had at that time just succeeded in getting my handicap

down into single figures, and I welcomed the opportunity of dilating on the noblest of pastimes. But I had barely begun my eulogy when he stopped me.

'It's a game, is it?'

'I suppose you could call it that,' I said, 'but it is an off-hand way of describing the holiest—'

'How do you play it?'

'Pretty well,' I said. 'At the beginning of the season I didn't seem able to keep 'em straight at all, but lately I've been doing fine. Getting better every day. Whether it was that I was moving my head or gripping too tightly with the right hand—'

'Keep the reminiscences for your grandchildren during the long winter evenings,' he interrupted, abruptly, as was his habit. 'What I want to know is what a fellow does when he plays golf. Tell me in as few words as you can just what it's all about.'

'You hit a ball with a stick till it falls into a hole.'

'Easy!' he snapped. 'Take dictation.'

I produced my pad.

'May the fifth, take up golf. What's an Amateur Championship?'

'It is the annual competition to decide which is the best player among the amateurs. There is also a Professional Championship, and an Open event.'

'Oh, there are golf professionals, are there? What do they do?'

'They teach golf.'

'Which is the best of them?'

'Sandy McHoots won both British and American Open events last year.'

'Wire him to come here at once.'

'But McHoots is in Inverlochty, in Scotland.'

'Never mind. Get him; tell him to name his own terms. When is the Amateur Championship?'

'I think it is on September the twelfth this year.'

'All right, take dictation. September twelfth, win Amateur Championship.'

I stared at him in amazement, but he was not looking at me.

'Got that?' he said. 'September thir— Oh, I was forgetting! Add September twelfth, corner wheat. September thirteenth, marry Amelia.'

'Marry Amelia,' I echoed, moistening my pencil.

'Where do you play this – what's-its-name – golf?'

'There are clubs all over the country. I belong to the Wissahicky Glen.'

'That a good place?'

'Very good.'

'Arrange to-day for my becoming a member.'

Sandy McHoots arrived in due course, and was shown into the private office.

'Mr McHoots?' said Vincent Jopp.

'Mphm!' said the Open Champion.

'I have sent for you, Mr McHoots, because I hear that you are the greatest living exponent of this game of golf.'

'Aye,' said the champion, cordially. 'I am that.'

'I wish you to teach me the game. I am already somewhat behind schedule owing to the delay incident upon your long journey, so let us start at once. Name a few of the most important points in connection with the game. My secretary will make notes of them, and I will memorize them. In this way we shall save time. Now, what is the most important thing to remember when playing golf?'

'Keep your heid still.'

'A simple task.'

'Na sae simple as it soonds.'

'Nonsense!' said Vincent Jopp, curtly. 'If I decide to keep my head still, I shall keep it still. What next?'

'Keep yer ee on the ba'.'

'It shall be attended to. And the next?'

'Dinna press.'

'I won't. And to resume.'

Mr McHoots ran through a dozen of the basic rules, and I took them down in shorthand. Vincent Jopp studied the list.

'Very good. Easier than I had supposed. On the first tee at Wissahicky Glen at eleven sharp to-morrow, Mr McHoots. Hi! You!'

'Sir?' I said.

'Go out and buy me a set of clubs, a red jacket, a cloth cap, a pair of spiked shoes, and a ball.'

'One ball?'

'Certainly. What need is there of more?'

'It sometimes happens,' I explained, 'that a player who is learning the game fails to hit his ball straight, and then he often loses it in the rough at the side of the fairway.'

'Absurd!' said Vincent Jopp. 'If I set out to drive my ball straight, I shall drive it straight. Good morning, Mr McHoots. You will excuse me now. I am busy cornering Woven Textiles.'

Golf is in its essence a simple game. You laugh in a sharp, bitter, barking manner when I say this, but nevertheless it is true. Where the average man goes wrong is in making the game difficult for himself. Observe the non-player, the man who walks round with you for the sake of the fresh air. He will hole out with a single care-free flick of his umbrella the twenty-foot putt over which you would ponder and hesitate for a full minute before sending it right off the line. Put a driver in his hands, and he pastes the ball into the next county without a thought. It is only when he takes to the game in earnest that he becomes self-conscious and anxious, and tops his shots even as you and I. A man who could retain through his golfing career the almost scornful confidence of the non-player would be unbeatable. Fortunately such an attitude of mind is beyond the scope of human nature.

It was not, however, beyond the scope of Vincent Jopp, the superman. Vincent Jopp was, I am inclined to think, the only golfer who ever approached the game in a spirit of Pure Reason. I have read of men who, never having swum in their lives, studied a textbook on their way down to the swimming bath, mastered its contents, and dived in and won the big race. In just such a spirit did Vincent Jopp start to play golf. He committed McHoots's hints to memory, and then went out on the links and put them into practice. He came to the tee with a clear picture in his mind of what he had to do, and he did it. He was not intimidated, like the average novice, by the thought that if he pulled in his hands he would slice, or if he gripped too tightly with the right he would pull. Pulling in the hands was an error, so he did not pull in his hands. Gripping too tightly was a defect, so he did not grip too tightly. With that weird concentration which had served him so well in business he did precisely what he had set out to do – no less and no more. Golf with Vincent Jopp was an exact science.

The annals of the game are studded with the names of those who have made rapid progress in their first season. Colonel Quill, we read in our Vardon, took up golf at the age of fifty-six, and by devising an ingenious machine consisting of a fishing-line and a sawn-down bedpost was enabled to keep his head so still that he became a scratch player before the end of the year. But no one, I imagine, except Vincent Jopp, has ever achieved scratch on his first morning on the links.

The main difference, we are told, between the amateur and the professional golfer is the fact that the latter is always aiming at the pin, while the former has in his mind a vague picture of getting somewhere reasonably near it. Vincent Jopp invariably went for the pin. He tried to hole out from anywhere inside two hundred and twenty yards. The only occasion on which I ever heard him express any chagrin or disappointment was during the afternoon round on his first day out, when from the tee on the two-hundred-and-eighty-yard seventh he laid his ball within six inches of the hole.

'A marvellous shot!' I cried, genuinely stirred.

'Too much to the right,' said Vincent Jopp, frowning.

He went on from triumph to triumph. He won the monthly medal in May, June, July, August, and September. Towards the end of May he was heard to complain that Wissahicky Glen was not a sporting course. The Greens Committee sat up night after night trying to adjust his handicap so as to give other members an outside chance against him. The golf experts of the daily papers wrote columns about his play. And it was pretty generally considered throughout the country that it would be a pure formality for anyone else to enter against him in the Amateur Championship – an opinion which was borne out when he got through into the final without losing a hole. A safe man to have betted on, you would have said. But mark the sequel.

The American Amateur Championship was held that year in Detroit. I had accompanied my employer there; for, though engaged on this nerve-wearing contest, he refused to allow his business to be interfered with. As he had indicated in his schedule, he was busy at the time cornering wheat; and it was my task to combine the duties of caddie and secretary. Each day I accompanied him round the links with my note-book and his bag of clubs, and the progress of his various matches was somewhat complicated by the arrival of a stream of telegraph-boys bearing important messages. He would read these between the strokes and dictate replies to me, never, however, taking more than the five minutes allowed by the rules for an interval between strokes. I am inclined to think that it was this that put the finishing touch on his opponents' discomfiture. It is not soothing for a nervous man to have the game hung up on the green while his adversary dictates to his caddie a letter beginning 'Yours of the 11th inst. received and contents noted. In reply would state—' This sort of thing puts a man off his game.

I was resting in the lobby of our hotel after a strenuous day's work, when I found that I was being paged. I answered the summons, and was informed that a lady wished to see me. Her card bore the name 'Miss Amelia Merridew.' Amelia! The name seemed familiar. Then I remembered. Amelia was the name of the girl Vincent Jopp intended to marry, the fourth of the long line of Mrs Jopps. I hurried to present myself, and found a tall, slim girl, who was plainly labouring under a considerable agitation.

'Miss Merridew?' I said.

'Yes,' she murmured. 'My name will be strange to you.'

'Am I right,' I queried, 'in supposing that you are the lady to whom Mr Jopp—'

'I am! I am!' she replied. 'And, oh, what shall I do?'

'Kindly give me particulars,' I said, taking out my pad from force of habit.

She hesitated a moment, as if afraid to speak.

'You are caddying for Mr Jopp in the final to-morrow?' she said at last.

'I am.'

'Then could you – would you mind – would it be giving you too much trouble if I asked you to shout "Boo!" at him when he is making his stroke, if he looks like winning?'

I was perplexed.

'I don't understand.'

'I see that I must tell you all. I am sure you will treat what I say as absolutely confidential.'

'Certainly.'

'I am provisionally engaged to Mr Jopp.'

'Provisionally?'

She gulped.

'Let me tell you my story. Mr Jopp asked me to marry him, and I would rather do anything on earth than marry him. But how could I say "No!" with those awful eyes of his boring me through? I knew that if I said "No," he would argue me out of it in two minutes. I had an idea. I gathered that he had never played golf, so I told him that I would marry him if he won the

Amateur Championship this year. And now I find that he has
been a golfer all along, and, what is more, a plus man! It isn't
fair!'

'He was not a golfer when you made that condition,' I said.
'He took up the game on the following day.'

'Impossible! How could he have become as good as he is in
this short time?'

'Because he is Vincent Jopp! In his lexicon there is no such
word as impossible.'

She shuddered.

'What a man! But I can't marry him,' she cried. 'I want
to marry somebody else. Oh, won't you help me? Do shout
"Boo!" at him when he is starting his down-swing!'

I shook my head.

'It would take more than a single "boo" to put Vincent Jopp
off his stroke.'

'But won't you try it?'

'I cannot. My duty is to my employer.'

'Oh, do!'

'No, no. Duty is duty, and paramount with me. Besides, I
have a bet on him to win.'

The stricken girl uttered a faint moan, and tottered away.

I was in our suite shortly after dinner that night, going over
some of the notes I had made that day, when the telephone
rang. Jopp was out at the time, taking a short stroll with his

after-dinner cigar. I unhooked the receiver, and a female voice spoke.

'Is that Mr Jopp?'

'Mr Jopp's secretary speaking. Mr Jopp is out.'

'Oh, it's nothing important. Will you say that Mrs Luella Mainprice Jopp called up to wish him luck? I shall be on the course to-morrow to see him win the final.'

I returned to my notes. Soon afterwards the telephone rang again.

'Vincent, dear?'

'Mr Jopp's secretary speaking.'

'Oh, will you say that Mrs Jane Jukes Jopp called up to wish him luck? I shall be there to-morrow to see him play.'

I resumed my work. I had hardly started when the telephone rang for the third time.

'Mr Jopp?'

'Mr Jopp's secretary speaking.'

'This is Mrs Agnes Parsons Jopp. I just called up to wish him luck. I shall be looking on to-morrow.'

I shifted my work nearer to the telephone-table so as to be ready for the next call. I had heard that Vincent Jopp had only been married three times, but you never knew.

Presently Jopp came in.

'Anybody called up?' he asked.

'Nobody on business. An assortment of your wives were on the wire wishing you luck. They asked me to say that they will be on the course to-morrow.'

For a moment it seemed to me that the man's iron repose was shaken.

'Luella?' he asked.

'She was the first.'

'Jane?'

'And Jane.'

'And Agnes?'

'Agnes,' I said, 'is right.'

'H'm!' said Vincent Jopp. And for the first time since I had known him I thought that he was ill at ease.

The day of the final dawned bright and clear. At least, I was not awake at the time to see, but I suppose it did; for at nine o'clock, when I came down to breakfast, the sun was shining brightly. The first eighteen holes were to be played before lunch, starting at eleven. Until twenty minutes before the hour Vincent Jopp kept me busy taking dictation, partly on matters connected with his wheat deal and partly on a signed article dealing with the final, entitled 'How I Won'. At eleven sharp we were out on the first tee.

Jopp's opponent was a nice-looking young man, but obviously nervous. He giggled in a distraught sort of way as he shook hands with my employer.

'Well, may the best man win,' he said.

'I have arranged to do so,' replied Jopp, curtly, and started to address his ball.

There was a large crowd at the tee, and, as Jopp started his down-swing, from somewhere on the outskirts of this crowd there came suddenly a musical 'Boo!' It rang out in the clear morning air like a bugle.

I had been right in my estimate of Vincent Jopp. His forceful stroke never wavered. The head of his club struck the ball, dispatching it a good two hundred yards down the middle of the fairway. As we left the tee I saw Amelia Merridew being led away with bowed head by two members of the Greens Committee. Poor girl! My heart bled for her. And yet, after all, Fate had been kind in removing her from the scene, even in custody, for she could hardly have borne to watch the proceedings. Vincent Jopp made rings round his antagonist. Hole after hole he won in his remorseless, machine-like way, until when lunchtime came at the end of the eighteenth he was ten up. All the other holes had been halved.

It was after lunch, as we made our way to the first tee, that the advance-guard of the Mrs Jopps appeared in the person of Luella Mainprice Jopp, a kittenish little woman with blonde hair and a Pekingese dog. I remembered reading in the papers that she had divorced my employer for persistent and aggravated mental cruelty, calling witnesses to bear out her statement that he had said he did not like her in pink, and that on two separate occasions had insisted on her dog eating the leg of a chicken instead of the breast; but Time, the great healer, seemed to have removed all bitterness, and she greeted him affectionately.

'Wassums going to win great big championship against nasty rough strong man?' she said.

'Such,' said Vincent Jopp, 'is my intention. It was kind of you, Luella, to trouble to come and watch me. I wonder if you know Mrs Agnes Parsons Jopp?' he said, courteously, indicating a kind-looking, motherly woman who had just come up. 'How are you, Agnes?'

'If you had asked me that question this morning, Vincent,' replied Mrs Agnes Parsons Jopp, 'I should have been obliged to say that I felt far from well. I had an odd throbbing feeling in the left elbow, and I am sure my temperature was above the normal. But this afternoon I am a little better. How are you, Vincent?'

Although she had, as I recalled from the reports of the case, been compelled some years earlier to request the Court to sever her marital relations with Vincent Jopp on the ground of calculated and inhuman brutality, in that he had callously refused, in spite of her pleadings, to take old Dr Bennett's Tonic Swamp-Juice three times a day, her voice, as she spoke, was kind and even anxious. Badly as this man had treated her – and I remember hearing that several of the jury had been unable to restrain their tears when she was in the witness-box giving her evidence – there still seemed to linger some remnants of the old affection.

'I am quite well, thank you, Agnes,' said Vincent Jopp.

'Are you wearing your liver-pad?'

A frown flitted across my employer's strong face.

'I am not wearing my liver-pad,' he replied, brusquely.

'Oh, Vincent, how rash of you!'

He was about to speak, when a sudden exclamation from his rear checked him. A genial-looking woman in a sports coat was standing there, eyeing him with a sort of humorous horror.

'Well, Jane,' he said.

I gathered that this was Mrs Jane Jukes Jopp, the wife who had divorced him for systematic and ingrowing fiendishness on the ground that he had repeatedly outraged her feelings by wearing a white waistcoat with a dinner-jacket. She continued to look at him dumbly, and then uttered a sort of strangled, hysterical laugh.

'Those legs!' she cried. 'Those legs!'

Vincent Jopp flushed darkly. Even the strongest and most silent of us have our weaknesses, and my employer's was the rooted idea that he looked well in knickerbockers. It was not my place to try to dissuade him, but there was no doubt that they did not suit him. Nature, in bestowing upon him a massive head and a jutting chin, had forgotten to finish him off at the other end. Vincent Jopp's legs were skinny.

'You poor dear man!' went on Mrs Jane Jukes Jopp. 'What practical joker ever lured you into appearing in public in knickerbockers?'

'I don't object to the knickerbockers,' said Mrs Agnes Parsons Jopp, 'but when he foolishly comes out in quite a strong east wind without his liver-pad—'

'Little Tinky-Ting don't need no liver-pad, he don't,' said

Mrs Luella Mainprice Jopp, addressing the animal in her arms, 'because he was his muzzer's pet, he was.'

I was standing quite near to Vincent Jopp, and at this moment I saw a head of perspiration spring out on his forehead, and into his steely eyes there came a positively hunted look. I could understand and sympathize. Napoleon himself would have wilted if he had found himself in the midst of a trio of females, one talking baby-talk, another fussing about his health, and the third making derogatory observations on his lower limbs. Vincent Jopp was becoming unstrung.

'May as well be starting, shall we?'

It was Jopp's opponent who spoke. There was a strange, set look on his face – the look of a man whose back is against the wall. Ten down on the morning's round, he had drawn on his reserves of courage and was determined to meet the inevitable bravely.

Vincent Jopp nodded absently, then turned to me.

'Keep those women away from me,' he whispered tensely. 'They'll put me off my stroke!'

'Put *you* off your stroke!' I exclaimed, incredulously.

'Yes, me! How the deuce can I concentrate, with people babbling about liver-pads, and – and knickerbockers all round me? Keep them away!'

He started to address his ball, and there was a weak uncertainty in the way he did it that prepared me for what was to come. His club rose, wavered, fell; and the ball, badly topped, trickled two feet and sank into a cuppy lie.

'Is that good or bad?' inquired Mrs Luella Mainprice Jopp.

A sort of desperate hope gleamed in the eye of the other competitor in the final. He swung with renewed vigour. His ball sang through the air, and lay within chip-shot distance of the green.

'At the very least,' said Mrs Agnes Parsons Jopp, 'I hope, Vincent, that you are wearing flannel next to your skin.'

I heard Jopp give a stifled groan as he took his spoon from the bag. He made a gallant effort to retrieve the lost ground, but the ball struck a stone and bounded away into the long grass to the side of the green. His opponent won the hole.

We moved to the second tee.

'Now, *that* young man,' said Mrs Jane Jukes Jopp, indicating her late husband's blushing antagonist, 'is quite right to wear knickerbockers. He can carry them off. But a glance in the mirror must have shown you that you—'

'I'm sure you're feverish, Vincent,' said Mrs Agnes Parsons Jopp, solicitously. You are quite flushed. There is a wild gleam in your eyes.'

'Muzzer's pet's got little buttons of eyes, that don't never have no wild gleam in zem because he's muzzer's own darling, he was!' said Mrs Luella Mainprice Jopp.

A hollow groan escaped Vincent Jopp's ashen lips.

I need not recount the play hole by hole, I think. There are some subjects that are too painful. It was pitiful to watch Vincent Jopp in his downfall. By the end of the first nine his lead had been reduced to one, and his antagonist, rendered a new man by success, was playing magnificent golf. On the next hole he drew level. Then with a superhuman effort Jopp contrived to halve the eleventh, twelfth, and thirteenth. It seemed as though his iron will might still assert itself, but on the fourteenth the end came.

He had driven a superb ball, outdistancing his opponent by a full fifty yards. The latter played a good second to within a few feet of the green. And then, as Vincent Jopp was shaping for his stroke, Luella Mainprice gave tongue.

'Vincent!'

'Well?'

'Vincent, that other man – bad man – not playing fair. When your back was turned just now, he gave his ball a great bang. *I* was watching him.'

'At any rate,' said Mrs Agnes Parsons Jopp, 'I do hope, when the game is over, Vincent, that you will remember to cool slowly.'

'Flesho!' cried Mrs Jane Jukes Jopp triumphantly. 'I've been trying to remember the name all the afternoon. I saw about it in one of the papers. The advertisements speak most highly of it. You take it before breakfast and again before retiring, and they guarantee it to produce firm, healthy flesh on the most sparsely-covered limbs in next to no time. Now, *will* you remember to get a bottle to-night? It comes in two sizes, the five-shilling (or large size) and the smaller at half-a-crown. G. K. Chesterton writes that he used it regularly for years.'

Vincent Jopp uttered a quavering moan, and his hand, as he took the mashie from his bag, was trembling like an aspen.

Ten minutes later, he was on his way back to the club-house, a beaten man.

And so (concluded the Oldest Member) you see that in golf there is no such thing as a soft snap. You can never be certain of the finest player. Anything may happen to the greatest expert at any stage of the game. In a recent competition George Duncan took eleven shots over a hole which eighteen-handicap men generally do in five. No! Back horses or go down to Throgmorton Street and try to take it away from the Rothschilds, and I will applaud you as a shrewd and cautious financier. But to bet at golf is pure gambling.

Indian Summer of an Uncle

Ask anyone at the Drones, and they will tell you that Bertram Wooster is a fellow whom it is dashed difficult to deceive. Old Lynx-Eye is about what it amounts to. I observe and deduce. I weigh the evidence and draw my conclusions. And that is why Uncle George had not been in my midst more than about two minutes before I, so to speak, saw all. To my trained eye the thing stuck out a mile.

And yet it seemed so dashed absurd. Consider the facts, if you know what I mean.

I mean to say, for years, right back to the time when I first went to school, this bulging relative had been one of the recognized eyesores of London. He was fat then, and day by day in every way has been getting fatter ever since, till now tailors measure him just for the sake of the exercise. He is what they call a prominent London clubman — one of those birds in tight morning coats and grey toppers whom you see toddling along

St James's Street on fine afternoons, puffing a bit as they make the grade. Slip a ferret into any good club between Piccadilly and Pall Mall, and you would start half a dozen Uncle Georges.

He spends his time lunching and dining at the Buffers and, between meals, sucking down spots in the smoking-room and talking to anyone who will listen about the lining of his stomach. About twice a year his liver lodges a formal protest and he goes off to Harrogate or Carlsbad to get planed down. Then back again and on with the programme. The last bloke in the world, in short, who you would think would ever fall a victim to the divine pash. And yet, if you will believe me, that was absolutely the strength of it.

This old pestilence blew in on me one morning at about the hour of the after-breakfast cigarette.

'Oh, Bertie,' he said.

'Hullo?'

'You know those ties you've been wearing. Where did you get them?'

'Blucher's, in the Burlington Arcade.'

'Thanks.'

He walked across to the mirror and stood in front of it, gazing at himself in an earnest manner.

'Smut on your nose?' I asked courteously.

Then I suddenly perceived that he was wearing a sort of horrible simper, and I confess it chilled the blood to no little extent. Uncle George, with face in repose, is hard enough on the eye. Simpering, he goes right above the odds.

'Ha!' he said.

He heaved a long sigh, and turned away. Not too soon, for the mirror was on the point of cracking.

'I'm not so old,' he said, in a musing sort of voice.

'So old as what?'

'Properly considered, I'm in my prime. Besides, what a young and inexperienced girl needs is a man of weight and years to lean on. The sturdy oak, not the sapling.'

It was at this point that, as I said above, I saw all.

'Great Scott, Uncle George!' I said. 'You aren't thinking of getting married?'

'Who isn't?' he said.

'You aren't,' I said.

'Yes, I am. Why not?'

'Oh, well—'

'Marriage is an honourable state.'

'Oh, absolutely.'

'It might make you a better man, Bertie.'

'Who says so?'

'I say so. Marriage might turn you from a frivolous young scallywag into – er – a non-scallywag. Yes, confound you, I *am* thinking of getting married, and if Agatha comes sticking her oar in I'll – I'll – well, I shall know what to do about it.'

He exited on the big line, and I rang the bell for Jeeves. The situation seemed to me one that called for a cosy talk.

'Jeeves,' I said.

'Sir?'

'You know my Uncle George?'

'Yes, sir. His lordship has been familiar to me for some years.'

'I don't mean do you know my Uncle George. I mean do you know what my Uncle George is thinking of doing?'

'Contracting a matrimonial alliance, sir.'

'Good Lord! Did he tell you?'

'No, sir. Oddly enough, I chance to be acquainted with the other party in the matter.'

'The girl?'

'The young person, yes, sir. It was from her aunt, with whom she resides, that I received the information that his lordship was contemplating matrimony.'

'Who is she?'

'A Miss Platt, sir. Miss Rhoda Platt. Of Wistaria Lodge, Kitchener Road, East Dulwich.'

'Young?'

'Yes, sir.'

'The old fathead!'

'Yes, sir. The expression is one which I would, of course, not have ventured to employ myself, but I confess to thinking his lordship somewhat ill-advised. One must remember, however, that it is not unusual to find gentlemen of a certain age yielding to what might be described as a sentimental urge. They appear to experience what I may term a sort of Indian summer, a kind of temporarily renewed youth. The phenomenon is particularly noticeable, I am given to understand, in the United

States of America among the wealthier inhabitants of the city of Pittsburgh. It is notorious, I am told, that sooner or later, unless restrained, they always endeavour to marry chorus-girls. Why this should be so, I am at a loss to say, but——'

I saw that this was going to take some time. I tuned out.

'From something in Uncle George's manner, Jeeves, as he referred to my Aunt Agatha's probable reception of the news, I gather that this Miss Platt is not of the *noblesse*.'

'No, sir. She is a waitress at his lordship's club.'

'My God! The proletariat!'

'The lower middle classes, sir.'

'Well, yes, by stretching it a bit, perhaps. Still, you know what I mean.'

'Yes, sir.'

'Rummy thing, Jeeves,' I said thoughtfully, 'this modern tendency to marry waitresses. If you remember, before he settled down, young Bingo Little was repeatedly trying to do it.'

'Yes, sir.'

'Odd!'

'Yes, sir.'

'Still, there it is, of course. The point to be considered now is, What will Aunt Agatha do about this? You know her, Jeeves. She is not like me. I'm broad-minded. If Uncle George wants to marry waitresses, let him, say I. I hold that the rank is but the penny stamp——'

'Guinea stamp, sir.'

'All right, guinea stamp. Though I don't believe there is

such a thing. I shouldn't have thought they came higher than five bob. Well, as I was saying, I maintain that the rank is but the guinea stamp and a girl's a girl for all that.'

' "For *a*' that", sir. The poet Burns wrote in the North British dialect.'

'Well, "a' that", then, if you prefer it.'

'I have no preference in the matter, sir. It is simply that the poet Burns—'

'Never mind about the poet Burns.'

'No, sir.'

'Forget the poet Burns.'

'Very good, sir.'

'Expunge the poet Burns from your mind.'

'I will do so immediately, sir.'

'What we have to consider is not the poet Burns but the Aunt Agatha. She will kick, Jeeves.'

'Very probably, sir.'

'And, what's worse, she will lug me into the mess. There is only one thing to be done. Pack the toothbrush and let us escape while we may, leaving no address.'

'Very good, sir.'

At this moment the bell rang.

'Ha!' I said. 'Someone at the door.'

'Yes, sir.'

'Probably Uncle George back again. I'll answer it. You go and get ahead with the packing.'

'Very good, sir.'

I sauntered along the passage, whistling carelessly, and there on the mat was Aunt Agatha. Herself. Not a picture.

A nasty jar.

'Oh, hullo!' I said, it seeming but little good to tell her I was out of town and not expected back for some weeks.

'I wish to speak to you, Bertie,' said the Family Curse. 'I am greatly upset.'

She legged it into the sitting-room and volplaned into a chair. I followed, thinking wistfully of Jeeves packing in the bedroom. That suitcase would not be needed now. I knew what she must have come about.

'I've just seen Uncle George,' I said, giving her a lead.

'So have I,' said Aunt Agatha, shivering in a marked manner. 'He called on me while I was still in bed to inform me of his intention of marrying some impossible girl from South Norwood.'

'East Dulwich, the *cognoscenti* inform me.'

'Well, East Dulwich, then. It is the same thing. But who told you?'

'Jeeves.'

'And how, pray, does Jeeves come to know all about it?'

'There are very few things in this world, Aunt Agatha,' I said gravely, 'that Jeeves doesn't know all about. He's met the girl.'

'Who is she?'

'One of the waitresses at the Buffers.'

I had expected this to register, and it did. The relative let out a screech rather like the Cornish Express going through a junction.

'I take it from your manner, Aunt Agatha,' I said, 'that you want this thing stopped.'

'Of course it must be stopped.'

'Then there is but one policy to pursue. Let me ring for Jeeves and ask his advice.'

Aunt Agatha stiffened visibly. Very much the *grande dame* of the old *régime*.

'Are you seriously suggesting that we should discuss this intimate family matter with your manservant?'

'Absolutely. Jeeves will find the way.'

'I have always known that you were an imbecile, Bertie,' said the flesh-and-blood, now down at about three degrees Fahrenheit, 'but I did suppose that you had some proper feeling, some pride, some respect for your position.'

'Well, you know what the poet Burns says.'

She squelched me with a glance.

'Obviously the only thing to do,' she said, 'is to offer this girl money.'

'Money?'

'Certainly It will not be the first time your uncle has made such a course necessary.'

We sat for a bit, brooding. The family always sits brooding when the subject of Uncle George's early romance comes up. I was too young to be actually in on it at the time, but I've had the details frequently from many sources, including Uncle

George. Let him get even the slightest bit pickled, and he will tell you the whole story, sometimes twice in an evening. It was a barmaid at the Criterion, just before he came into the title. Her name was Maudie and he loved her dearly, but the family would have none of it. They dug down into the sock and paid her off. Just one of those human-interest stories, if you know what I mean.

I wasn't so sold on this money-offering scheme.

'Well, just as you like, of course,' I said, 'but you're taking an awful chance. I mean, whenever people do it in novels and plays, they always get the dickens of a welt. The girl gets the sympathy of the audience every time. She just draws herself up and looks at them with clear, steady eyes, causing them to feel not a little cheesy. If I were you, I would sit tight and let Nature take its course.'

'I don't understand you.'

'Well, consider for a moment what Uncle George looks like. No Greta Garbo, believe me. I should simply let the girl go on looking at him. Take it from me, Aunt Agatha, I've studied human nature and I don't believe there's a female in the world who could see Uncle George fairly often in those waistcoats he wears without feeling that it was due to her better self to give him the gate. Besides, this girl sees him at mealtimes, and Uncle George with head down among the food-stuffs is a spectacle which——'

'If it is not troubling you too much, Bertie, I should be greatly obliged if you would stop drivelling.'

'Just as you say. All the same, I think you're going to find it dashed embarrassing, offering this girl money.'

'I am not proposing to do so. *You* will undertake the negotiations.'

'Me?'

'Certainly. I should think a hundred pounds would be ample. But I will give you a blank cheque, and you are at liberty to fill it in for a higher sum if it becomes necessary. The essential point is that, cost what it may, your uncle must be released from this entanglement.'

'So you're going to shove this off on me?'

'It is quite time you did something for the family.'

'And when she draws herself up and looks at me with clear, steady eyes, what do I do for an encore?'

'There is no need to discuss the matter any further. You can get down to East Dulwich in half an hour. There is a frequent service of trains. I will remain here to await your report.'

'But, listen!'

'Bertie, you will go and see this woman immediately.'

'Yes, but dash it!'

'Bertie!'

I threw in the towel.

'Oh, right-ho, if you say so.'

'I do say so.'

'Oh, well, in that case, right-ho.'

*

I don't know if you have ever tooled off to East Dulwich to offer a strange female a hundred smackers to release your Uncle George. In case you haven't, I may tell you that there are plenty of things that are lots better fun. I didn't feel any too good driving to the station. I didn't feel any too good in the train. And I didn't feel any too good as I walked to Kitchener Road. But the moment when I felt least good was when I had actually pressed the front-door bell and a rather grubby-looking maid had let me in and shown me down a passage and into a room with pink paper on the walls, a piano in the corner and a lot of photographs on the mantelpiece.

Barring a dentist's waiting-room, which it rather resembles, there isn't anything that quells the spirit much more than one of these suburban parlours. They are extremely apt to have stuffed birds in glass cases standing about on small tables, and if there is one thing which gives the man of sensibility that sinking feeling it is the cold, accusing eye of a ptarmigan or whatever it may be that has had its interior organs removed and sawdust substituted.

There were three of these cases in the parlour of Wistaria Lodge, so that, wherever you looked, you were sure to connect. Two were singletons, the third a family group, consisting of a father bullfinch, a mother bullfinch, and little Master Bullfinch, the last-named of whom wore an expression that was definitely that of a thug, and did more to damp my *joie de vivre* than all the rest of them put together.

I had moved to the window and was examining the

aspidistra in order to avoid this creature's gaze, when I heard the door open and, turning, found myself confronted by something which, since it could hardly be the girl, I took to be the aunt.

'Oh, what-ho,' I said. 'Good morning.'

The words came out rather roopily, for I was feeling a bit on the stunned side. I mean to say, the room being so small and this exhibit so large, I had got that sensation of wanting air. There are some people who don't seem to be intended to be seen close to, and this aunt was one of them. Billowy curves, if you know what I mean. I should think that in her day she must have been a very handsome girl, though even then on the substantial side. By the time she came into my life, she had taken on a good deal of excess weight. She looked like a photograph of an opera singer of the 'eighties. Also the orange hair and the magenta dress.

However, she was a friendly soul. She seemed glad to see Bertram. She smiled broadly.

'So here you are at last!' she said.

I couldn't make anything of this.

'Eh?'

'But I don't think you had better see my niece just yet. She's just having a nap.'

'Oh, in that case——'

'Seems a pity to wake her, doesn't it?'

'Oh, absolutely,' I said, relieved.

'When you get the influenza, you don't sleep at night, and

then if you doze off in the morning – well, it seems a pity to wake someone, doesn't it?'

'Miss Platt has influenza?'

'That's what we think it is. But, of course, you'll be able to say. But we needn't waste time. Since you're here, you can be taking a look at my knee.'

'Your knee?'

I am all for knees at their proper time and, as you might say, in their proper place, but somehow this didn't seem the moment. However, she carried on according to plan.

'What do you think of that knee?' she asked, lifting the seven veils.

Well, of course, one has to be polite.

'Terrific!' I said.

'You wouldn't believe how it hurts me sometimes.'

'Really?'

'A sort of shooting pain. It just comes and goes. And I'll tell you a funny thing.'

'What's that?' I said, feeling I could do with a good laugh.

'Lately I've been having the same pain just here, at the end of the spine.'

'You don't mean it!'

'I do. Like red-hot needles. I wish you'd have a look at it.'

'At your spine?'

'Yes.'

I shook my head. Nobody is fonder of a bit of fun than myself, and I am all for Bohemian camaraderie and making

a party go, and all that. But there is a line, and we Woosters
know when to draw it.

'It can't be done,' I said austerely. 'Not spines. Knees, yes.
Spines, no,' I said.

She seemed surprised.

'Well,' she said, 'you're a funny sort of doctor, I must say.'

I'm pretty quick, as I said before, and I began to see that
something in the nature of a misunderstanding must have
arisen.

'Doctor?'

'Well, you call yourself a doctor, don't you?'

'Did you think I was a doctor?'

'Aren't you a doctor?'

'No. Not a doctor.'

We had got it straightened out. The scales had fallen from
our eyes. We knew where we were.

I had suspected that she was a genial soul. She now endorsed
this view. I don't think I have ever heard a woman laugh so
heartily.

'Well, that's the best thing!' she said, borrowing my
handkerchief to wipe her eyes. 'Did you ever! But, if you aren't
the doctor, who are you?'

'Wooster's the name. I came to see Miss Platt.'

'What about?'

This was the moment, of course, when I should have
come out with the cheque and sprung the big effort. But
somehow I couldn't make it. You know how it is. Offering

people money to release your uncle is a scaly enough job at
best, and when the atmosphere's not right the shot simply
isn't on the board.

'Oh, just came to see her, you know.' I had rather a bright
idea. 'My uncle heard she was seedy, don't you know, and asked
me to look in and make enquiries,' I said.

'Your uncle?'

'Lord Yaxley.'

'Oh! So you are Lord Yaxley's nephew?'

'That's right. I suppose he's always popping in and out of
here, what?'

'No. I've never met him.'

'You haven't?'

'No. Rhoda talks a lot about him, of course, but for some
reason she's never so much as asked him to look in for a cup of
tea.'

I began to see that this Rhoda knew her business. If I'd
been a girl with someone wanting to marry me and knew that
there was an exhibit like this aunt hanging around the home,
I, too, should have thought twice about inviting him to call
until the ceremony was over and he had actually signed on the
dotted line. I mean to say, a thoroughly good soul – heart of
gold beyond a doubt – but not the sort of thing you wanted to
spring on Romeo before the time was ripe.

'I suppose you were all very surprised when you heard
about it?' she said.

'Surprised is right.'

'Of course, nothing is definitely settled yet.'

'You don't mean that? I thought—'

'Oh, no. She's thinking it over.'

'I see.'

'Of course, she feels it's a great compliment. But then sometimes she wonders if he isn't too old.'

'My Aunt Agatha has rather the same idea.'

'Of course, a title *is* a title.'

'Yes, there's that. What do you think about it yourself?'

'Oh, it doesn't matter what I think. There's no doing anything with girls these days, is there?'

'Not much.'

'What I often say is, I wonder what girls are coming to. Still, there it is.'

'Absolutely.'

There didn't seem much reason why the conversation shouldn't go on for ever. She had the air of a woman who had settled down for the day. But at this point the maid came in and said the doctor had arrived.

I got up.

'I'll be tooling off, then.'

'If you must.'

'I think I'd better.'

'Well, pip pip.'

'Toodle-oo,' I said, and out into the fresh air.

*

Knowing what was waiting for me at home, I would have preferred to have gone to the club and spent the rest of the day
there. But the thing had to be faced.

'Well?' said Aunt Agatha, as I trickled into the sitting-room.

'Well, yes and no,' I replied.

'What do you mean? Did she refuse the money?'

'Not exactly.'

'She accepted it?'

'Well, there, again, not precisely.'

I explained what had happened. I wasn't expecting her to
be any too frightfully pleased, and it's as well that I wasn't,
because she wasn't. In fact, as the story unfolded, her comments
became fruitier and fruitier, and when I had finished she
uttered an exclamation that nearly broke a window. It sounded
something like 'Gor!' as if she had started to say 'Gorblimey!'
and had remembered her ancient lineage just in time.

'I'm sorry,' I said. 'And can a man say more? I lost my nerve.
The old *morale* suddenly turned blue on me. It's the sort of
thing that might have happened to anyone.'

'I never heard of anything so spineless in my life.'

I shivered, like a warrior whose old wound hurts him.

'I'd be most awfully obliged, Aunt Agatha,' I said, 'if you
would not use that word spine. It awakens memories.'

The door opened. Jeeves appeared.

'Sir?'

'Yes, Jeeves?'

'I thought you called, sir.'

'No, Jeeves.'

'Very good, sir.'

There are moments when, even under the eye of Aunt Agatha, I can take the firm line. And now, seeing Jeeves standing there with the light of intelligence simply fizzing in every feature, I suddenly felt how perfectly footling it was to give this pre-eminent source of balm and comfort the go-by simply because Aunt Agatha had prejudices against discussing family affairs with the staff. It might make her say 'Gor!' again, but I decided to do as we ought to have done right from the start – put the case in his hands.

'Jeeves,' I said, 'this matter of Uncle George.'

'Yes, sir.'

'You know the circs?'

'Yes, sir.'

'You know what we want.'

'Yes, sir.'

'Then advise us. And make it snappy. Think on your feet.'

I heard Aunt Agatha rumble like a volcano just before it starts to set about the neighbours, but I did not wilt. I had seen the sparkle in Jeeves's eye which indicated that an idea was on the way.

'I understand that you have been visiting the young person's home, sir?'

'Just got back.'

'Then you no doubt encountered the young person's aunt?'

'Jeeves, I encountered nothing else but.'

'Then the suggestion which I am about to make will, I feel sure, appeal to you, sir. I would recommend that you confronted his lordship with this woman. It has always been her intention to continue residing with her niece after the latter's marriage. Should he meet her, this reflection might give his lordship pause. As you are aware, sir, she is a kind-hearted woman, but definitely of the people.'

'Jeeves, you are right! Apart from anything else, that orange hair!'

'Exactly, sir.'

'Not to mention the magenta dress.'

'Precisely, sir.'

'I'll ask her to lunch to-morrow, to meet him. You see,' I said to Aunt Agatha, who was still fermenting in the background, 'a ripe suggestion first crack out of the box. Did I or did I not tell you—'

'That will do, Jeeves,' said Aunt Agatha.

'Very good, madam.'

For some minutes after he had gone, Aunt Agatha strayed from the point a bit, confining her remarks to what she thought of a Wooster who could lower the prestige of the clan by allowing menials to get above themselves. Then she returned to what you might call the main issue.

'Bertie,' she said, 'you will go and see this girl again tomorrow, and this time you will do as I told you.'

'But, dash it! With this excellent alternative scheme, based firmly on the psychology of the individual—'

'That is quite enough, Bertie. You heard what I said. I am going. Good-bye.'

She buzzed off, little knowing of what stuff Bertram Wooster was made. The door had hardly closed before I was shouting for Jeeves.

'Jeeves,' I said, 'the recent aunt will have none of your excellent alternative schemes, but none the less I propose to go through with it unswervingly. I consider it a ball of fire. Can you get hold of this female and bring her here for lunch to-morrow?'

'Yes, sir.'

'Good. Meanwhile, I will be 'phoning Uncle George. We will do Aunt Agatha good despite herself. What is it the poet says, Jeeves?'

'The poet Burns, sir?'

'Not the poet Burns. Some other poet. About doing good by stealth.'

' "These little acts of unremembered kindness", sir?'

'That's it in a nutshell, Jeeves.'

I suppose doing good by stealth ought to give one a glow, but I can't say I found myself exactly looking forward to the binge in prospect. Uncle George by himself is a mouldy enough luncheon companion, being extremely apt to collar the conversation and confine it to a description of his symptoms, he being one of those birds who can never be brought to believe that the general public isn't agog to hear all about the lining of his stomach. Add the aunt, and you have a little gathering which might well dismay the stoutest. The moment I woke, I felt conscious of some impending doom, and the cloud, if you know what I mean, grew darker all the morning. By the time Jeeves came in with the cocktails, I was feeling pretty low.

'For two pins, Jeeves,' I said, 'I would turn the whole thing up and leg it to the Drones.'

'I can readily imagine that this will prove something of an ordeal, sir.'

'How did you get to know these people, Jeeves?'

'It was through a young fellow of my acquaintance, sir, Colonel Mainwaring-Smith's personal gentleman's gentleman. He and the young person had an understanding at the time, and he desired me to accompany him to Wistaria Lodge and meet her.'

'They were engaged?'

'Not precisely engaged, sir. An understanding.'

'What did they quarrel about?'

'They did not quarrel, sir. When his lordship began to pay his addresses, the young person, naturally flattered, began to waver between love and ambition. But even now she has not formally rescinded the understanding.'

'Then, if your scheme works and Uncle George edges out, it will do your pal a bit of good?'

'Yes, sir. Smethurst – his name is Smethurst – would consider it a consummation devoutly to be wished.'

'Rather well put, that, Jeeves. Your own?'

'No, sir. The Swan of Avon, sir.'

An unseen hand without tootled on the bell, and I braced myself to play the host. The binge was on.

'Mrs Wilberforce, sir,' announced Jeeves.

'And how I'm to keep a straight face with you standing behind and saying "Madam, can I tempt you with a potato?" is more than I know,' said the aunt, sailing in, looking larger and pinker and matier than ever. 'I know him, you know,' she said, jerking a thumb after Jeeves. 'He's been round and taken tea with us.'

'So he told me.'

She gave the sitting-room the once-over.

'You've got a nice place here,' she said. 'Though I like more pink about. It's so cheerful. What's that you've got there? Cocktails?'

'Martini with a spot of absinthe,' I said, beginning to pour.

She gave a girlish squeal.

'Don't you try to make me drink that stuff! Do you know what would happen if I touched one of those things? I'd be racked with pain. What they do to the lining of your stomach!'

'Oh, I don't know.'

'I do. If you had been a barmaid as long as I was, you'd know, too.'

'Oh – er – were you a barmaid?'

'For years, when I was younger than I am. At the Criterion.'

I dropped the shaker.

'There!' she said, pointing the moral. 'That's through drinking that stuff. Makes your hand wobble. What I always used to say to the boys was, "Port, if you like. Port's wholesome. I appreciate a drop of port myself. But these newfangled messes from America, no." But they would never listen to me.'

I was eyeing her warily. Of course, there must have been thousands of barmaids at the Criterion in its time, but still it gave one a bit of a start. It was years ago that Uncle George's dash at a mesalliance had occurred – long before he came into the title – but the Wooster clan still quivered at the name of the Criterion.

'Er – when you were at the Cri.,' I said, 'did you ever happen to run into a fellow of my name?'

'I've forgotten what it is. I'm always silly about names.'

'Wooster.'

'Wooster! When you were there yesterday I thought you said Foster. Wooster! Did I run into a fellow named Wooster? Well! Why, George Wooster and me – Piggy, I used to call him – were going off to the registrar's, only his family heard of it and interfered. They offered me a lot of money to give him up, and, like a silly girl, I let them persuade me. If I've wondered once what became of him, I've wondered a thousand times. Is he a relation of yours?'

'Excuse me,' I said. 'I just want a word with Jeeves.'

I legged it for the pantry.

'Jeeves!'

'Sir?'

'Do you know what's happened?'

'No, sir.'

'This female—'

'Sir?'

'She's Uncle George's barmaid!'

'Sir?'

'Oh, dash it, you must have heard of Uncle George's barmaid. You know all the family history. The barmaid he wanted to marry years ago.'

'Ah, yes, sir.'

'She's the only woman he ever loved. He's told me so a million times. Every time he gets to the fourth whisky-and-potash, he always becomes maudlin about this female. What a dashed bit of bad luck! The first thing we know, the call of the past will be echoing in his heart. I can feel it, Jeeves. She's just his sort. The first thing she did when she came in was to start talking about the lining of her stomach. You see the hideous significance of that, Jeeves? The lining of his stomach is Uncle George's favourite topic of conversation. It means that he and she are kindred souls. This woman and he will be like—'

'Deep calling to deep, sir?'

'Exactly.'

'Most disturbing, sir.'

'What's to be done?'

'I could not say, sir.'

'I'll tell you what I'm going to do – 'phone him and say the lunch is off.'

'Scarcely feasible, sir. I fancy that is his lordship at the door now.'

And so it was. Jeeves let him in, and I followed him as he navigated down the passage to the sitting-room. There was a stunned silence as he went in, and then a couple of the startled yelps you hear when old buddies get together after long separation.

'Piggy!'

'Maudie!'

'Well, I never!'

'Well, I'm dashed!'

'Did you ever!'

'Well, bless my soul!'

'Fancy you being Lord Yaxley!'

'Came into the title soon after we parted.'

'Just to think!'

'You could have knocked me down with a feather!'

I hung about in the offing, now on this leg, now on that. For all the notice they took of me, I might just have well been the late Bertram Wooster, disembodied.

'Maudie, you don't look a day older, dash it!'

'Nor do you, Piggy.'

'How have you been all these years?'

'Pretty well. The lining of my stomach isn't all it should be.'

'Good Gad! You don't say so? I have trouble with the lining of *my* stomach.'

'It's a sort of heavy feeling after meals.'

'*I* get a sort of heavy feeling after meals. What are you trying for it?'

'I've been taking Perkins' Digestine.'

'My dear girl, no use! No use at all. Tried it myself for years and got no relief. Now, if you really want something that is some good—'

I slid away. The last I saw of them, Uncle George was down beside her on the Chesterfield, buzzing hard.

'Jeeves,' I said, tottering into the pantry.

'Sir?'

'There will only be two for lunch. Count me out. If they notice I'm not there, tell them I was called away by an urgent 'phone message. The situation has got beyond Bertram, Jeeves. You will find me at the Drones.'

'Very good, sir.'

It was lateish in the evening when one of the waiters came to me as I played a distrait game of snooker pool and informed me that Aunt Agatha was on the 'phone.

'Bertie!'

'Hullo?'

I was amazed to note that her voice was that of an aunt who feels that things are breaking right. It had the birdlike trill.

'Bertie, have you that cheque I gave you?'

'Yes.'

'Then tear it up. It will not be needed.'

'Eh?'

'I say it will not be needed. Your uncle has been speaking to me on the telephone. He is not going to marry that girl.'

'Not?'

'No. Apparently he has been thinking it over and sees how unsuitable it would have been. But what is astonishing is that he *is* going to be married!'

'He is?'

'Yes, to an old friend of his, a Mrs Wilberforce. A woman of a sensible age, he gave me to understand. I wonder which Wilberforces that would be. There are two main branches of the family – the Essex Wilberforces and the Cumberland Wilberforces. I believe there is also a cadet branch somewhere in Shropshire.'

'And one in East Dulwich.'

'What did you say?'

'Nothing,' I said. 'Nothing.'

I hung up. Then back to the old flat, feeling a trifle sandbagged.

'Well, Jeeves,' I said, and there was censure in the eyes. 'So I gather everything is nicely settled?'

'Yes, sir. His lordship formally announced the engagement between the sweet and cheese courses, sir.'

'He did, did he?'

'Yes, sir.'

I eyed the man sternly.

'You do not appear to be aware of it, Jeeves,' I said, in a cold, level voice, 'but this binge has depreciated your stock very considerably. I have always been accustomed to look upon you as a counsellor without equal. I have, so to speak, hung upon your lips. And now see what you have done. All this is the direct consequence of your scheme, based on the psychology of the individual. I should have thought, Jeeves, that, knowing the woman – meeting her socially, as you might say, over the afternoon cup of tea – you might have ascertained that she was Uncle George's barmaid.'

'I did, sir.'

'What!'

'I was aware of the fact, sir.'

'Then you must have known what would happen if she came to lunch and met him.'

'Yes, sir.'

'Well, I'm dashed!'

'If I might explain, sir. The young man Smethurst, who is greatly attached to the young person, is an intimate friend of mine. He applied to me some little while back in the hope that I might be able to do something to ensure that the young person followed the dictates of her heart and refrained from permitting herself to be lured by gold and the glamour of his lordship's position. There will now be no obstacle to their union.'

'I see. "Little acts of unremembered kindness", what?'

'Precisely, sir.'

'And how about Uncle George? You've landed him pretty nicely in the cart.'

'No, sir, if I may take the liberty of opposing your view. I fancy that Mrs Wilberforce should make an ideal mate for his lordship. If there was a defect in his lordship's mode of life, it was that he was a little unduly attached to the pleasures of the table—'

'Ate like a pig, you mean?'

'I would not have ventured to put it in quite that way, sir, but the expression does meet the facts of the case. He was also inclined to drink rather more than his medical adviser would have approved of. Elderly bachelors who are wealthy and without occupation tend somewhat frequently to fall into this error, sir. The future Lady Yaxley will check this. Indeed, I overheard her ladyship saying as much as I brought in the fish. She was commenting on a certain puffiness of the face which had been absent in his lordship's appearance in the earlier days of their acquaintanceship, and she observed that his lordship needed looking after. I fancy, sir, that you will find the union will turn out an extremely satisfactory one.'

It was – what's the word I want? – it was plausible, of course, but still I shook the onion.

'But, Jeeves!'

'Sir?'

'She *is*, as you remarked not long ago, definitely of the people.'

He looked at me in a reproachful sort of way.

'Sturdy lower middle class stock, sir.'

'H'm!'

'Sir?'

'I said "H'm!" Jeeves.'

'Besides, sir, remember what the poet Tennyson said: "Kind hearts are more than coronets".'

'And which of us is going to tell Aunt Agatha that?'

'If I might make the suggestion, sir, I would advise that we omitted to communicate with Mrs Spenser Gregson in any way. I have your suitcase practically packed. It would be a matter of but a few minutes to bring the car round from the garage—'

'And off over the horizon to where men are men?'

'Precisely, sir.'

'Jeeves,' I said, 'I'm not sure that even now I can altogether see eye to eye with you regarding your recent activities. You think you have scattered light and sweetness on every side. I am not so sure. However, with this latest suggestion you have rung the bell. I examine it narrowly and I find no flaw in it. It is the goods. I'll get the car at once.'

'Very good, sir.'

'Remember what the poet Shakespeare said, Jeeves.'

'What was that, sir?'

' "Exit hurriedly, pursued by a bear". You'll find it in one of his plays. I remember drawing a picture of it on the side of the page, when I was at school.'

Romance at Droitgate Spa

When young Freddie Fitch-Fitch went down to Droitgate Spa, that celebrated cure resort in the west of England, to ask his uncle and trustee, Major-General Sir Aylmer Bastable, to release his capital in order that he might marry Annabel Purvis, he was fully alive to the fact that the interview might prove a disagreeable one. However, his great love bore him on, and he made the journey and was shown into the room where the old man sat nursing a gouty foot.

'Hullo-ullo-ullo, uncle,' he cried, for it was always his policy on these occasions to be buoyant till thrown out. 'Good morning, good morning, good morning.'

'Gaw!' said Sir Aylmer, with a sort of long, shuddering sigh. 'It's you, is it?'

And he muttered something which Freddie did not quite catch, though he was able to detect the words 'last straw'.

Freddie's heart sank a little. He could see that his flesh and blood was in a difficult mood, and he guessed what must have happened. No doubt Sir Aylmer had been to the Pump Room earlier in the day to take the waters, and while there had met and been high-hatted by some swell whom the doctors had twice given up for dead. These snobs, he knew, were always snubbing the unfortunate old man.

On coming to settle in Droitgate Spa, Sir Aylmer Bastable had had a humiliating shock. The head of a fine old family and the possessor of a distinguished military record, he had expected on his arrival to be received with open arms by the best people and welcomed immediately into the inner-set. But when it was discovered that all he had wrong with him was a touch of gout in the right foot, he found himself cold-shouldered by the men who mattered and thrust back on the society of the asthma patients and the fellows with slight liver trouble.

For though few people are aware of it – so true is it that half the world does not know how the other half lives – there is no section of the community in which class-consciousness is so rampant as among invalids. The ancient Spartans, one gathers, were far from cordial towards their Helots, and the French aristocrat of pre-Revolution days tended to be a little stand-offish with his tenantry, but their attitude was almost back-slapping compared with that of – let us say – the man who has been out in Switzerland taking insulin for his diabetes towards one who is simply undergoing treatment from the village doctor for an in-growing toe-nail. And this is particularly so, of course, in those places where invalids collect in gangs – Baden-Baden, for example, or Hot Springs, Virginia, or, as in Sir Aylmer's case, Droitgate Spa.

In such resorts the atmosphere is almost unbelievably cliquey. The old aristocracy, the top-notchers with maladies that get written up in the medical journals, keep themselves to themselves pretty rigidly, and have a very short way with the smaller fry.

It was this that had soured Sir Aylmer Bastable's once sunny disposition and caused him now to glare at Freddie with an unfriendly eye.

'Well,' he said, 'what do you want?'

'Oh, I just looked in,' said Freddie. 'How's everything?'

'Rotten,' replied Sir Aylmer. 'I've just lost my nurse.'

'Dead?'

'Worse. Married. The cloth-headed girl has gone off and got spliced to one of the *canaille* – a chap who's never even had so much as athlete's foot. She must be crazy.'

'Still, one sees her point of view.'

'No, one doesn't.'

'I mean,' said Freddie, who felt strongly on this subject, 'it's love that makes the world go round.'

'It isn't anything of the kind,' said Sir Aylmer. Like so many fine old soldiers, he was inclined to be a little literal-minded. 'I never heard such dashed silly nonsense in my life. What makes the world go round is ... Well, I've forgotten at the moment, but it certainly isn't love. How the dooce could it?'

'Oh, right-ho. I see what you mean,' said Freddie. 'But put

it another way. Love conquers all. Love's all right. Take it from me.'

The old man looked at him sharply.

'Are you in love?'

'Madly.'

'Of all the young cuckoos! And I suppose you've come to ask for money to get married on?'

'Not at all. I just dropped round to see how you were. Still, as the subject has happened to crop up—'

Sir Aylmer brooded for a moment, snorting in an undertone.

'Who's the girl?' he demanded.

Freddie coughed, and fumbled with his collar. The crux of the situation, he realized, had now been reached. He had feared from the first that this was where the good old snag might conceivably sidle into the picture. For his Annabel was of humble station, and he knew how rigid were his relative's views on the importance of birth. No bigger snob ever swallowed a salicylate pill.

'Well, as a matter of fact,' he said, 'she's a conjurer's stooge.'

'A what?'

'A conjurer's assistant, don't you know. I saw her first at a charity matinee. She was abetting a bloke called The Great Boloni.'

'In what sense, abetting?'

'Well, she stood there up-stage, don't you know, and every now and then she would skip down-stage, hand this chap a bowl of goldfish or something, beam at the audience, do a sort of dance step and skip back again. You know the kind of thing.'

A dark frown had come into Sir Aylmer's face.

'I do,' he said grimly. 'My only nephew has been ensnared by a bally, beaming goldfish-handler! Ha!'

'I wouldn't call it ensnared exactly,' said Freddie deferentially.

'I would,' said Sir Aylmer. 'Get out of here.'

'Right,' said Freddie, and caught the two-thirty-five express back to London. And it was during the journey that an idea flashed upon him.

The last of the Fitch-Fitches was not a great student of literature, but he occasionally dipped into a magazine: and everybody who has ever dipped into a magazine has read a story about a hard-hearted old man who won't accept the hero's girl at any price, so what do they do but plant her on him without telling him who she is and, by Jove, he falls under her spell completely, and then they tear off their whiskers and there they are. There was a story of this nature in the magazine which Freddie had purchased at the bookstall at Droitgate Spa Station, and, as he read it, he remembered what his uncle had told him about his nurse handing in her portfolio.

By the time the train checked in at Paddington, his plans were fully formed.

'Listen,' he said to Annabel Purvis, who had met him at the terminus, and Annabel said: 'What?'

'Listen,' said Freddie, and Annabel again said: 'What?'

'Listen,' said Freddie, clasping her arm tenderly and steering her off in the direction of the refreshment-room, where it was his intention to have a quick one. 'To a certain extent I am compelled to admit that my expedition has been a wash-out . . .'

Annabel caught her breath sharply.

'No blessing?'

'No blessing.'

'And no money?'

'No money. The old boy ran entirely true to stable form. He listened to what I had to say, snorted in an unpleasant manner and threw me out. The old routine. But what I'm working round to is that the skies are still bright and the blue bird on the job. I have a scheme. Could you be a nurse?'

'I used to nurse my Uncle Joe.'

'Then you shall nurse my Uncle Aylmer. The present incumbent, he tells me, has just tuned out, and he needs a successor. I will 'phone him that I am dispatching immediately a red-hot nurse whom he will find just the same as Mother makes, and you shall go down to Droitgate Spa and ingratiate yourself.'

'But how?'

'Why, cluster round him. Smooth his pillow. Bring him cooling drinks. Coo to him, and give him the old oil. Tell him you are of gentle birth, if that's the expression I want. And when the time is ripe, when you have entwined yourself about his heart and he looks upon you as a daughter, shoot me a wire and I'll come down and fall in love with you and he will give us his consent, blessing and the stuff. I guarantee this plan. It works.'

So Annabel went to Droitgate Spa, and about three weeks later a telegram arrived for Freddie, running as follows:

'Have ingratiated self. Come at once. Love and kisses. Annabel'

Within an hour of its arrival, Freddie was on his way to Podagra Lodge, his uncle's residence. He found Sir Aylmer in his study. Annabel was sitting by his side, reading aloud to him from a recently published monograph on certain obscure ailments of the medulla oblongata. For the old man, though a mere gout patient, had pathetic aspirations towards higher things. There was a cooling drink on the table, and, as Freddie entered, the girl paused in her reading to smooth her employer's pillow.

'Gaw!' said Sir Aylmer. 'You again?'

'Here I am,' said Freddie.

'Well, by an extraordinary chance, I'm glad to see you. Leave us for a moment, Miss Purvis. I wish to speak to my nephew here, such as he is, on a serious and private matter. Did you notice that girl?' he said, as the door closed.

'I did, indeed.'

'Pretty.'

'An eyeful.'

'And as good,' said Sir Aylmer, 'as she is beautiful. You should see her smooth pillows. And what a cooling drink she mixes!

Excellent family, too, I understand. Her father is a colonel. Or, rather, was. He's dead.'

'Ah, well, all flesh is as grass.'

'No, it isn't. It's nothing of the kind. The two things are entirely different. I've seen flesh and I've seen grass. No resemblance whatever. However, that is not the point at issue. What I wanted to say was that if you were not a damn fool, that's the sort of girl you would be in love with.'

'I am.'

'A damn fool?'

'No. In love with that girl.'

'What! You have fallen in love with Miss Purvis? Already?'

'I have.'

'Well, that's the quickest thing I ever saw. What about your beaming goldfish?'

'Oh, that's all over. A mere passing boyish fancy.'

Sir Aylmer took a deep swig at his cooling drink, and regarded him in silence for a moment.

'Well,' he said, at length, breathing heavily, 'if that's the airy, casual way in which you treat life's most sacred emotions, the sooner you are safely married and settled down, the better. If you're allowed to run around loose much longer, indulging those boyish fancies of yours, I foresee the breach of promise case of the century. However, I'm not saying I'm not relieved. I am relieved. I suppose she wore tights, this goldfish girl?'

'Pink.'

'Disgusting. Thank God it's all over. Very good, then. You

are free, I understand, to have a pop at Miss Purvis. Do you propose to do so?'

'I do.'

'Excellent. You get that sweet, refined, most-suitable-in-all-respects girl to marry you, and I'll hand over that money of yours, every penny of it.'

'I will start at once.'

'Heaven speed your wooing,' said Sir Aylmer.

And ten minutes later Freddie was able to inform his uncle that his whirlwind courtship had been successful, and Sir Aylmer said that when he had asked Heaven to speed his wooing he had had no notion that it would speed it to quite that extent. He congratulated Freddie warmly and said he hoped that he appreciated his good fortune, and Freddie said he certainly did, because his love was like a red, red rose, and Sir Aylmer said 'No, she wasn't,' and when Freddie added that he was walking on air Sir Aylmer said he couldn't be – the thing was physically impossible.

However, he gave his blessing and promised to release Freddie's capital as soon as the necessary papers were drawn up, and Freddie went back to London to see his lawyer about this.

His mood, as the train sped through the quiet countryside, was one of perfect tranquillity and happiness. It seemed to him that his troubles were now definitely ended. He looked down the vista of the years and saw nothing but joy and sunshine. If somebody had told Frederick Fitch-Fitch at that moment that even now a V-shaped depression was coming along which would shortly blacken the skies and lower the general temperature to freezing-point, he would not have believed him.

Nor when, two days later, as he sat in his club, he was informed that a Mr Rackstraw was waiting to see him in the small smoking-room, did he have an inkling that here was the V-shaped depression in person. His heart was still light as he went down the passage, wondering idly, for the name was unfamiliar to him, who this Mr Rackstraw might be. He entered the room, and found there a tall, thin man with pointed black moustaches who was pacing up and down, nervously taking rabbits out of his top hat as he walked.

'Mr Rackstraw?'

His visitor spun round, dropping a rabbit. He gazed at Freddie piercingly. He had bright, glittering, sinister eyes.

'That is my name. Mortimer Rackstraw.'

Freddie's mind had flown back to the charity matinee at which he had first seen Annabel, and he recognized the fellow now.

'The Great Boloni, surely?'

'I call myself that professionally. So you are Mr Fitch? So *you* are Mr Fitch? Ha! Fiend!'

'Eh?'

'I am not mistaken. You are Frederick Fitch?'

'Frederick Fitch-Fitch.'

'I beg your pardon. In that case, I should have said "Fiend! Fiend!"'

He produced a pack of cards and asked Freddie to take one
– any one – and memorize it and put it back. Freddie did so
absently. He was considerably fogged. He could make nothing
of all this.

'How do you mean – Fiend-Fiend?' he asked.

The other sneered unpleasantly.

'Cad!' he said, twirling his moustache.

'Cad?' said Freddie, mystified.

'Yes, sir. Cad. You have stolen the girl I love.'

'I don't understand.'

'Then you must be a perfect ass. It's quite simple, isn't it?
I can't put it any plainer, can I? I say you have stolen ... Well,
look here,' said Mortimer Rackstraw. 'Suppose this top hat
is me. This rabbit,' he went on, producing it from the lining,
'is the girl I love. You come along and – presto – the rabbit
vanishes.'

'It's up your sleeve.'

'It is not up my sleeve. And if it were, if I had a thousand
sleeves and rabbits up every one of them, that would not alter
the fact that you have treacherously robbed me of Annabel
Purvis.'

Freddie began to see daylight. He was able to appreciate the
other's emotion. 'So you love Annabel, too?'

'I do.'

'I don't wonder. Nice girl, what? I see, I see. You worshipped
her in secret, never telling your love.'

'I did tell my love. We were engaged.'

'Engaged?'

'Certainly. And this morning I get a letter from her saying that it's all off, because she has changed her mind and is going to marry you. She has thrown me over.'

'Oh, ah? Well, I'm frightfully sorry – deepest sympathy, and all that, but I don't see what's to be done about it, what?'

'I do. There still remains – revenge.'

'Oh, I say, dash it! You aren't going to be stuffy about it?'

'I am going to be stuffy about it. For the moment you triumph. But do not imagine that this is the end. You have not heard the last of me. Not by any means. You may have stolen the woman I love with your underhand chicanery, but I'll fix you.'

'How?'

'Never mind how. You will find out how quite soon enough. A nasty jolt you're going to get, my good fiend, and almost immediately. As sure,' said Mortimer Rackstraw, illustrating by drawing one from Freddie's back hair, 'as eggs are eggs. I wish you a very good afternoon.'

He took up his top hat, which in his emotion he had allowed to fall to the ground, brushed it on his coat-sleeve, extracted from it a cage of love-birds and strode out.

A moment later, he returned, bowed a few times to right and left and was gone again.

To say that Freddie did not feel a little uneasy as the result of this scene would be untrue. There had been something in the confident manner in which the other had spoken of revenging himself that he had not at all liked. The words had had a sinister ring, and all through the rest of the day he pondered thoughtfully, wondering what a man so trained in the art of having things up his sleeve might have up it now. It was in meditative mood that he dined, and only on the following morning did his equanimity return to him.

Able, now that he had slept on it, to review the disturbing conversation in its proper perspective, he came to the conclusion that the fellow's threats had been mere bluff. What, after all, he asked himself, could this conjurer do? It was not as if they had been living in the Middle Ages, when chaps of that sort used to put spells on you and change you into things.

No, he decided, it was mere bluff, and with his complacency completely restored had just lighted a cigarette and fallen to dreaming of the girl he loved, when a telegram was brought to him.

It ran as follows:

Come at once. All lost. Ruin stares face. Love and kisses. Annabel.

Half an hour later he was in the train, speeding towards Droitgate Spa.

It had been Freddie's intention, on entering the train, to devote the journey to earnest meditation. But, as always happens when one wishes to concentrate and brood during a railway journey, he found himself closeted with a talkative fellow-traveller.

The one who interrupted Freddie's thoughts was a flabby, puffy man of middle age, wearing a red waistcoat, brown shoes, a morning coat and a bowler hat. With such a Grade A bounder, even had his mind been at rest, Freddie would have had little in common, and he sat chafing while the prismatic fellow prattled on. Nearly an hour passed before he was freed from the infliction of the other's conversation, but eventually the man's head began to nod, and presently he was snoring and Freddie was able to give himself up to his reverie.

His thoughts became less and less agreeable as the train rolled on. And what rendered his mental distress so particularly acute was the lack of detail in Annabel's telegram. It seemed to him to offer so wide a field for uncomfortable speculation.

'All lost,' for instance. A man could do a lot of thinking about a phrase like that. And 'Ruin stares face.' Why, he asked himself, did ruin stare face? While commending Annabel's thriftiness in keeping the thing down to twelve words, he could not help wishing that she could have brought herself to spring another twopence and be more lucid.

But of one thing he felt certain. All this had something to do with his recent visitor. Behind that mystic telegram he seemed to see the hand of Mortimer Rackstraw, that hand whose quickness deceived the eye, and he knew that in lightly dismissing the other as a negligible force he had been too sanguine.

By the time he reached Podagra Lodge, the nervous strain had become almost intolerable. As he rang the bell he was quivering like some jelly set before a diet-patient, and the sight of Annabel's face as she opened the door did nothing to alleviate his perturbation. The girl was obviously all of a twitter.

'Oh, Freddie!' she cried. 'The worst has happened.'

Freddie gulped.

'Rackstraw?'

'Yes,' said Annabel. 'But how did you know about him?'

'He came to see me, bubbling over a good deal with veiled menaces and what not,' explained Freddie. He frowned, and eyed her closely. 'Why didn't you tell me you had been engaged to that bird?'

'I didn't think you would be interested. It was just a passing girlish fancy.'

'You're sure? You didn't really love this blighted prestidigitator?'

'No, no. I was dazzled for a while, as any girl might have been when he sawed me in half, but then you came along and I saw that I had been mistaken, and that you were the only man in the world for me.'

'Good egg,' said Freddie, relieved.

He kissed her fondly and, as he did so, there came to his ears the sound of rhythmic hammering from somewhere below. 'What's that?' he asked.

Annabel wrung her hands. 'It's Mortimer!'

'Is he here?'

'Yes. He arrived on the one-fifteen. I locked him in the cellar.'

'Why?'

'To stop him going to the Pump Room.'

'Why shouldn't he go to the Pump Room?'

'Because Sir Aylmer has gone there to listen to the band, and they must not meet. If they do, we are lost. Mortimer has hatched a fearful plot.'

Freddie's heart seemed to buckle under within him. He had tried to be optimistic, but all along he had known that Mortimer Rackstraw would hatch some fearful plot. He could have put his shirt on it. A born hatcher.

'What plot?'

Annabel wrung her hands again.

'He means to introduce Sir Aylmer to my Uncle Joe. He wired Uncle Joe to come to Droitgate Spa. He had arranged to meet him at the Pump Room, and then he was going to intro-duce him to Sir Aylmer.'

Freddie was a little fogged. It did not seem to him much of a plot.

'Now that I can never be his, all he wants is to make himself unpleasant and prevent our marriage. And he knows that Sir Aylmer will never consent to your marrying me if he finds out that I have an uncle like Uncle Joe.'

Freddie ceased to be fogged. He saw the whole devilish scheme now – a scheme worthy of the subtle brain that could put the ace of spades back in the pack, shuffle, cut three times, and then produce it from the inside of a lemon.

'Is he so frightful?' he quavered.

'Look,' said Annabel simply. She took a photograph from

her bosom and extended it towards him with a trembling hand. 'That is Uncle Joe, taken in the lodge regalia of a Grand Exalted Periwinkle of the Mystic Order of Whelks.'

Freddie glanced at the photograph and started back with a hoarse cry. Annabel nodded sadly.

'Yes,' she said. 'That is how he takes most people. The only faint hope I have is that he won't have been able to come. But if he has—'

'He has,' cried Freddie, who had been fighting for breath. 'We travelled down in the train together.'

'What?'

'Yes. He must be waiting at the Pump Room now.'

'And at any moment Mortimer will break his way out of the cellar. The door is not strong. What shall we do?'

'There is only one thing to do. I have all the papers ...'

'You have no time to read now.'

'The legal papers, the ones my uncle has to sign in order to release my money. There is just a chance that if I rush to the Pump Room I may get him to put his name on the dotted line before the worst happens.'

'Then rush,' cried Annabel.

'I will,' said Freddie. He kissed her quickly, grabbed his hat, and was off the mark like a jack rabbit.

A man who is endeavouring to lower the record for the distance between Podagra Lodge, which is in Arterio-Sclerosis

Avenue, and the Droitgate Spa Pump Room has little leisure
for thinking, but Freddie managed to put in a certain amount
as his feet skimmed the pavement. And the trend of his thought
such as to give renewed vigour to his legs. He could scarcely
have moved more rapidly if he had been a character in a two-
reel film with the police after him.

And there was need for speed. Beyond a question, Annabel
had been right when she had said that Sir Alymer would never
consent to their union if he found out that she had an uncle like
her Uncle Joe. Uncle Joe would get right in amongst him. Let
them but meet, and nothing was more certain than that the
haughty old man would veto the proposed nuptials.

A final burst of speed took him panting up the Pump Room
steps and into the rotunda where all that was best and most
refined in Droitgate Spa was accustomed to assemble of an
afternoon and listen to the band. He saw Sir Aylmer in a distant
seat and hurried towards him.

'Gaw!' said Sir Aylmer. 'You?'

Freddie could only nod.

'Well, stop puffing like that and sit down,' said Sir Aylmer.
'They're just going to play "Poet and Peasant".'

Freddie recovered his breath.

'Uncle,' he began. But it was too late. Even as he spoke,
the conductor's baton fell and Sir Aylmer's face assumed that
reverent doughlike expression of attention so familiar to the
rotundas of cure resorts.

'S'h,' he said.

Of all the uncounted millions who in their time have listened to bands playing 'Poet and Peasant', few can ever have listened with such a restless impatience as did Frederick Fitch-Fitch on this occasion. Time was flying. Every second was precious. At any moment disaster might befall. And the band went on playing as if it had taken on a life-job. It seemed to him an eternity before the final oom-pom-pa.

'Uncle,' he cried, as the echoes died away.

'S'h,' said Sir Aylmer testily, and Freddie, with a dull despair, perceived that they were going to get an encore.

Of all the far-flung myriads who year in and year out have listened to bands playing the overture to 'Raymond', few can ever have chafed as did Frederick Fitch-Fitch now. This suspense was unmanning him, this delay was torture. He took the papers and a fountain-pen from his pocket and toyed with them nervously. He wondered dully as he sat there how the opera 'Raymond' had ever managed to get itself performed, if the overture was as long as this. They must have rushed it through in the last five minutes of the evening as the audience groped for its hats and wraps.

But there is an end to all things, even to the overture from 'Raymond'. Just as the weariest river winds somewhere safe to the sea, so does this overture eventually finish. And when it did, when the last notes faded into silence and the conductor stood bowing and smiling with that cool assumption, common to all conductors, that it is they and not the perspiring orchestra who have been doing the work, he started again.

'Uncle,' he said, 'may I trouble you for a moment? . . . These papers.'

Sir Aylmer cocked an eye at the documents. 'What papers are those?'

'The ones you have to sign, releasing my capital.'

'Oh, those,' said Sir Aylmer genially. The music had plainly mellowed him. 'Of course, yes. Certainly, certainly. Give me . . .'

He broke off, and Freddie saw that he was looking at a distinguished, silvery-haired man with thin, refined features, who was sauntering by.

'Afternoon, Rumbelow,' he said.

There was an unmistakable note of obsequiousness in Sir Aylmer's voice. His voice had become pink, and he was shuffling his feet and twiddling his fingers. The man to whom he had spoken paused and looked down. Seeing who it was that accosted him, he raised a silvery eyebrow. His manner was undisguisedly supercilious.

'Ah, Bastable,' he said distantly.

A duller man than Sir Aylmer Bastable could not have failed to detect the cold hauteur in his voice. Freddie saw the flush on his uncle's face deepen. Sir Aylmer mumbled something about hoping that the distinguished-looking man was feeling better to-day.

'Worse,' replied the other curtly. 'Much worse. The doctors are baffled. Mine is a very complicated case.' He paused for a moment, and his delicately chiselled lip curled in a sneer. 'And how is the gout, Bastable? Gout! Ha, ha!'

Without waiting for a reply he passed on and joined a group that stood chatting close by. Sir Aylmer choked down a mortified oath.

'Snob!' he muttered. 'Thinks he's everybody just because he's got telangiectasis. I don't see what's so wonderful about having telangiectasis. Anybody could have ... What on earth are you doing? What the devil's all this you're waving under my nose? Papers? Papers? I don't want any papers. Take them away, sir!'

And before Freddie could burst into the impassioned plea which trembled on his lips, a commotion in the doorway distracted his attention. His heart missed a beat, and he sat there, frozen.

On the threshold stood Mortimer Rackstraw. He was making some inquiry of an attendant, and Freddie could guess only too well what that inquiry was. Mortimer Rackstraw was asking which of those present was Major-General Aylmer Bastable. Attached to his arm, obviously pleading with him and appealing to his better self, Annabel Purvis gazed up into his face with tear-filled eyes.

A moment later, the conjurer strode up, still towing the girl. He halted before Sir Aylmer and threw Annabel aside like a soiled glove. His face was cold and hard and remorseless. With one hand he was juggling mechanically with two billiard balls and a bouquet of roses.

'Sir Aylmer Bastable?'

'Yes.'

'I forbid the banns.'

'What banns?'

'Their banns,' said Mortimer Rackstraw, removing from his lips the hand with which he had been coldly curling his moustache and jerking it in the direction of Annabel and Freddie, who stood clasped in each other's arms, waiting for they knew not what.

'They're not up yet,' said Annabel.

The conjurer seemed a little taken aback.

'Oh?' he said. 'Well, when they are, I forbid them. And so will you, Sir Aylmer, when you hear all.'

Sir Aylmer puffed.

'Who is this tight bounder?' he asked irritably.

Mortimer Rackstraw shook his head and took the two of clubs from it.

'A bounder, maybe,' he said, 'but not tight. I have come here, Sir Aylmer, in a spirit of altruism to warn you that if you allow your nephew to marry this girl the grand old name of Bastable will be mud.'

Sir Aylmer started. 'Mud?'

'Mud. She comes from the very dregs of society.'

'I don't,' cried Annabel.

'Of course she doesn't,' cried Freddie.

'Certainly she does not,' assented Sir Aylmer warmly. 'She told me herself that her father was a colonel.'

Mortimer Rackstraw uttered a short, sneering laugh and took an egg from his left elbow.

'She did, eh? Did she add that he was a colonel in the Salvation Army?'

'What!'

'And that before he saw the light he was a Silver Ring bookie, known to all the heads as Rat-Faced Rupert, the Bermondsey Twister?'

'Good God!'

Sir Aylmer turned to the girl with an awful frown. 'Is this true?'

'Of course it's true,' said Mortimer Rackstraw. 'And if you want further proof of her unfitness to be your nephew's bride, just take a look at her Uncle Joe, who is now entering left-centre.'

And Freddie, listless now and without hope, saw that his companion of the train was advancing towards them. He heard Sir Aylmer gasp and was aware that Annabel had stiffened in his arms. He was not surprised. The sun, filtering through the glass of the rotunda, lit up the man's flabby puffiness, his morning coat, his red waistcoat and his brown shoes, and rarely if ever, thought Freddie, could the sun of Droitgate Spa have shone on a more ghastly outsider.

There was nothing, however, in the newcomer's demeanour to suggest that he felt himself out of place in these refined surroundings. His manner had an easy self-confidence. He sauntered up and without *gêne* slapped the conjurer on the back and patted Annabel on the shoulder.

''Ullo, Mort. 'Ullo, Annie, my dear.'

Sir Aylmer, who had blinked, staggered and finally recovered himself, spoke in a voice of thunder. 'You, sir! Is this true?'

'What's that, old cock?'

'Are you this girl's uncle?'

'That's right.'

'Gaw!' said Sir Aylmer.

He would have spoken further, but at this point the band burst into 'Pomp and Circumstance', and conversation was temporarily suspended. When it became possible once more for the human voice to make itself heard, it was Annabel's Uncle Joe who took the floor. He had recognized Freddie.

'Why, I've met you,' he said. 'We travelled down in the train together. Who's this young feller, Annie, that's huggin' and squeezin' you?'

'He is the man I am going to marry,' said Annabel.

'He is not the man you are going to marry,' said Sir Aylmer.

'Yes, I am the man she is going to marry,' said Freddie.

'No, you're not the man she is going to marry,' said Mortimer Rackstraw.

Annabel's Uncle Joe seemed puzzled. He appeared not to know what to make of this conflict of opinion.

'Well, settle it among yourselves,' he said genially. 'All I know is that whoever does marry you, Annie, is going to get a good wife.'

'That's me,' said Freddie.

'No, it isn't,' said Sir Aylmer.

'Yes, it is,' said Annabel.

'No, it's not,' said Mortimer Rackstraw.

'Because I'm sure no man,' proceeded Uncle Joe, 'ever had a better niece. I've never forgotten the way you used to come and smooth my pillow and bring me cooling drinks when I was in the hospital.'

There was the sound of a sharp intake of breath. Sir Aylmer, who was saying, 'It isn't, it isn't, it isn't,' had broken off abruptly.

'Hospital?' he said. 'Were you ever in a hospital?'

Mr Boffin laughed indulgently. 'Was I ever in a hospital! That's a good 'un. That would make the boys on the Medical Council giggle. Ask them at St Luke's if Joe Boffin was ever in a hospital. Ask them at St Christopher's. Why, I've spent most of my life in hospitals. Started as a child with Congenital Pyloric Hypertrophy of the Stomach and never looked back.'

Sir Aylmer was trembling violently. A look of awe had come into his face, the look which a small boy wears when he sees a heavyweight champion of the world.

'Did you say your name was Joe Boffin?'

'That's right.'

'Not *the* Joe Boffin? Not the man there was that interview with in the Christmas number of *The Lancet*?'

'That's me.'

Sir Aylmer started forward impulsively. 'May I shake your hand?'

'Put it there.'

'I am proud to meet you, Mr Boffin. I am one of your greatest admirers.'

'Nice of you to say so, old man.'

'Your career has been an inspiration to me. Is it really true ... that you have Thrombosis of the Heart *and* Vesicular Emphysema of the Lungs?'

'That's right.'

'And that your temperature once went up to 107.5?'

'Twice. When I had Hyperpyrexia.'

Sir Aylmer sighed.

'The best I've ever done is 102.2.'

Joe Boffin patted him on the back.

'Well, that's not bad,' he said. 'Not bad at all.'

'Excuse me,' said a well-bred voice.

It was the distinguished-looking man with the silvery hair who had approached them, the man Sir Aylmer had addressed as Rumbelow. His manner was diffident. Behind him stood an eager group, staring and twiddling their fingers.

'Excuse me, my dear Bastable, for intruding on a private conversation, but I fancied ... and my friends fancied ...'

'We all fancied,' said the group.

'That we overheard the name Boffin. Can it be, sir, that you are Mr Joseph Boffin?'

'That's right.'

'Boffin of St Luke's?'

'That's right.'

The silvery-haired man seemed overcome by a sudden shyness. He giggled nervously.

'Then may we say – my friends and I – how much . . . We felt we would just like . . . Unwarrantable intrusion, of course, but we are all such great admirers. I suppose you have to go through a good deal of this sort of thing, Mr Boffin . . . People coming up to you, I mean, and . . . Perfect strangers, I mean to say . . .'

'Quite all right, old man, quite all right. Always glad to meet the fans.'

'Then may I introduce myself. I am Lord Rumbelow. These are my friends, the Duke of Mull, the Marquis of Peckham, Lord Percy . . .'

''Ow are you, 'ow are you? Come and join us, boys. My niece, Miss Purvis.'

'Charmed.'

'The young chap she's going to marry.'

'How do you do?'

'And his uncle, Sir Aylmer Bastable.'

All heads were turned towards the Major-General. Lord Rumbelow spoke in an awed voice.

'Is this really so, Bastable? Your nephew is actually going to marry Mr Boffin's niece? I congratulate you, my dear fellow. A most signal honour.' A touch of embarrassment came into his manner. He coughed. 'We were just talking about you, oddly enough, Bastable, my friends and I. Saying what a pity it was that we saw so little of you. And we were wondering – it was the Duke's suggestion – if you would care to become a member of a little club we have – quite a small affair – rather exclusive, we like to feel – the Twelve Jolly Stretcher-Cases . . .'

'My dear Rumbelow!'

'We have felt for a long time that our company was incomplete without you. So you will join us? Capital, capital! Perhaps you will look in there to-night? Mr Boffin, of course,' he went on deprecatingly, 'would, I am afraid, hardly condescend to allow himself to be entertained by so humble a little circle. Otherwise—'

Joe Boffin slapped him affably on the back. 'My dear feller, I'd be delighted. There's nothing stuck-up about me.'

'Well, really! I hardly know what to say . . .'

'We can't all be Joe Boffins. That's the way I look at it.'

'The true democratic spirit.'

'Why, I was best man at a chap's wedding last week, and all he'd got was emotional dermatitis.'

'Amazing! Then you and Sir Aylmer will be with us to-night? Delightful. We can give you a bottle of lung tonic which I think you will appreciate. We pride ourselves on our cellar.'

A babble of happy chatter had broken out, almost drowning the band, and Mr Boffin, opening his waistcoat, was showing the Duke of Mull the scar left by his first operation. Sir Aylmer, watching them with throbbing heart, was dizzily aware of a fountain-pen being thrust into his hand.

'Eh?' he said. 'What? What's this? What, what?'

'The papers,' said Freddie. 'The merry old documents in the case. You sign here, where my thumb is.'

'Eh? What? Eh? Ah, yes, to be sure. Yes, yes, yes,' said Sir Aylmer, absently affixing his signature.

'Thank you, uncle, a thousand ...'

'Quite, quite. But don't bother me now, my boy. Busy. Got a lot to talk about to those friends of mine. Take the girl away and give her a sulphur water.'

And, brushing aside Mortimer Rackstraw, who was offering him a pack of cards, he joined the group about Joe Boffin. Freddie clasped Annabel in a fond embrace. Mortimer Rackstraw stood glaring for a moment, twisting his moustache. Then he took the flags of all nations from Annabel's back hair and, with a despairing gesture, strode from the room.

Sundered Hearts

In the smoking-room of the club-house a cheerful fire was burning, and the Oldest Member glanced from time to time out of the window into the gathering dusk. Snow was falling lightly on the links. From where he sat, the Oldest Member had a good view of the ninth green; and presently, out of the greyness of the December evening, there appeared over the brow of the hill a golf-ball. It trickled across the green, and stopped within a yard of the hole. The Oldest Member nodded approvingly. A good approach-shot.

A young man in a tweed suit clambered on to the green, holed out with easy confidence, and, shouldering his bag, made his way to the club-house. A few moments later he entered the smoking-room, and uttered an exclamation of rapture at the sight of the fire.

'I'm frozen stiff!'

He rang for a waiter and ordered a hot drink. The Oldest

Member gave a gracious assent to the suggestion that he should join him.

'I like playing in winter,' said the young man. 'You get the course to yourself, for the world is full of slackers who only turn out when the weather suits them. I cannot understand where they get the nerve to call themselves golfers.'

'Not everyone is as keen as you are, my boy,' said the Sage, dipping gratefully into his hot drink. 'If they were, the world would be a better place, and we should hear less of all this modern unrest.'

'I *am* pretty keen,' admitted the young man.

'I have only encountered one man whom I could describe as keener. I allude to Mortimer Sturgis.'

'The fellow who took up golf at thirty-eight and let the girl he was engaged to marry go off with someone else because he hadn't the time to combine golf with courtship? I remember. You were telling me about him the other day.'

'There is a sequel to that story, if you would care to hear it,' said the Oldest Member.

'You have the honour,' said the young man. 'Go ahead!'

Some people (began the Oldest Member) considered that Mortimer Sturgis was too wrapped up in golf, and blamed him for it. I could never see eye to eye with them. In the days of King Arthur nobody thought the worse of a young knight if he suspended all his social and business engagements in favour of a search for the Holy Grail. In the Middle Ages a man could devote his whole life to the Crusades, and the public fawned upon him. Why, then, blame the man of to-day for a zealous attention to the modern equivalent, the Quest of Scratch? Mortimer Sturgis never became a scratch player, but he did eventually get his handicap down to nine, and I honour him for it.

The story which I am about to tell begins in what might be called the middle period of Sturgis's career. He had reached the stage when his handicap was a wobbly twelve; and, as you are no doubt aware, it is then that a man really begins to golf in the true sense of the word. Mortimer's fondness for the game until then had been merely tepid compared with what it now became. He had played a little before, but now he really buckled to and got down to it. It was at this point, too, that he began once more to entertain thoughts of marriage. A profound statistician in this one department, he had discovered that practically all the finest exponents of the art are married men; and the thought that there might be something in the holy state which improved a man's game, and that he was missing a good thing, troubled him a great deal. Moreover, the paternal instinct had awakened in him. As he justly pointed out, whether marriage improved your game or not, it was to Old Tom Morris's marriage that the existence of young Tommy Morris, winner of the British Open Championship four times in succession, could be directly traced. In fact, at the age of forty-two, Mortimer Sturgis was in just the frame of mind to take some nice girl aside and ask her to become a step-mother to his eleven drivers, his baffy, his twenty-eight putters, and the rest of the ninety-four clubs which he had accumulated in the course of his golfing career. The sole stipulation, of course, which he made when dreaming his daydreams was that the future Mrs Sturgis must be a golfer. I can still recall the horror in his face when one girl, admirable in other respects, said that she had never heard of Harry Vardon, and didn't he mean Dolly Varden? She has since proved an excellent wife and mother, but Mortimer Sturgis never spoke to her again.

With the coming of January, it was Mortimer's practice to leave England and go to the South of France, where there was sunshine and crisp dry turf. He pursued his usual custom this year. With his suitcase and his ninety-four clubs he went off to Saint Brule, staying as he always did at the Hotel Superbe, where they knew him, and treated with an amiable tolerance his habit of practising chip-shots in his bedroom. On the first evening, after breaking a statuette of the Infant Samuel in Prayer, he dressed and went down to dinner. And the first thing he saw was Her.

Mortimer Sturgis, as you know, had been engaged before, but Betty Weston had never inspired the tumultuous rush of emotion which the mere sight of this girl had set loose in him. He told me later that just to watch her holing out her soup gave him a sort of feeling you get when your drive collides with a rock in the middle of a tangle of rough and kicks back into the middle of the fairway. If golf had come late in life to Mortimer

Sturgis, love came later still, and just as the golf, attacking him in middle life, had been some golf, so was the love considerable love. Mortimer finished his dinner in a trance, which is the best way to do it at some hotels, and then scoured the place for someone who would introduce him. He found such a person eventually and the meeting took place.

She was a small and rather fragile-looking girl, with big blue eyes and a cloud of golden hair. She had a sweet expression, and her left wrist was in a sling. She looked up at Mortimer as if she had at last found something that amounted to something. I am inclined to think it was a case of love at first sight on both sides.

'Fine weather we're having,' said Mortimer, who was a capital conversationalist.

'Yes,' said the girl.

'I like fine weather.'

'So do I.'

'There's something about fine weather!'

'Yes.'

'It's – it's – well, fine weather's so much finer than weather that isn't fine,' said Mortimer.

He looked at the girl a little anxiously, fearing he might be taking her out of her depth, but she seemed to have followed his train of thought perfectly.

'Yes, isn't it?' she said. 'It's so – so fine.'

'That's just what I meant,' said Mortimer. 'So fine. You've just hit it.'

He was charmed. The combination of beauty with intelligence is so rare.

'I see you've hurt your wrist,' he went on, pointing to the sling.

'Yes. I strained it a little playing in the championship.'

'The championship?' Mortimer was interested. 'It's awfully rude of me,' he said, apologetically, 'but I didn't catch your name just now.'

'My name is Somerset.'

Mortimer had been bending forward solicitously. He overbalanced and nearly fell off his chair. The shock had been stunning. Even before he had met and spoken to her, he had told himself that he loved this girl with the stored-up love of a lifetime. And she was Mary Somerset! The hotel lobby danced before Mortimer's eyes.

The name will, of course, be familiar to you. In the early rounds of the Ladies' Open Golf Championship of that year nobody had paid much attention to Mary Somerset. She had survived her first two matches, but her opponents had been nonentities like herself. And then, in the third round, she had met and defeated the champion. From that point on, her name was on everybody's lips. She became favourite. And she had justified the public confidence by sailing into the final and winning easily. And here she was, talking to him like an ordinary person, and, if he could read the message in her eyes, not altogether indifferent to his charms, if you could call them that.

'Golly!' said Mortimer, awed.

Their friendship ripened rapidly, as friendships do in the South of France. In that favoured clime, you find the girl and Nature does the rest. On the second morning of their acquaintance Mortimer invited her to walk round the links with him and watch him play. He did it a little diffidently, for his golf was not of the calibre that would be likely to extort admiration from a champion. On the other hand, one should never let slip the opportunity of acquiring wrinkles on the game, and he thought that Miss Somerset, if she watched one or two of his shots, might tell him just what he ought to do. And sure enough, the opening arrived on the fourth hole, where Mortimer, after a drive which surprised even himself, found his ball in a nasty cuppy lie.

He turned to the girl.

'What ought I to do here?' he asked.

Miss Somerset looked at the ball. She seemed to be weighing the matter in her mind.

'Give it a good hard knock,' she said.

Mortimer knew what she meant. She was advocating a full iron. The only trouble was that, when he tried anything more ambitious than a half-swing, except off the tee, he almost invariably topped. However, he could not fail this wonderful girl, so he swung well back and took a chance. His enterprise was rewarded. The ball flew out of the indentation in the turf as cleanly as though John Henry Taylor had been behind it, and rolled, looking neither to left nor to right, straight for the pin. A few moments later Mortimer Sturgis had holed out one under bogey, and it was only the fear that, having known him for so short a time, she might be startled and refuse him that kept him from proposing then and there. This exhibition of golfing generalship on her part had removed his last doubts. He knew that, if he lived for ever, there could be no other girl in the world for him. With her at his side, what might he not do? He might get his handicap down to six – to three – to scratch – to plus something! Good heavens, why, even the Amateur Championship was not outside the range of possibility. Mortimer Sturgis shook his putter solemnly in the air, and vowed a silent vow that he would win this pearl among women.

Now, when a man feels like that, it is impossible to restrain him long. For a week Mortimer Sturgis's soul sizzled within him: then he could contain himself no longer. One night, at one of the informal dances at the hotel, he drew the girl out on to the moonlit terrace.

'Miss Somerset—' he began, stuttering with emotion like an imperfectly-corked bottle of ginger-beer. 'Miss Somerset – may I call you Mary?'

The girl looked at him with eyes that shone softly in the dim light.

'Mary?' she repeated. 'Why, of course, if you like—'

'If I like!' cried Mortimer. 'Don't you know that it is my dearest wish? Don't you know that I would rather be permitted to call you Mary than do the first hole at Muirfield in two? Oh, Mary, how I have longed for this moment! I love you! I love you! Ever since I met you I have known that you were the one girl in this vast world whom I would die to win! Mary, will you be mine? Shall we go round together? Will you fix up a match with me on the links of life which shall end only when the Grim Reaper lays us both a stymie?'

She drooped towards him.

'Mortimer!' she murmured.

He held out his arms, then drew back. His face had grown suddenly tense, and there were lines of pain about his mouth.

'Wait!' he said, in a strained voice. 'Mary, I love you dearly, and because I love you so dearly I cannot let you trust your sweet life to me blindly. I have a confession to make. I am not – I have not always been' – he paused – 'a good man,' he said, in a low voice.

She started indignantly.

'How can you say that? You are the best, the kindest, the bravest man I have ever met! Who but a good man would have risked his life to save me from drowning?'

'Drowning?' Mortimer's voice seemed perplexed. 'You? What do you mean?'

'Have you forgotten the time when I fell in the sea last week, and you jumped in with all your clothes on –'

'Of course, yes,' said Mortimer. 'I remember now. It was the day I did the long seventh in five. I got off a good tee-shot straight down the fairway, took a baffy for my second, and— But that is not the point. It is sweet and generous of you to think so highly of what was the merest commonplace act of ordinary politeness, but I must repeat that, judged by the standards of your snowy purity, I am not a good man. I do not come to you clean and spotless as a young girl should expect her husband to come to her. Once, playing in a foursome, my ball fell in some long grass. Nobody was near me. We had no caddies, and the others were on the fairway. God knows—' His voice shook. 'God knows I struggled against the temptation. But I fell. I kicked the ball on to a little bare mound, from which it was an easy task with a nice half-mashie to reach the green for a snappy seven. Mary, there have been times when, going round by myself, I have allowed myself ten-foot putts on three holes in succession, simply in order to be able to say I had done the course in under a hundred. Ah! you shrink from me! You are disgusted!'

'I'm not disgusted! And I don't shrink! I only shivered because it is rather cold.'

'Then you can love me in spite of my past?'

'Mortimer!'

She fell into his arms.

'My dearest,' he said, presently, 'what a happy life ours will be. That is, if you do not find that you have made a mistake.'

'A mistake!' she cried, scornfully.

'Well, my handicap is twelve, you know, and not so darned twelve at that. There are days when I play my second from the fairway of the next hole but one, days when I couldn't putt into a coal-hole with "Welcome!" written over it. And you are a Ladies' Open Champion. Still, if you think it's all right – Oh, Mary, you little know how I have dreamed of some day marrying a really first-class golfer! Yes, that was my vision – of walking up the aisle with some sweet plus two girl on my arm. You shivered again. You are catching cold.'

'It is a little cold,' said the girl. She spoke in a small voice.

'Let me take you in, sweetheart,' said Mortimer. 'I'll just put you in a comfortable chair with a nice cup of coffee, and then I think I really must come out again and tramp about and think how perfectly splendid everything is.'

They were married a few weeks later, very quietly, in the little village church of Saint Brule. The secretary of the local golf-club acted as best man for Mortimer, and a girl from the hotel was the only bridesmaid. The whole business was rather a disappointment to Mortimer, who had planned out a somewhat florid ceremony at St George's, Hanover Square, with the Vicar of Tooting (a scratch player excellent at short approach-shots) officiating, and 'The Voice That Breathed O'er St Andrews' booming from the organ. He had even had the idea of copying the military wedding and escorting his bride out of the church under an arch of crossed cleeks. But she would have none of this pomp. She insisted on a quiet wedding, and for the honeymoon trip preferred a tour through Italy. Mortimer, who had wanted to go to Scotland to visit the birthplace of James Braid, yielded amiably, for he loved her dearly. But he did not think much of Italy. In Rome, the great monuments of the past left him cold. Of the Temple of Vespasian, all he thought was that it would be a devil of a place to be bunkered behind. The Colosseum aroused a faint spark of interest in him, as he speculated whether Abe Mitchell would use a full brassey to carry it. In Florence, the view over the Tuscan Hills from the Torre Rosa, Fiesole, over which his bride waxed enthusiastic, seemed to him merely a nasty bit of rough which would take a deal of getting out of.

And so, in the fullness of time, they came home to Mortimer's cosy little house adjoining the links.

Mortimer was so busy polishing his ninety-four clubs on the evening of their arrival that he failed to notice that his wife was preoccupied. A less busy man would have perceived at a glance that she was distinctly nervous. She started at sudden noises, and once, when he tried the newest of his mashie-niblicks and broke one of the drawing-room windows, she screamed sharply. In short her manner was strange, and, if Edgar Allan Poe had put her into 'The Fall of the House of Usher', she would have fitted it like the paper on the wall. She had the air of one waiting tensely for the approach of some imminent doom. Mortimer, humming gaily to himself as he sandpapered the blade of his twenty-second putter, observed nothing of this. He was thinking of the morrow's play.

'Your wrist's quite well again now, darling, isn't it?' he said.

'Yes. Yes, quite well.'

'Fine!' said Mortimer. 'We'll breakfast early — say at half-past seven — and then we'll be able to get in a couple of rounds before lunch. A couple more in the afternoon will about see us through. One doesn't want to over-golf oneself the first day.' He swung the putter joyfully. 'How had we better play do you think? We might start with you giving me a half.'

She did not speak. She was very pale. She clutched the arm of her chair tightly till the knuckles showed white under the skin.

To anybody but Mortimer her nervousness would have been even more obvious on the following morning, as they reached the first tee. Her eyes were dull and heavy, and she started when a grasshopper chirruped. But Mortimer was too occupied with thinking how jolly it was having the course to themselves to notice anything.

He scooped some sand out of the box, and took a ball out of her bag. His wedding-present to her had been a brand-new golf-bag, six dozen balls, and a full set of the most expensive clubs, all born in Scotland.

'Do you like a high tee?' he asked.

'Oh, no,' she replied, coming with a start out of her thoughts. 'Doctors say it's indigestible.'

Mortimer laughed merrily.

'Deuced good!' he chuckled. 'Is that your own or did you read it in a comic paper? There you are!' He placed the ball on a little hill of sand, and got up. 'Now let's see some of that championship form of yours!'

She burst into tears.

'My darling!'

Mortimer ran to her and put his arms round her. She tried weakly to push him away.

'My angel! What is it?'

She sobbed brokenly. Then, with an effort, she spoke.

'Mortimer, I have deceived you!'

'Deceived me?'

'I have never played golf in my life! I don't even know how to hold the caddie!'

Mortimer's heart stood still. This sounded like the gibberings of an unbalanced mind, and no man likes his wife to begin gibbering immediately after the honeymoon.

'My precious! You are not yourself!'

'I am! That's the whole trouble! I'm myself and not the girl you thought I was!'

Mortimer stared at her, puzzled. He was thinking that it was a little difficult and that, to work it out properly, he would need a pencil and a bit of paper.

'My name is not Mary!'

'But you said it was.'

'I didn't. You asked if you could call me Mary, and I said you

340

might, because I loved you too much to deny your smallest whim. I was going on to say that it wasn't my name, but you interrupted me.'

'Not Mary!' The horrid truth was coming home to Mortimer. 'You were not Mary Somerset?'

'Mary is my cousin. My name is Mabel.'

'But you said you had sprained your wrist playing in the championship.'

'So I had. The mallet slipped in my hand.'

'The mallet!' Mortimer clutched at his forehead. 'You didn't say "the mallet"?'

'Yes, Mortimer! The mallet!'

A faint blush of shame mantled her cheek, and into her blue eyes there came a look of pain, but she faced him bravely.

'I am the Ladies' Open Croquet Champion!' she whispered.

Mortimer Sturgis cried aloud, a cry that was like the shriek of some wounded animal.

'Croquet!' He gulped, and stared at her with unseeing eyes. He was no prude, but he had those decent prejudices of which no self-respecting man can wholly rid himself, however broad-minded he may try to be. 'Croquet!'

There was a long silence. The light breeze sang in the pines above them. The grasshoppers chirruped at their feet.

She began to speak again in a low, monotonous voice.

'I blame myself! I should have told you before, while there was yet time for you to withdraw. I should have confessed this to you that night on the terrace in the moonlight. But you

swept me off my feet, and I was in your arms before I realized
what you would think of me. It was only then that I understood
what my supposed skill at golf meant to you, and then it was
too late. I loved you too much to let you go! I could not bear
the thought of you recoiling from me. Oh, I was mad – mad! I
knew that I could not keep up the deception for ever, that you
must find me out in time. But I had a wild hope that by then we
should be so close to one another that you might find it in your
heart to forgive. But I was wrong. I see it now. There are some
things that no man can forgive. Some things,' she repeated,
dully, 'which no man can forgive.'

She turned away. Mortimer awoke from his trance.

'Stop!' he cried. 'Don't go!'

'I must go.'

'I want to talk this over.'

She shook her head sadly and started to walk slowly across
the sunlit grass. Mortimer watched her, his brain in a whirl of
chaotic thoughts. She disappeared through the trees.

Mortimer sat down on the tee-box, and buried his face in
his hands. For a time he could think of nothing but the cruel
blow he had received. This was the end of those rainbow visions
of himself and her going through life side by side, she lovingly
criticizing his stance and his back-swing, he learning wisdom
from her. A croquet-player! He was married to a woman who
hit coloured balls through hoops. Mortimer Sturgis writhed in
torment. A strong man's agony.

The mood passed. How long it had lasted, he did not

know. But suddenly, as he sat there, he became once more aware of the glow of the sunshine and the singing of the birds. It was as if a shadow had lifted. Hope and optimism crept into his heart.

He loved her. He loved her still. She was part of him, and nothing that she could do had power to alter that. She had deceived him, yes. But why had she deceived him? Because she loved him so much that she could not bear to lose him. Dash it all, it was a bit of a compliment.

And, after all, poor girl, was it her fault? Was it not rather the fault of her upbringing? Probably she had been taught to play croquet when a mere child, hardly able to distinguish right from wrong. No steps had been taken to eradicate the virus from her system, and the thing had become chronic. Could she be blamed? Was she not more to be pitied than censured?

Mortimer rose to his feet, his heart swelling with generous forgiveness. The black horror had passed from him. The future seemed once more bright. It was not too late. She was still young, many years younger than he himself had been when he took up golf, and surely, if she put herself into the hands of a good specialist and practised every day, she might still hope to become a fair player. He reached the house and ran in, calling her name.

No answer came. He sped from room to room, but all were empty.

She had gone. The house was there. The furniture was there. The canary sang in its cage, the cook in the kitchen. The pictures still hung on the walls. But she had gone. Everything was at home except his wife.

Finally, propped up against the cup he had once won in a handicap competition, he saw a letter. With a sinking heart he tore open the envelope.

It was a pathetic, a tragic letter, the letter of a woman endeavouring to express all the anguish of a torn heart with one of those fountain-pens which suspend the flow of ink about twice in every three words. The gist of it was that she felt she had wronged him; that, though he might forgive, he could never forget; and that she was going away, away out into the world alone.

Mortimer sank into a chair, and stared blankly before him. She had scratched the match.

I am not a married man myself, so have had no experience of how it feels to have one's wife whizz off silently into the unknown; but I should imagine that it must be something like taking a full swing with a brassey and missing the ball. Something, I take it, of the same sense of mingled shock, chagrin, and the feeling that nobody loves one, which attacks a man in such circumstances, must come to the bereaved husband. And one can readily understand how terribly the incident must have shaken Mortimer Sturgis. I was away at the time, but I am told by those who saw him that his game went all to pieces.

He had never shown much indication of becoming anything

in the nature of a first-class golfer, but he had managed to acquire one or two decent shots. His work with the light iron was not at all bad, and he was a fairly steady putter. But now, under the shadow of this tragedy, he dropped right back to the form of his earliest period. It was a pitiful sight to see this gaunt, haggard man with the look of dumb anguish behind his spectacles taking as many as three shots sometimes to get past the ladies' tee. His slice, of which he had almost cured himself, returned with such virulence that in the list of ordinary hazards he had now to include the tee-box. And, when he was not slicing, he was pulling. I have heard that he was known, when driving at the sixth, to get bunkered in his own caddie, who had taken up his position directly behind him. As for the deep sand-trap in front of the seventh green, he spent so much of his time in it that there was some informal talk among the members of the committee of charging him a small weekly rent.

A man of comfortable independent means, he lived during these days on next to nothing. Golf-balls cost him a certain amount, but the bulk of his income he spent in efforts to discover his wife's whereabouts. He advertised in all the papers. He employed private detectives. He even, much as it revolted his finer instincts, took to travelling about the country, watching croquet matches. But she was never among the players. I am not sure that he did not find a melancholy comfort in this, for it seemed to show that, whatever his wife might be and whatever she might be doing, she had not gone right under.

Summer passed. Autumn came and went. Winter arrived. The days grew bleak and chill, and an early fall of snow, heavier than had been known at that time of the year for a long while, put an end to golf. Mortimer spent his days indoors, staring gloomily through the window at the white mantle that covered the earth.

It was Christmas Eve.

The young man shifted uneasily on his seat. His face was long and sombre.

'All this is very depressing,' he said.

'These soul tragedies,' agreed the Oldest Member, 'are never very cheery.'

'Look here,' said the young man, firmly, 'tell me one thing frankly, as man to man. Did Mortimer find her dead in the snow, covered except for her face, on which still lingered that faint, sweet smile which he remembered so well? Because, if he did, I'm going home.'

'No, no,' protested the Oldest Member. 'Nothing of that kind.'

'You're sure? You aren't going to spring it on me suddenly?'

'No, no!'

The young man breathed a relieved sigh.

'It was your saying that about the white mantle covering the earth that made me suspicious.'

The Sage resumed.

*

It was Christmas Eve. All day the snow had been falling, and now it lay thick and deep over the countryside. Mortimer Sturgis, his frugal dinner concluded – what with losing his wife and not being able to get any golf, he had little appetite these days – was sitting in his drawing-room, moodily polishing the blade of his jigger. Soon wearying of this once congenial task, he laid down the club and went to the front door, to see if there was any chance of a thaw. But no. It was freezing. The snow, as he tested it with his shoe, crackled crisply. The sky above was black and full of cold stars. It seemed to Mortimer that the sooner he packed up and went to the South of France, the better. He was just about to close the door, when suddenly he thought he heard his own name called.

'Mortimer!'

Had he been mistaken? The voice had sounded faint and far away.

'Mortimer!'

He thrilled from head to foot. This time there could be no mistake. It was the voice he knew so well, his wife's voice, and it had come from somewhere down near the garden-gate. It is difficult to judge distance where sounds are concerned, but Mortimer estimated that the voice had spoken about a short mashie-niblick and an easy putt from where he stood.

The next moment he was racing down the snow-covered path. And then his heart stood still. What was that dark something on the ground just inside the gate? He leaped towards it.

He passed his hands over it. It was a human body. Quivering, he struck a match. It went out. He struck another. That went out, too. He struck a third, and it burnt with a steady flame; and, stooping, he saw that it was his wife who lay there, cold and stiff. Her eyes were closed, and on her face still lingered that faint, sweet smile which he remembered so well.

The young man rose with a set face. He reached for his golf-bag.

'I call that a dirty trick,' he said, 'after you promised—'

The Sage waved him back to his seat. 'Have no fear! She had only fainted.'

'You said she was cold.'

'Wouldn't you be cold if you were lying in the snow?'

'And stiff.'

'Mrs Sturgis was stiff because the train-service was bad, it being the holiday-season, and she had had to walk all the way from the junction, a distance of eight miles. Sit down and allow me to proceed.'

Tenderly, reverently Mortimer Sturgis picked her up and began to bear her into the house. Half-way there, his foot slipped on a piece of ice and he fell heavily, barking his shin and shooting his lovely burden out on to the snow.

The fall brought her to. She opened her eyes.

'Mortimer, darling!' she said.

Mortimer had just been going to say something else, but he checked himself.

'Are you alive?' he asked.

'Yes,' she replied.

'Thank God!' said Mortimer, scooping some of the snow out of the back of his collar.

Together they went into the house, and into the drawing-room. Wife gazed at husband, husband at wife. There was a silence.

'Rotten weather!' said Mortimer.

'Yes, isn't it!'

The spell was broken. They fell into each other's arms. And presently they were sitting side by side on the sofa, holding hands, just as if that awful parting had been but a dream.

It was Mortimer who made the first reference to it.

'I say, you know,' he said, 'you oughtn't to have nipped away like that!'

'I thought you hated me!'

'Hated *you*! I love you better than life itself! I would sooner have smashed my pet driver than have had you leave me!'

She thrilled at the words.

'Darling!'

Mortimer fondled her hand.

'I was just coming back to tell you that I loved you still. I was going to suggest that you took lessons from some good professional. And I found you gone!'

'I wasn't worthy of you, Mortimer!'

'My angel!' He pressed his lips to her hair, and spoke solemnly. 'All this has taught me a lesson, dearest. I knew all along, and I know it more than ever now, that it is you – you that I want. Just you! I don't care if you don't play golf. I don't care—' He hesitated, then went on manfully. 'I don't care even if you play croquet, so long as you are with me!'

For a moment her face showed a rapture that made it almost angelic. She uttered a low moan of ecstasy. She kissed him. Then she rose.

'Mortimer, look!'

'What at?'

'Me. Just look!'

The jigger which he had been polishing lay on a chair close by. She took it up. From the bowl of golf-balls on the mantelpiece she selected a brand-new one. She placed it on the carpet. She addressed it. Then, with a merry cry of 'Fore!' she drove it hard and straight through the glass of the china-cupboard.

'Good God!' cried Mortimer, astounded. It had been a bird of a shot.

She turned to him, her whole face alight with that beautiful smile.

'When I left you, Mortie,' she said, 'I had but one aim in life, somehow to make myself worthy of you. I saw your advertisements in the papers, and I longed to answer them, but I was not ready. All this long, weary while I have been in the village of Auchtermuchtie, in Scotland, studying under Tammas McMickle.'

'Not the Tammas McMickle who finished fourth in the Open Championship of 1911, and had the best ball in the foursome in 1912 with Jock McHaggis, Andy McHeather, and Sandy McHoots!'

'Yes, Mortimer, the very same. Oh, it was difficult at first. I missed my mallet, and longed to steady the ball with my foot and use the toe of the club. Wherever there was a direction post I aimed at it automatically. But I conquered my weakness. I practised steadily. And now Mr McMickle says my handicap would be a good twenty-four on any links.' She smiled apologetically. 'Of course, that doesn't sound much to you! You were a twelve when I left you, and now I suppose you are down to eight or something.'

Mortimer shook his head.

'Alas, no!' he replied, gravely. 'My game went right off for some reason or other, and I'm twenty-four, too.'

'For some reason or other!' She uttered a cry. 'Oh, I know what the reason was! How can I ever forgive myself! I have ruined your game!'

The brightness came back to Mortimer's eyes. He embraced her fondly.

'Do not reproach yourself, dearest,' he murmured. 'It is the best thing that could have happened. From now on, we start level, two hearts that beat as one, two drivers that drive as one. I could not wish it otherwise. By George! It's just like that thing of Tennyson's.'

He recited the lines softly:

>   *My bride,*
> *My wife, my life. Oh, we will walk the links*
> *Yoked in all exercise of noble end,*
> *And so thro' those dark bunkers off the course*
> *That no man knows. Indeed, hove thee: come,*
> *Yield thyself up: our handicaps are one;*
> *Accomplish thou my manhood and thyself,*
> *Lay thy sweet hands in mine and trust to me.*

She laid her hands in his.

'And now, Mortie, darling,' she said, 'I want to tell you all about how I did the long twelfth at Auchtermuchtie in one under bogey.'

'Had P.G.Wodehouse's only contribution to literature been Lord Emsworth and Blandings Castle, his place in history would have been assured. Had he written of none but Mike and Psmith, he would be cherished today as the best and brightest of our comic authors. If Jeeves and Wooster had been his solitary theme, still he would be hailed as The Master. If he had given us only Ukridge, or nothing but the recollections of the Mulliner family, or a pure diet of golfing stories, Wodehouse would never the less be considered immortal. That he gave us all those and more – so much more – is our good fortune and a testament to the most industrious, prolific and beneficent author ever to have sat down, scratched his head and banged out a sentence.'   Stephen Fry

We hope you have enjoyed this book. The stories in this book come from various collections. 'Jeeves and the Yule-Tide Spirit', 'Indian Summer of an Uncle', 'The Spot of Art' and 'The Ordeal of Young Tuppy' come from Very Good, Jeeves; *'One Touch of Nature' is from* The Man With Two Left Feet; *'Romance at Droitwich Spa' from* Eggs, Beans and Crumpets; *'Uncle Fred Flits By' from* Young Men in Spats; *'The Story of William' and 'Honeysuckle Cottage' from* Meet Mr Mulliner; *'Ukridge's Dog College' from* Ukridge; *'How's That, Umpire' from* Nothing Serious; *and 'The Heel of Achilles' and 'Sundered Hearts' from* The Clicking of Cuthbert. *With over ninety novels and around 300 short stories to choose from, you may be wondering which Wodehouse to choose next. It is our pleasure to introduce . . .*

UNCLE FRED

Uncle Dynamite

Meet Frederick Altamount Cornwallis Twistleton, Fifth Earl of Ickenham. Better known as Uncle Fred, an old boy of such a sunny and youthful nature that explosions of sweetness and light detonate all around him.

Cocktail Time

Frederick, Earl of Ickenham, remains young at heart. So his jape of using a catapult to ping the silk top hat off his grumpy half-brother-in-law is nothing out of the ordinary but the consequences abound with possibilities.

UKRIDGE

Ukridge

Money makes the world go round for Stanley Featherstonehaugh Ukridge – looking like an animated blob of mustard in his bright yellow raincoat – and when there isn't enough of it, the world just has to spin a bit faster.

MR MULLINER

Meet Mr Mulliner

Sitting in the Angler's Rest, drinking hot scotch and lemon, Mr Mulliner has fabulous stories to tell of the extraordinary behaviour of his far flung family. This includes Wilfred, whose formula for Buck-U-Uppo enables elephants to face tigers with the necessary nonchalance.

Mr Mulliner Speaking

Holding court in the bar-parlour of the Angler's Rest, Mr Mulliner reveals what happened to

The Man Who Gave Up Smoking, what the Something Squishy was that the butler had on a silver salver, and what caused the dreadful Unpleasantness at Bludleigh Court.

MONTY BODKIN

The Luck of the Bodkins

Monty Bodkin, besotted with 'precious dream-rabbit' Gertrude Butterwick, Reggie and Ambrose Tennyson (the latter mistaken for the late Poet Laureate), and Hollywood starlet Lotus Blossom, complete with pet alligator, all embark on a voyage of personal discovery aboard the luxurious liner *S. S. Atlantic*.

JEEVES

The Novels

Thank You, Jeeves

Bertie disappears to the country as a guest of his chum Chuffy – only to find his peace shattered by the arrival of his ex-fiancée Pauline Stoker, her formidable father and the eminent loony-doctor Sir Roderick Glossop. When Chuffy falls in love with Pauline and Bertie seems to be caught in flagrante, a situation boils up which only Jeeves (whether employed or not) can simmer down . . .

Jeeves and the Feudal Spirit

A moustachioed Bertie must live up to 'Stilton' Cheesewright's expectations in the Drones Club darts tournament, or risk being beaten to a pulp by 'Stilton', jealous of his fiancée Florence's affections . . .

Much Obliged, Jeeves

What happens when the Book of Revelations, the Junior Ganymede Club's recording of their masters' less than perfect habits falls into potentially hostile hands?

Aunts Aren't Gentlemen

Under doctor's orders, Bertie moves with Jeeves to a countryside cottage. But Jeeves can cope with anything – even Aunt Dahlia.

Jeeves in the Offing

When Jeeves goes on holiday to Herne Bay, Bertie's life collapses; finding his mysterious engagement announced in *The Times* and encountering his nemesis Sir Roderick Glossop in disguise, Bertie hightails it to Herne Bay. Then the fun really starts . . .

The Code of the Woosters

Purloining an antique cow creamer under the instruction of the indomitable Aunt Dahlia is the least of Bertie's tasks, for he has to play Cupid while feuding with Spode.

The Mating Season

In an idyllic Tudor manor in a picture-perfect English village, Bertie is in disguise as Gussie Fink-Nottle, Gussie is in disguise as Bertram Wooster and Jeeves, also in disguise, is the only one who can set things right . . .

Ring for Jeeves

Patch Perkins and his clerk are not the 'honest bookies' they seem, but Bill, the rather impoverished 9th Earl of Rowcester, and his temporary butler Jeeves. When they abscond with the freak winnings of Captain Biggar, Jeeves's resourcefulness is put to the test . . .

Stiff Upper Lip, Jeeves

Bertie Wooster visits Major Plank in an attempt to return a work of art which Stiffy had told Bertie had been effectively stolen from Plank by Sir Watkyn Bassett. Thank goodness for Chief Inspector Witherspoon – but is he all he seems?

Right Ho, Jeeves

Bertie assumes his alter-ego of Cupid and arranges the engagement of Gussie Fink-Nottle to Tuppy Glossop. Thankfully, Jeeves is ever present to correct the blundering plans hatched by his master.

Joy in the Morning

Trapped in rural Steeple Bumpleigh with old flame Florence Craye, her new and suspicious fiancé Stilton Cheesewright, and two-faced Edwin the Boy Scout, Bertie desperately needs Jeeves to save him . . .

JEEVES

The Collections

Carry on, Jeeves

In his new role as valet to Bertie Wooster, Jeeves's first duty is to create a miracle hangover cure. From that moment, the partnership that is Jeeves and Wooster never looks back . . .

Very Good, Jeeves

Endeavouring to give satisfaction, Jeeves embarks on a number of rescue missions, including rescuing Bingo Little and Tuppy Glossop from the soup . . . Twice each.

The Inimitable Jeeves

In pages stalked by the carnivorous Aunt Agatha, Bingo Little embarks on a relationship rollercoaster and Bertie needs Jeeves's help to narrowly evade the clutches of terrifying Honoria Glossop . . .

The World of Jeeves

A complete collection of the Jeeves and Wooster short stories, described by Wodehouse as 'the ideal paperweight'.

BLANDINGS

Something Fresh

The first Blandings novel, featuring the delightfully dotty Lord Emsworth and introducing the first of many impostors who are to visit the Castle.

Pigs Have Wings

Can the Empress of Blandings avoid a pignapping to win the Fat Pigs class at the Shropshire Show for the third year running?

Leave it to Psmith

Lady Constance Keeble, sister of Lord Emsworth of Blandings Castle, has both an imperious manner and a valuable diamond necklace. The precarious peace of Blandings is shattered when her necklace becomes the object of dark plottings, for within the castle lurk some well-connected jewel thieves – among them a pair of American crooks, Lord Emsworth's younger son Freddie, desperate for money to establish a bookie's business, and Psmith, hoping to use a promised commission to finance his old school friend Mike's purchase of a farm to secure his future happiness.

Service with a Smile

When Clarence, Ninth Earl of Emsworth, must travel to London for the opening of Parliament, he grudgingly leaves beloved pig, the Empress of Blandings, at home. When he returns, he must call upon Uncle Fred to restore normality to the chaos instilled during his absence . . .

Summer Lightning

The first appearance in a novel of The Empress of Blandings, the prize-winning pig and all-consuming passion of Clarence, Ninth Earl of Emsworth, which has disappeared. Suspects within the Castle abound . . . Did the butler do it?

Full Moon

When the moon is full at Blandings, strange things happen. Including a renowned painter being miraculously revivified to paint a portrait of the beloved pig The Empress of Blandings, decades after his death . . .

Uncle Fred in the Springtime

Uncle Fred believes he can achieve anything in the springtime; however, disguised as a loony-doctor and trying to prevent prize pig, the Empress of Blandings, from falling into the hands of the unscrupulous Duke of Dunstable, he is stretched to his limit . . .

A Pelican at Blandings

Skulduggery is afoot, involving the sale of a modern nude painting, which in Lord Emsworth's eyes, resembles a pig. Inundated with unwelcome guests, Clarence is embarking on the short journey to the end of his wits. Fortunately Galahad Threepwood is on hand to solve all the mysteries . . .

The World of Blandings (Omnibus)

This wonderfully fat omnibus (containing three short stories and two full novels) spans the dimensions of the Empress of Blandings herself, surely the fattest pig in England . . .

Blandings Castle

The Empress of Blandings, potential silver medal winner in the Fat Pigs Class at the Shropshire Agricultural show, is off her food. Clarence, absent-minded Ninth Earl of Emsworth, is engaged in a feud with Head Gardener McAllister. But first of all, the vexed matter of the custody of the pumpkin must be resolved. This collection also includes Mr Mulliner's stories about Hollywood.

And Some Other Treats . . .

What Ho!

Introduced by Stephen Fry, this is a bumper anthology, providing the cream of the crop of Wodehouse's hilarious stories, together with verse, articles and all manner of treasures.

The Heart of a Goof

From his favourite chair on the terrace above the ninth hole, the Oldest Member reveals the stories behind his club's players, from notorious 'golfing giggler' Evangeline to poor, inept Rollo Podmarsh.

The Clicking of Cuthbert

A collection of stories, including that of Cuthbert, golfing ace, hopelessly in love with Adeline, who only cares for rising young writers. But enter a Great Russian Novelist with a strange passion, and Cuthbert's prospects might be looking up . . .

Big Money

Berry Conway, employee of dyspeptic American millionaire Torquil Patterson Frisby, has inherited a large number of shares in the Dream Come True copper mine. Of course they're worthless . . . aren't they?

Hot Water

In the heady atmosphere of a 1930s French Château, J Wellington Gedge only wants to return to his life in California, where everything is as it seems . . .